DEC 2 2 2017 YAD
MLN

RECEIVED

P9-DNI-473

PLYMOUTH PUBLIC LIBRARY
PLYMOUTH, MA 02360

PLYMOUTH PUBLIC LIBRARY
PLYMOUTH, MA 02360

Nobody's Lady
The Never Veil Series Book Two

Amy McNulty

DISCARDED

PLYMOUTH PUBLIC LIBRARY
PLYMOUTH, MA 02360

www.patchwork-press.com

COPYRIGHT

Nobody's Lady by Amy McNulty

© 2016 by Amy McNulty. All rights reserved.

Second edition.

No part of this book may be reproduced or transmitted in any form, including written, electronic, recording, or photocopying, without written permission of the author. The exception would be in the case of brief quotations embodied in critical articles or reviews.

Published by Patchwork Press and Amy McNulty

Cover by Makeready Designs. Photography provided by Meet Cute Photography, featuring Sakinah Caradine.

The characters and events appearing in this work are fictitious. Existing brands and businesses are used in a fictitious manner, and the author claims no ownership of or affiliation with trademarked properties. Any resemblance to real persons, living or dead, is purely coincidental, and not intended by the author.

ISBN-13: 978-1-927940-69-3

*To all the readers who were kind enough to tell me they loved
my first book.*

.

Chapter One

WHEN I THOUGHT I UNDERSTOOD real friendship, I was a long-lost queen. When I discovered there was so much more to my life than love and hate, that those around me were just pawns in a game whose rules I'd unwittingly put in place, I discovered I was a long-forgotten goddess. But goddess or not, powerless or powerful, my feet were taking me someplace I wasn't sure I wanted to go. What did I hope to find? Did I truly believe I could hear him call me—that he'd want to call me? Yes, I did. I wanted to see him again. I wanted to hope, even if I wasn't sure I was allowed. If I deserved to. I headed down the familiar dirt path beneath the lattice of trees overhead, pausing beside the bush with a partially snapped stem that jutted outward like a broken limb. The one that pointed to the secret cavern.

Only, it's not much of a secret anymore, is it?

My feet picked themselves up. Glowing pools would never again tempt me.

I reached the black, towering fortress that had for so long shaken and screamed at the power of my glance.

For the first time in this lifetime, I stared up at it, and nothing moved. My legs, unused to such steady footing while in the sight of the lord's castle, twitched in anticipation of a fall that never came.

There was no need. My feet dragged me forward.

At the grand wooden door, I raised a fist to knock.

But I stopped. I felt like if I touched it, the entire castle might crumble. It had done so once before. Not at my touch exactly. But I couldn't shake the feeling that I was responsible for whatever destruction I'd find in this place. But that was presumptuous of me. He was strong-willed, and he wouldn't crumble at the prospect of freedom. If anything, he'd be triumphant over it.

You can't stop now. I pulled my sleeves over my wrists and propped both elbows against the door, pushing until it gave way.

The darkness inside the foyer tried to deceive me into thinking night had fallen. The stream of light that trickled from the familiar crack in the garden door called the darkness a liar.

I gripped the small iron handles, the material of my sleeves guarding the cold metal from my touch, and pulled.

My touch had come to the garden before me.

The rose bushes that surrounded the enclosed circular area were torn, ripped, trodden, and plucked. The blooms lay withered, scattered and turned to dust, their once-white petals a sickly shade of yellowish brown, smooth blooms turned coarse and wrinkled.

The fountain at the center no longer trickled with water. Its shallow pool was stagnant, piles of brown festering in mildewing green liquid. Dotted amongst the brown was pallid stone rubble. The tears of the weeping elf child statue, which belonged at the top of the fountain, had ceased at last. But the gash across its face told me the child's tears had not been staunched by joy. I wondered if Ailill had had it carved to represent the pain I'd inflicted on him as a child. And I wondered if now he could no longer bear to remind himself of what I'd done.

I hadn't done this. But I felt as if I had. If Ailill had gone on a rampage after he came back to the castle, it was because of what I'd done to him. Everything I touched turned sour. I yanked and pulled, trying to draw my hands further into my sleeves, but there wasn't enough material to cover them entirely.

"Well, what a surprise."

I gazed into the shadow beside the doorway. How could I have not seen? The stone table was occupied. The place where I'd sat alone for hours, days, and months was littered with crumpled and decaying leaves, branches, and petals, obscuring the scars left by a dagger or knife striking time and time again across its surface. The matching bench that once nestled on the opposite side was toppled over, leaving only dark imprints in the dirt.

"A pity you could not make yourself at home here when you were welcome."

My breath caught in my throat.

The man at the table was clad entirely in black, as I knew he would be. The full-length jacket had been swapped for a jerkin, but I could see the embossing of roses hadn't been discarded in the exchange. He wore dark leather gloves, the fingers of which were crossed like the wings of a bird in flight. His pale elbows rested on the table amongst the leaves and branches and thorns. He wore the hat I was used to seeing him wear, a dark, pointed top resting on a wide brim. Its black metal band caught a ray of the sunlight almost imperceptibly. But I noticed. I always did.

His face was entirely uncovered. Those large and dark eyes, locked on me, demanded my attention. They were the same eyes of the boy I'd left alone to face my curse—not so long ago from my point of view. He was more frightened then, but there was no mistaking the hurt in those eyes both then and now.

"You are not welcome here, Olivière."

His words sliced daggers through my stomach.

"I... I thought I heard you call me."

He cocked his head to the side, his brown eyes moving askance. "You heard me call you?"

3

"Yes..." I realized how foolish it sounded. I was a fool to come. Why had I let myself fall for that sound again, for my name whispered on the wind? Why was I so certain it was he who'd said my name?

He smiled, not kindly. "And where, pray tell, have you been lurking? Under a rose bush? Behind the garden door? Or do those rounded female ears possess a far greater sense of hearing than my jagged male ones?"

I brushed the tips of my ears self-consciously. Elric had been so fascinated by them, by what he saw as a mutilation. This lord—*Ailill*—wasn't like that. He'd touched them once, as a child. He'd tried to heal them, thinking they were meant to be pointed.

The boy with a heart was the man sitting there before me. Even after all we'd been through, he'd still done me a kindness by healing my mother. "No, I just thought—"

"No, you did *not* think, or you would not have come."

I clenched my jaw. My tongue was threatening to spew the vile anger that had gotten us into this mess to begin with.

He sighed and crossed his arms across his chest. "I gave explicit instructions that I not be disturbed." He leaned back against the wall behind him, his chin jutting outward slightly.

I wiped my sweaty fingertips on my skirt. I wouldn't let the rest of my hands out from the insides of my sleeves. The sweat had already soaked through them. "I needed to thank you."

He scoffed. "Thank me for what? For your prolonged captivity, or for not murdering both your mother and your lover when I had the chance?"

So you admit you took Jurij to punish me? You admit they were both in danger in your "care"? Quickly, I had to clench my jaw to keep down the words that threatened to spill over. *He's not who I thought he was. He wouldn't have harmed them.*

4

I loosened the muscles in my jaw one hair's breadth at a time.

"For healing me when you were a child. For accepting me into your castle instead of putting me to death for trespassing in it. For... For forgiving me for cursing you, even though you were innocent." My voice was quiet, but I was determined to make it grow louder. "For saving my mother's life."

He waved one hand lazily in the air. "Unfinished projects irk me."

"But you didn't have to."

A shrug. "The magic was nearly entirely spent on the churl anyway."

"I beg your pardon?"

He leaned forward and placed both palms across the rotted forest remnants on the table. "My apologies," he said, his lips curled into a sneer. "I simply meant that I wasted years and years and let the magic wither from my body to save a person of no consequence. You may thank me for that if you like. I would rather not be reminded of it."

How odd it was to see the face I'd imagined come to life. The mocking, the condescending—it was all there. I just hadn't known the canvas before.

And what a strange and beautiful canvas it was. That creamy peach skin, the brownish tint of his shoulder-length tresses. He was so much paler than any person I had ever seen. Save for the specters.

Despite the paleness, part of me felt I wasn't wrong to have mistaken one brother for another. Elric had been dark-skinned, but they seemed almost like reflections of the same person; they shared the same brows, the same lips, and even eyes of a similar shape if not color. Perhaps the face before me was a bit gaunter, the nose a bit longer. It was easier to focus on the differences. Thinking of the similarities made me want to punch the face in front of me all the more—and that would undermine everything I had set out to do when I made my way to him. *I wanted to see if you were really restored to life. Say it. I wanted to know if you really forgave me. Say it. I wanted to know why I... Why I feel this way about you, why I keep thinking about you, when I used to be unable to stand the sight of you. Say it, Noll!* I dug my nails into my palm and shook the thoughts from my head. He'd called my mother a "churl." I couldn't just tell him everything I was thinking. "Have you no sense of empathy?"

"What a coincidence that you should mention that. I am sending Ailill to the village with an edict. He can escort you there."

"Ailill?" *But aren't you him? Could I have been mistaken? Oh, goddess, help me, why do I do this to myself? Why do I think I know everything?*

He waved his hand, and one of the specters appeared beside me from the foyer.

The specters. There were about a hundred of them in the castle. Pale as snow in skin and hair with red, burning eyes. Mute servants who seemed to anticipate the lord's every command. Only now I knew who they really were.

Oh. "You call him by your own name?" I asked.

He raised an eyebrow. "I call them all by my name. They are me, remember?"

His icy stare sent another invisible dagger through my stomach. "Yes, but—"

"A shame you never cared to ask my name when you were my guest," he said. "I have a feeling things might have turned out much differently—for all of us."

"You knew what would happen! Why didn't you warn me?" I had to squeeze my fists and teeth together to stop myself from screaming. This wasn't going at all like I had hoped. But what had I hoped? What could I have possibly expected? *I thought I'd be forgiven. I thought that Ailill and I might start over, that we could be friends, perhaps even... What a fool I've been.*

Ailill turned slightly, his attention suddenly absorbed in a single white petal that remained on a half-

6

trodden bush beside him. "I was not entirely in control of my emotions," he said, "as you may well know."

"I tried to give you a way out!" My jaw wouldn't stay shut.

Ailill laughed and reached over to pluck the petal from its thorns. "Remind me exactly when that was? Perhaps between condemning me to an eternal life of solitude and wretchedness and providing yourself with a way to feel less guilty about the whole affair? And then you just popped right back to the present, I suppose, skipping over those endless years in a matter of moments." He crushed the petal in his hand.

"A way to let *myself* feel less guilty?" He wasn't entirely wrong. But it wasn't as if he had done nothing wrong.

Ailill bolted upright, slamming the fist that gripped the petal against the twigs and grass on the table. "Your last words to me were entirely for your own benefit, as well you know!"

If, after your own Returning, you can find it in your heart to forgive me, the last of the men whose blood runs with his own power will free all men bound by my curse.

"How is wishing to break the curse on the village for *my* benefit?"

"Perhaps because the curse was your doing? Perhaps because you only wanted the curse broken to free your lover from it in the first place?"

"Stop calling Jurij my 'lover.' He's not—"

"And you did free him with those words. You knew I would forgive you."

"How could I have known? I didn't think it possible you'd forgive me, not after all we've been through."

"You knew because you knew I wanted to be free myself. That I would do anything—even forgive you for half a moment—to earn that freedom." His voice grew quieter. "You never wanted anything from me, not really. I was just a pawn in your game, a way to free the other men in your village, a way to punish the men from mine."

I fought back what I couldn't believe was threatening to spring to my eyes. No tears, not in front of him.

"The men of the old village deserved everything they got," I spat at last, knowing full well that wasn't the whole story.

Ailill scoffed and put both hands on his hips, his arms akimbo. Oh, how I tired of that pose. The crushed petal remained on the table. Its bright white added a bit of life to the decay.

"There were plenty of young boys not yet corrupted," he said. "And some that might have never been." He took a deep breath. "But, of course, you are not entirely to blame. I blame myself every day for ever taking a childish interest in you. That should not have counted as love."

I swallowed. Of course. Before the curse of the village had broken, a woman had absolute power over the one man who loved or yearned for her. When I visited the past through the pool in the secret cavern, I discovered a horde of lusty men who knew nothing of love but were overcome with desire. Since so many had lusted for any female who walked before them, and I had carried the power from my own version of the village with me, it had been child's play to control the men. But why had that power extended to Ailill? He had only been a boy then, broken, near silent—and kindhearted. He couldn't have regarded me with more than a simple crush on an older sisterly figure, but it had been enough.

"But you did forgive me." Why couldn't I stop the words from flowing?

Ailill shook his head and let a weary smile spread across his features. "Forgive *you*? I could never forgive you. No more than I could forgive myself for daring to think, if just for a moment, that I..." He stopped.

8

I shook my head. "The curse wouldn't have been broken. The men in the village wouldn't now be walking around without masks. Nor you without your veil. If you hadn't forgiven me."

Ailill tilted his head slightly. His dark eyes searched mine, perhaps for some answer he thought could be found there. "I would still need the veil even now?" he asked, his voice quiet. "Are you certain?"

Removing the veil before the curse was broken would have required the Returning, a ritual in which I freely and earnestly bestowed my heart and affection to him. It would have never happened, not with the man I knew at the time to be mine. So yes, he would still need the veil to survive the gaze of women. I was sure of it. He'd been arrogant, erratic, and even cruel. Perhaps not so much as Elric, Ailill's even more volatile older brother, the one who wound up with a mob of angry, murderous women in his castle and a gouge through his heart. But even so.

It was my turn to cross my arms and sneer. "I said you could break the curse after your own Returning, and I specified that you didn't need my affection to have a Returning. All you needed to do was crawl out of whatever abyss I'd sent you to." I shifted uncomfortably in place. "And I suppose I should be grateful—for my mother's sake—that you did."

Ailill waved a hand at the specter beside me and brushed aside a pile of clippings on the table to reveal a hand-written letter. It was yellowed and a tad soggy. "Yes, well, the endless droning that made up your curse gets a bit foggy in my mind—assuming it even made sense in *your* mind to begin with. I am afraid I lack the ability to retain exact memories of an event that took place a hundred lifetimes ago when I was but a scarred child terrified of the monster before him." He looked up to face me as the specter retrieved the letter from his extended hand. "But I suppose it was not all that long ago for the monster, was it?"

9

He turned again to the table, shuffling brush about aimlessly. "Take her with you to the market," he said.

The specter made to grab my arm as he passed. I slipped out of his reach only to back into another specter who had appeared quick as lightning from the foyer. He grabbed one arm, and the first specter seized the other.

"Let go of me!" I shouted as they began to drag me away.

The specters didn't pause, as they once would have.

"Stop!" called Ailill from behind me. The specters did as they were told.

Ailill spoke. "I forgot to inform you that my retainers lost all desire to follow your orders when I did." He waved his fingers in the air. "Carry on."

I struggled against the grip the specters had on my arms. *Again. He has me under his thumb again.* "I can walk by myself!" I screamed as my toes slid awkwardly against the dark foyer floor. "I don't need to go to the market!"

A black carriage awaited us outside the castle doorway. A third specter opened the carriage door, and my captors heaved me up into the seat like a sack of grain. The one with the letter slid in and took the seat across from me. He stared vacantly at the top of the seat behind me.

I leaned forward, whipping my hand out to stop the carriage door as one of the specters moved to close it. I didn't care what I touched in the castle anymore. Let the whole thing crumble.

A black-gloved hand covered mine. I jumped back. Ailill stuck his head inside the carriage. His face stopped right before mine, the brim of his hat practically shading me under it. The sight of his face so close to mine, unveiled and painted with disdain, caused a thunderous racing of my heart. It was as if I'd just run the length of the entire village.

"You kept your hair short," he said. He reached his free hand toward it, then pulled back.

I'd once let the bushy mess of black hair grow as long as it wanted, but once I cropped it closely to my scalp, I found it easier to deal with. "There hasn't been enough time for it to grow, anyway. Not for me."

He snorted. "Of course. But it makes me remember you as you were, long ago. When you cursed me and every man whether he deserved it or not." He leaned back a bit, putting more space between our faces. "I think you will be most interested in going with my servants to the market," he said. "But there will be no need to thank me in person afterward. I would rather not see you again." His eyes drifted upwards, thoughtfully. "In fact, remind the villagers that I am closed to all audiences. My servants will be out there to see that my edict is obeyed."

Before I could speak, he leaned back and let my hand fall from his. He reached around the door to close it.

"Wait—"

And slammed it in my face.

Chapter Two

*Y*OU FOOL.
YOU MISERABLE, SIMPERING fool.
If you let so much as one tear fall, I'll never forgive you.

I stared at the specter seated before me and laughed. I had been directing my thoughts to the raging idiot rattling around inside my heart, but I kind of liked the idea of pretending it had been the specter who had earned my ire. Him? Cry? I'd seen more life in that stone version of little Ailill that had spent all of those years sobbing atop the castle's garden fountain.

The specter really did look like Ailill. Paler, for certain, and with crow's feet around his eyes. This one was maybe in his forties or fifties. I had seen younger and older—mostly older. They were all versions of Ailill that had died, turned into ghastly shades to serve the new one.

I had a feeling I wouldn't have the opportunity to ask.

Not that I wanted the opportunity.

And he would probably just tell me I ought to know, since I was the one who cursed him to never die. Well, I used a myth I guessed to be true and commanded him not to meet his goddess—the one woman he would ever love— for many, many lifetimes. Apparently the men got to live long enough to meet their goddesses, no matter how long it took. Luckily for most men, it took far, far less time.

Luckily or unluckily? Eternal life had its advantages, I supposed, but it hadn't been meant as a blessing. And it hadn't even been meant for him. Not for the little boy I had befriended who had known nothing but pain.

And now that I thought about it, I always knew I would turn out to be his goddess, so I'd outright doomed myself, too. Put a sword, a weapon of tales of old, in my hands and I was bound to grow a little overly passionate and foolish. It was a lesson sorely learned. And a lesson I was foolish to think he would ever let me forget.

I sighed and rubbed my temples, tearing my eyes from the specter's face. I was used to the red eyes, but I wasn't yet used to the resemblance to Ailill. Odd that I spent so long wondering what was under the lord's veil when all the while his face was plastered across every servant in the castle.

I glanced out the carriage window just as we put the woods surrounding the castle behind us. I never used to be able to look up at the eastern mountains. Someone once decided that no woman or girl could look at the castle that soared up above the woods without causing the earth to shake. That someone, I was astonished to learn, was me. Ailill was right—I couldn't keep it all straight, even though I had done it.

We passed the small house on the edge of the woods belonging to my parents, Gideon the woodcarver and his wife, Aubree. We lived snug with the trees so Father wouldn't have to travel far for the wood he needed for his work. Of course, he had done very little work while my mother was held captive in Ailill's castle. I thought her dead, and Father didn't dare correct me. Ailill was healing her, but the road to recovery from her illness was nearly two years long.

The carriage dipped down and up the small series of lily-covered hills that separated my home from the heart of the village. Master and Mistress Tailor's—no, I'd forgotten. Master Tailor and *Siofra's* tailoring shop was the next home we passed. That was where Jurij had lived with his parents before he wed my sister. Now Master Tailor lived there alone, except when his younger son, Luuk, and Luuk's former goddess, Nissa, were visiting. Although his former wife still helped him run his business.

With Mother restored to us and newlywed Elfriede and Jurij living at home, it was getting rather crowded. I couldn't blame my sister, as she and her husband originally had the place to themselves. Mother and I had both been in the castle, and Father was a drunken lout more likely to be at the tavern than at home. It had only been a few weeks since I'd emerged from the glowing pool and all of these changes had taken place. I was pining for my own space. I had thought of the castle. How stupid. But there were those stolen moments in the garden and the food far finer than anything I'd eaten at home. Even the lovely dresses, although unsuited to me, had grown on me now that I'd spent weeks wearing the same old rags. But that was Ailill's place, not mine—and it was a prison once, even despite all the fine things. Once, I might have lived with Alvilda, the lady woodcarver in the village who had picked up all of the slack my father had left behind. But she was practically a newlywed herself, and I never quite felt comfortable around her lover, Siofra, even if she had shown me kindness from time to time. I still remembered her as I did as a child, a towering woman, gruff and surly.

We made our way through the heart of the village, and men and women, girls and boys alike jumped backward to make way for their lord's black carriage. I was still not used to seeing so many faces on display. Before the curse broke, only the men who had earned the love of their goddesses had been able to remove their masks. More than once, I'd shut my eyes quickly before reminding myself I could keep them open.

In the distance were the western mountains, bearing down over the crop fields. The commune beside the fields was now empty, devoid of the unloved and unmarried men who once called it their home. But the place carried too many unpleasant memories for me, too. I had lived briefly in two versions of the same wretched and fading spot.

The southern mountains served as a backdrop for the livestock fields and farmers. The farmers had never been fond of me. As a child, I led a small group of boys around the village as their "elf queen" and attacked far too many cows and sheep with a tree branch sword I called Elgar.

That left the north. There was a quarry there, but more importantly, there was an empty shack. I might have accidentally killed the old crone who lived there a couple of years back. It wasn't really my fault—it was the earthquake's. But now that I knew I was responsible for the earthquakes, I guess it was my fault after all. My face flushed. One more black mark in my book.

The carriage ground to a sudden and sharp halt. Through the window, I saw the villagers who had been looking at the various stalls of goods for sale turn around to face us in wonder. More than one dropped the apple or blanket or whatever it was they were examining and stared slack-jawed, almost as still as the specters when they were awaiting orders. Did the lord of the village really still inspire such awe?

Their faces softened when one of the specters outside of the carriage opened the door and the specter inside the carriage disembarked before me. For all they knew, though, the other passenger could have been Ailill. His visits to the village were no longer unheard of.

I stepped outside, ignoring the proffered hand of the specter who had been driving the carriage. All around me, jaws slackened again. The villagers might have been just as scared to see me emerge from that carriage as they would have been to see Ailill.

Or perhaps they just didn't expect to see any evidence that I still carried their lord's favor. *Well, neither did I.*

"Noll!" cried a familiar voice. *Alvilda, shopping in the market?* She was wearing a golden, frilly dress, too, and carrying a basket across one elbow.

Alvilda swooped deftly through the crowd and stood beside me. She shot the specters a murderous look. *Ah, there she is.* They had a bit of history, although I'd never be able to say for certain whether it was these three specters in particular with whom she quarreled fruitlessly.

"Step aside," she grumbled to the nearest one. She had never learned that they would neither talk nor acknowledge her. Or perhaps it was her way of not acknowledging them not acknowledging her.

She looped her free arm through mine. "Watching you come out of his lordship's carriage has to be one of the last things I expected to see today."

The yellow monstrosity of a gown she wore was so bright, it almost blinded me. "And seeing you in such a lavish dress has to be the last thing I expected to see in my lifetime."

Alvilda pinched my arm and batted her long, dark eyelashes. "Oh, stop. You know I can't live with a tailor and not expect to be dressed up like a doll occasionally." She grinned. "Besides, we have a deal: she can dress me like a lady from time to time, and she has to shut her mouth for an hour or two that night."

I thought it best not to comment.

Alvilda watched the specters warily. The one who had ridden with me in the carriage approached the Great Hall door. As I had seen time and time before, he produced precisely what he needed from a pocket within his jacket. A nail appeared in one hand and a hammer in another, and he quickly posted the letter to the door.

Before anyone had a chance to read it, he was back in the carriage and the two others jumped up to the driver's seat. And then they were gone.

"That's... disturbing," remarked Alvilda. "Have any idea what they're up to now?"

I shook my head. "Ai—the lord said he was sending an edict to the village."

Villagers pulled away from their small clusters, and a few started shuffling over toward the Great Hall door.

Alvilda steered us both toward the growing crowd. "So you were visiting with him?" Her voice seemed too unconcerned, almost as if she was trying hard to seem nonchalant. But the slight grimace on her lips was unmistakable.

I bit my lip. "I had to thank him for what he did for my mother. And he was none too happy to see me."

Alvilda snorted. "That moron should thank *you* for putting up with his nonsense while letting him walk around with all of his limbs intact."

My eyes scanned the edge of the crowd uneasily. I still couldn't shake the feeling that he was always watching, that he had an eye to everything that went on around me.

"Don't—" I started. I could see Alvilda search my face skeptically. I turned my head away from her, staring intently at the crowd closest to the posted edict. "It's more complicated than that."

"If you say so," said Alvilda. Her tone made her disgust far clearer. Fat lot of help that was now. Where was her utter disgust with the man when I was looking for any way out of my coupling with him? I knew there were few places I could have hidden in our village wrapped in mountains, but surely she could have helped persuade someone to let me have my right as a woman to refuse him.

But it wasn't a matter of a woman's rights any longer. A man now had the right—no, he finally had the *ability*—to refuse love. As Ailill had so aptly demonstrated.

"I guess I shouldn't be so hard on the man. I'm upset with how he treated you, but I don't even know him. And I'm thankful I can watch the sunrise in the morning now. I suppose I have him to thank if he broke the curse like everyone's saying." Alvilda blew out a hard breath, which ruffled the hair that hung over her face. "Have you seen one yet? I always thought they must be like sunsets, only in reverse. Nothing special. But being able to look up at the eastern sky, not caring if you happen to see that castle, and watching the red light stretch out from the darkness over the mountaintops... Sunrises are so much more hopeful than sunsets."

"I never stopped to think about it," I admitted. "But you're right—"

"No!" screamed a woman in the crowd.

"That's ridiculous!"

The crowd turned into a mess of buzzing creatures. A gasp, a shout.

A woman slapped a man with her bare hand.

Everyone stilled for a moment.

"What are you doing, woman?" asked the man she'd hit. He cradled his cheek. "Have you gone mad?"

"I... I don't know." The woman stared at her hand like it was someone else's entirely. "But you..." She squeezed her hands into fists on either side of her. "How could you say such a thing?" Everyone began speaking at once again. Alvilda let go of my arm and shoved forward past the men and women toward the Great Hall door, clipping a boy on the head with her basket. It was easy enough to follow the path left in her wake, but once the people shoved aside had a moment to register their surprise, I had to put up with a few accusing stares as I made my way past them.

"Huh," barked Alvilda brusquely as I at last returned to her side. "I suppose my brother and Siofra were the first in a new trend." She arched an eyebrow, indicating that she had never once cared that Siofra had been married when she moved in with Alvilda. Siofra and Master Tailor had announced they were separating, but there had been no formal way to break off the original union.

My eyes at last fell upon the yellowed and water-stained paper. How long had Ailill had it there, under the damp and dirty remnants of the garden I'd once treasured? Only to send it out as soon as I entered? It was like he'd been waiting for me to come, even despite his disdain at my arrival.

It read:

READ THESE WORDS AND OBEY THE EDICT OF YOUR LORD:

Due to the release of this village from the curse that plagued it for years eternal, I hereby release all men from their unions, formal and informal alike. As of today, there are no husbands and wives, there are no goddesses and their men. If a former coupling wishes to maintain their union, they will have to wed once more. My servants, acting in my stead, are the only people capable of blessing a new union.

I heard a few more palms hitting tender cheeks behind me.

Chapter Three

EVERYTHING WAS CHAOS. SPECTERS APPEARED out of the crowd to drag women away from men, and Alvilda and I soon discovered these women had all hit their men after they'd exclaimed joy at the edict. They'd *hit* them. Like the men had hit the women in this village long ago. Perhaps not so hard as that—they'd followed that lead woman's example and slapped their palms against the men's cheeks at first. But then one even started pounding her fists on a man's chest. He didn't seem very hurt. Just puzzled. We all were. I'd seen violence, but not here. And no one else had seen much violence at all.

People sometimes had whispered about a woman or two who had hurt her man, but so few claimed to have witnessed it. Alvilda said a young woman in her day—not her Siofra, despite how obviously unhappy she was—had treated her man coldly every time they were in public, and that man came to sport a bruise or two he never would explain. No one thought hard about it, considering the specters were sure to step in thanks to the "always-watching" lord if anything truly untoward had occurred. So they thought. If it was her, the man's silence made sense— his goddess could do no wrong, even if she hurt him.

These men got extremely angry.

"Leave me alone, you cow!" said the man being pummeled, grabbing her by both shoulders and shoving her backwards.

The specters swooped in to grab the fist-pounding woman by the arms before she fell, and two others pulled the man back, letting them both snarl fruitlessly until they calmed down.

No one was very calm for long. They screamed at each other, at the specters, at their neighbors, at their friends. Then someone's voice rang out loud over the others. "He should know what his edict is doing, shouldn't he? Isn't he always watching? Well, it's time he came out from that stinkin' castle and gave us some answers!"

I tried to warn the crowd that Ailill would have no visitors, but they wouldn't heed me. Still, I followed the castle-bound mob out of curiosity, hoping to see Ailill step out of his castle to address them. I dug my fingernails into my palm as I kicked myself for admitting, even if just in my mind, that I hoped to see him at all.

Following a horde of women up the dirt path through the village, up and down the hills and into the woods, brought up rather unpleasant memories of a previous mob, although that one hadn't included any men. Last time, I led them with a glowing sword held high above my head. This time, I dragged my feet at the back of the crowd and kept my arms crossed tightly across my chest.

What awaited us at the castle was an unbreakable line of specters, their legs spread slightly apart, their hands clutched tightly behind their backs.

"Let us through!" called one of the women at the front.

"We demand to speak to his lordship!" shouted another. *Oh, dear.* I was sure Ailill would appear to remind her that no one *demanded* anything of him. But he didn't.

The specters didn't move. One of the men pushed at the chest of the nearest specter, but he didn't waver. A few men and women followed suit.

"He can't cheapen our unions!" called Elweard, once he threw up his hands in disgust at the unmovable object that was Ailill's servant. "Why does he get to decide if our vows hold true?"

Vena, his wife—or, his former wife—slipped forward and tentatively put an arm around his waist. She didn't seem at all herself. She was known from the quarries to the fields of livestock to be the true tavern master, a woman who enjoyed bossing her husband around almost as much as he enjoyed letting her. But perhaps even in the face of his outspoken outrage at the situation, there was now room for doubts, even for her.

Because the men had all been compelled to love. With that taken away, with even their unions stripped from them, what was left to hold a coupling together?

"I love Vena!" shouted Elweard over the heads of the specters as he slipped an arm around her shoulders. "And I'd wed her a thousand times to prove it!"

Vena's eyes glistened, and she raised herself on her tiptoes to kiss him on the cheek. "My darling." Her voice shook. "I would wed you every day for the rest of my life."

The nearest specter pulled parchment, quill, and a bottle of ink from his pocket.

"And now what nonsense is this?" demanded Elweard, ripping the parchment from the specter's hands. "An arrest order for declaring my love against his lordship's wishes?"

While Elweard continued to wish for the nearest specter's death with his steady glare, Vena leaned over his shoulder and pored over the paper.

"Dearest," said Vena, "it's a declaration of our marriage!"

The crowd began whispering and pointing. Those nearest the coupling strained to read the parchment as well.

"It's true!" said one woman. "All we have to do is declare our love for one another, sign a paper, and the whole mess will be behind us!"

Elweard and Vena grinned as they gazed into each other's eyes. After a quick kiss, Elweard snatched the quill, and Vena grabbed the ink from the specter. They used the flat surface of a nearby rock to sign it.

So they were once again husband and wife, whatever that meant now. Did the specters producing the paper count as the lord's blessing? Why were we skipping over the wedding? Was it because Vena and Elweard had already had theirs? Or was that all meaningless now, as meaningless as the edicts of the first goddess? As far as Vena and Elweard were concerned, this new marriage would give them an excuse to throw yet another feast at the Great Hall to celebrate, because that's just who they were—simple people, happy with simple pleasures. Maybe they didn't have to think about marriage too much—they just knew they wanted to be the only one for each other. If only it were so simple for everyone else.

The mob didn't make any headway after that. A few more men and women came forth to proclaim their desire to be wed once more, and a few more parchments were signed. I saw at least two women pinch, prod, or poke their former husbands into speaking up. When those men spoke their desire to be wed again, their voices were unsteady, and the specters didn't pull anything from their pockets. The couplings left the mob, former wives stomping ahead of former husbands and former husbands searching the mob for something. One's eyes rested a moment on a woman near me, and she blushed.

ŋ ŋ ŋ

The village had become far too chaotic for my tastes—not that it was ever a place that willingly drew me to it. I had to make my way through it almost daily to help Alvilda with her woodworking, but most of the time, she let me escape to the woods right away to chop wood for her future projects. I sometimes met my father there, sitting on a tree stump, his shiny, unscratched axe lying lifeless beside him. He'd nod at me and pick up a flask I knew he often stashed inside his pocket. When I announced my intention to move into the empty shack, it went somewhat unnoticed. Mother and Father were still together, but Father had made no proclamations of undying love, and Mother had followed his example. Frankly, I couldn't have left at a more suitable moment. It made me yearn for the days when I had been so revolted by the way they kissed and kissed and could only pull their arms from each other's backs with a great and wretched show of sadness.

Now that I was finally on my own, I preferred to work more delicately with a chisel, a gouge, and a small block of wood to felling a tree with my axe. Children especially seemed to enjoy the little animals I crafted, so I called them toys and said they were meant to be played with. I sold them around town a few days a week. The first day I'd asked Master Tailor if I could sell some outside of the Tailor Shop.

Helping me gave Nissa some distraction. I think what she really wanted was an excuse to see Luuk, who always seemed to want to spend the night with whichever parent she wasn't currently staying with. It wasn't that Luuk didn't like Nissa, but he was no longer sure he was ready for romance. Nissa decided to break it off between them, although I was sure her heart wasn't in it. Theirs was just one of many messy partings, and theirs wasn't even that messy, considering how young they were.

So I avoided the messiness of the village whenever possible. I felt more comfortable staying at my lone cottage outside the quarry.

I was fully used to rejection, so there was no need for screaming and crying out with me. The few villagers who bothered to pass by were quarry workers, mostly men, the rest women who had rejected love before the curse had broken. There were few men in the village who would shed a tear over the lord's edict.

"Morning!" called one such tearless man. I looked up from the stool I'd set on my porch. One of the quarry workers, a pickaxe slung casually over his shoulder, waved as he walked by. His face had a familiar pattern to it. I'd probably met him when he came to chastise Ingrith, the woman who'd once lived in my cottage. Since I knew his face, that meant he had once been Returned. Not that that mattered any more. I nodded my greeting before turning back to work.

This morning, I was halfway through making a cat's rotund hindquarters out of a scrap block of oak left over from the new table Alvilda and I had finished crafting for Vena and Elweard at the tavern.

Alvilda had been on her way home from the market to work on that table when a specter appeared out of nowhere and—much to Alvilda's consternation—followed her home. The next time I saw her, she stood cross-armed and smirking in her shop's doorway with a piece of parchment stating that his lordship recognized Alvilda and Siofra as each other's wives. She said the confounded white creature had pulled it out of his inner jacket pocket as soon as Alvilda had explained the situation in the market and Siofra had expressed her desire to wed Alvilda as well. All it took was their signatures and they were united, on paper as they were at heart.

I wished I had been there to see it.

"It's a beautiful day, lady carver!"

My hand slipped. Now my wooden cat had a chunk missing out of its tail.

I looked up. Another of the quarry workers. I couldn't place his face. But he might not have had it out in the open until recently.

He took my curt nod as an invitation. His trousers brushed against the bushes separating my new home from the dirt road. I remembered those bushes as a safe place from which to get a good look at the old, husbandless crone who once lived in my shack. She had killed the one man who would ever love her. All it took was a look at his unmasked face. And no one else remembered he ever existed. I figured this out only after I had done the same.

The worker brushed the bush's fine needles off the front of his trousers with one hand and swung the pickaxe he had been carrying over his shoulder with the other. He put his free hand on his hip and spread his lips wide to reveal a set of perfectly white teeth. The effect it had on his richly dark face stirred something unexpected in my belly. I quickly looked back down at the damage his greeting had caused my cat.

"I hear you've been selling those in the village," he said.

His hand appeared in my narrowly focused range of vision.

"Do you mind?" he asked.

I looked up. And quickly looked back down, numbly putting the wooden cat into his outstretched hand and laying my tools beside me on the stool. What was wrong with me? I'd had enough of these feelings to last a lifetime, and I had only ever bothered with one man before. Or two.

"Let me see. A butt. But whose?"

I laughed despite myself. "There's no real-life model."

He grinned. "Oh, I don't know. Maybe you haven't seen my former wife's ass. If not for the tail, it might be a perfect match."

I shifted uncomfortably and stretched my smile into my cheeks as far as my lips would let me. It took an effort.

The worker handed the cat back to me and held his hand out to shake mine. "I'm Sindri, one of the baker's sons. Don't know if you remember me."

I felt the uneasiness in my stomach cease instantly. Sindri, one of the boys I used to play with as a girl. I shook

26

his hand eagerly, a much easier smile on my face. "Sindri! I'm so sorry! Of course. How could I have forgotten?"

It was Sindri's turn to pull an uneasy smile onto his face. "Well, you've never seen my face, so I'm not that surprised."

Bile rose in my throat again. Another face I'd doomed to masking.

"Who was your goddess again?" I asked.

Sindri swung the pickaxe off his shoulder and let it scuff the ground by his feet. He leaned on it and glanced over my head, his eyes squinting at the promise of a still-brighter morning.

"Marden, Tanner's daughter."

One of Elfriede's friends. I'd never been that close to the girls. None of them wanted to swing sticks at pigs or roll on the hills and get their dresses caked in dirt. And Sindri had found his goddess early on in the process of maturing. I'd played with his brother Darwyn for far longer. I'd lost all track of Sindri and his goddess obsession soon after he stopped being one of the elf queen's loyal retainers.

"You got married?" I asked, picking up my chisel and going to work again. That was a rather stupid question, but I didn't remember the marriage.

"Yup," said Sindri, punctuating the end of the word sharply. "Never got Returned to. Not that I care now. When I think of how stupid I was, I want to strangle my past self. All of that trauma over that cold-hearted, selfish bi—"

He stopped. I thought of my recent bizarre feelings for Ailill and nodded. The chisel slipped awkwardly. Fur was starting to look more like scarring. Perhaps the fat cat would be a tomcat, complete with alleyway battle scars.

"You know," Sindri picked up again, "his lordship's edict has been a real blessing."

A dog barked sharply, cutting him short.

"Noll!"

My eyes snapped up at the dulcet, airy tones of my sister's voice. It was a little off-tune and shaky. She was coming through the fields from the east, taking a shortcut from our childhood home to my new one. Skipping beside her to one side was Bow, Jurij's old, sandy-furred retriever, and on the other side was Arrow, Bow's perky and easily distracted golden-colored son. He stopped twice within a matter of moments to sniff the grassy field at his paws before galloping to catch up.

Elfriede hadn't visited me since I moved. I'd thought it best to stay away from whatever was going on with her and her husband. And that included staying away from knowing whether or not they had convinced a specter to produce a paper for them to sign from his ever-useful inner jacket pocket.

She was crying now, her golden hair limp against her flushed and fair oak-toned face. I felt a sharp pain slide into my stomach.

"What's wrong?" I stood, knocking the gouge off the stool. Arrow jumped in place, yapping.

Elfriede took first one deep breath and then another but, much to my impatience, didn't speak. Her gaze fell on Sindri, a cold blast of something I could only describe as annoyance sparking in her face. But this was Elfriede, my sweet and much-loved elder sister. She could hardly express that side of herself with witnesses.

"Uh, see you around, Noll," said Sindri, who had clearly picked up on something, too.

"Sure," I mumbled. He took off through the bushes and up the dirt path toward the quarry, jogging to join a pack of working men a few paces ahead of him.

Bow growled. I turned back to my sister, but not before putting the chisel and the half cat down on the stool behind me. Her wary eyes, puffed and darkened lids surrounding pale hazel, hadn't torn themselves from Sindri's back. Golden fur covered her wrinkled dress and apron. Her skin was perhaps in need of scrubbing. She looked as if she hadn't cared what she looked like for days at least.

"What is it?" I snapped at last. If I waited for her to open her mouth and stop sending death wishes after a young man she hardly knew, I was bound to waste all of the morning.

Elfriede's gaze turned reluctantly in my direction.

"Was that Marden's husband?" she asked.

"Former husband," I pointed out.

Now Elfriede's icy stare shot directly into me. "It won't do to be seen with a traitor like him."

"He just stopped to say hello." I could hardly believe the young woman before me was my sister. Had she spent the past few weeks locked up in a dark and desolate dungeon? No, my frail and carefree sister had not yet had the pleasure of that experience. I was sure my stay at the castle counted as something close enough.

"Well, don't say anything back," she barked.

I scoffed. Like I cared about the who-should-blame-whom of one of her giddy friend's couplings.

I put my hands on my hips. "I'll speak to whomever I like."

"Don't you have enough men after you?"

"What are you talking about?"

"Where's Jurij?" Elfriede asked the question with such volume and tenacity, I thought she imagined him in some crystal-encased cage around the back of my moldering shack. Arrow whimpered, even as Bow growled.

"How should I know?" I asked.

Elfriede stood on her toes to crane around my shoulders. *She really is looking for some cage!*

"He's been gone for days," she said, her voice cracking.

I plopped down on the stool, shoving the fat cat and the chisel to the ground beside the gouge. I cradled my face in my hands and heard the soft patter of paws. One of the dogs' noses brushed my knees.

Why did she have to involve me in this? Can't she see that I'm here to get away from all of this drama?

"Did you try his father's?" I mumbled through my palms.

"Yes. And his mother's place, too. Both were as surprised as I was that he had gone missing."

"His friends?"

"He doesn't have any friends," she spat. "Only you."

I rubbed my hands over my face. Arrow sat down beside me, looking upward expectantly. Odd. He could never be bothered with anyone but Elfriede before.

"Well, I haven't seen him, either." It was true. I hadn't seen him in weeks. Not since he kissed me and told me he loved me amongst the lilies on the hills. I thought it best not to mention that to his wife—former wife—who stood before me and was no doubt just waiting for an excuse to lurch forward and strangle me.

"Aren't you the least bit worried?" She paced back and forth, flailing her hands up and down. Up and down. Bow's head bobbed with her as she walked back and forth. All of the motion was making me ill.

"Should I be?" I asked. She stopped moving and shot me a look of pure and utter annoyance. "Look, whatever happened between you, he probably just needs some time to himself. I mean, how far could he go? There aren't a lot of places to hide."

"He should have told me!" she said, resuming her Bow-escorted back-and-forth trek to nowhere. "I would have let him be, but he should have told me!"

I sighed and reached out a hand to stroke Arrow's head. He actually let me touch him. His mouth opened, and his tongue spilled forth as I stroked him.

Did I dare ask what had happened? Clearly they had signed no paper blessing their second union. Perhaps that was all I needed to know. Thinking too much about it made my chest ache.

"Do you want me to help search?" I asked.

"No!" Elfriede snapped almost the same moment I asked the question. Arrow yelped and jumped backward out of my reach at the sound.

"Then what would you have me do?"

She marched onto the porch and shoved open the door to my shack, Bow and Arrow both at her heels. I hadn't known her capable of knocking over a small building with her bare hands, but I feared briefly for the welfare of my new home.

"Jurij!" came Elfriede's voice from inside the shack.

I jumped up and followed her.

"He's not here! What are you doing?"

Elfriede was on her hands and knees, leering into the area under my bed. Bow sniffed the ground beside her. Arrow had decided to lend his investigative ability to pinpointing my food stores. Elfriede jumped up almost as quickly as a specter and pasted herself against the wall, peeking behind my cupboard. Arrow barked and pawed the door, perhaps hoping Elfriede would soon pull out a nice, long sausage.

"What? Are you looking for him back there? Behind about half a foot's length of space? Jurij is thin, Elfriede, but not so thin he might slide into nooks and crannies unnoticed."

Elfriede said nothing, her eyes darting frantically around the shack, but there were no more places he might be hiding. She let out a strange, shaky roar and plunked herself down in one of the two chairs around my small dining table. Bow sat down beside her and howled. Arrow's ears went back, and he lunged for the area beneath the table, pressing himself flat against the floor.

"Friede..."

She brought both hands up and then down, slamming them on her lap. Tears started flowing, and a series of chokes burst from her quivering lips.

I moved closer. She swung a hand wildly in my direction.

"Stay away from me!" She took a deep breath, choked with a sob. "You hussy!"

"*Hussy?*"

Elfriede sent me a cold, piercing look. "He told me he loved you. And you kissed him!" So she knew about that day on the hills after all. "And on my wedding day!"

Oh. *That* kiss. The one that had ended with an earthquake and Jurij getting a permanent gash over one of his eyes.

"Friede." *What can I say? I'm sorry? I am. I just...*

"I know you've always loved him," sobbed Elfriede. She rubbed her dripping nose on her sleeve. "You had no right!"

I threw my hands up in disgust. "I had no *right*? He was my friend before he was your man! And if I recall correctly, you didn't really want him at the start!"

That probably wasn't the best way to prove my innocence in the matter.

Elfriede jumped up from the table. "Don't blame me now for misgivings I entertained briefly as a child! He was *my* man, not yours!"

"Yes, *was*," I spat. "In case you haven't noticed, most of the town is in chaos. The past doesn't matter." I swallowed a lump forming in my throat. To me, the past was all that mattered, but she would never understand what I meant. "He loves you, too," I whispered.

Elfriede sniffled. "I know." She wiped first one eye and then the other with the heel of her palm. "But I don't want to share that love with you."

I turned away. What right did I have to deny any of it? "You're right. Once I would have given anything to steal him from you. I never wanted to hurt you. But I was tired of being the only one who felt a complete and utter mess inside. The only one whose feelings never mattered. But I feel fine now. I'm doing all right. Now you can all try dealing with those emotions I lived with for so long. Just leave me out of it."

Elfriede slipped past me, her sobs clogged, silent. Behind her trailed Bow, but it wasn't until Bow barked curtly that Arrow got up and followed. I twisted my body to watch Elfriede drag herself out my doorway and down my porch. She paused to look back at me, rubbing her hand over Bow's ear. Arrow started homeward without them.

"You know," Elfriede said, each word shaky, "I felt sorry for you then. But I don't think I can ever forgive you."

One after the other, she picked up the iron weights of her feet and left. Bow glanced at me but made no noise before following. Perhaps she didn't find me worthy even of a growl.

"I don't think I can ever forgive you." What a familiar line that was beginning to be. I wondered how many more I would wind up crossing off my ever-shortening list of loved ones. My decision to move to the old crone's shack was beginning to make more and more sense with each passing hour.

Still, I felt I should get going. Time to cross off one more.

Chapter Four

THE PERSON I USED TO be wouldn't have hesitated to cross the cavern threshold. She also wouldn't have come with a candle in hand.

Leave the candle. Make your way through darkness. You know the way by heart.

But I also knew now that there was more to this cavern than I ever would have imagined. Even when I was imagining sticks as swords and monsters flickering on the walls. Even when I fashioned myself an elf queen.

No, you're no queen. You're only the first goddess.

I shook my head and steadied the candle as I took note of my trembling hand. There were no goddesses anymore. It didn't matter if I was the first, or even the last. Everything was put right now.

So why does everything feel so wrong?

I lifted the candle higher to look for signs of Jurij, even though I was just guessing he came here. *Where else is there to go to be alone? Where else is there to go at all?*

I hoped the glowing light hadn't drawn him into the water. But maybe that was something it did only for me.

I told myself I'd never set foot in the cavern again. But if Jurij was in there, I had to know.

I stopped, bringing the candle closer to my chest. I heard the drip, drip, drop of the water trickling up ahead.

And just at the edge of darkness, I saw a light. I was expecting that enticing violet glow, the light that always called me whenever I was near. The light that nearly drowned me more than once.

But the light I saw was red, dim and dark instead of bright.

I can't go there. A pain sheered through my chest. I swallowed. It didn't matter. There was nothing left for me there.

I blew out the candle and turned, forgetting why I came in the first place, focusing on nothing but getting out and pretending I was never there. My foot found a growth I didn't remember, and I stumbled.

"Whoa. I'm sorry."

A hand on my thigh and another on my ankle steadied me, the grip gentle but sturdy, enough to keep me from falling over without making it feel like I was caught against my will. I regained my feet, and the hands fell. I looked down, blinking to adjust to the darkness.

"Jurij?"

I wasn't sure how I hadn't noticed him as I passed.

"You found me," he said, a sheepish smile hidden in his voice. The sound of a scratch against a rock sent a shiver up my back, and Jurij's face alit with warm light. He smiled awkwardly as he placed a lit candle beside him on the ground and displayed the flint between his fingers. "You want me to light yours?"

I sat down on the ground beside him and slid my candlestick over to him. "Thank you." I wasn't even sure why I blew it out in the first place. Like the red glow wouldn't be able to find me in the darkness. Like that pool ever needed to *see* me to call my name—or keep me away. I took a deep breath. *Enough. Enough of that pool and all that came with it. Remember why you're here.* "You could have said something when I passed by the first time."

Jurij guided his flint to the candle's wick. "I thought maybe you wouldn't notice I was here. You seemed pretty transfixed by the pool." He dropped the flint into the sediment to let the flame die out. "I thought maybe you weren't even here for me."

Because I have a habit of jumping in this pool. "Elfriede's looking for you."

"I know." Jurij set my candlestick down on the ground between us. "Why do you think I'm here?"

I shrugged and bit my lip to avoid stating the obvious. I didn't come to commiserate with him, or to encourage him to continue acting like a fool. I came to put an end to his estrangement, so I could get back to my cottage and live in peace. Because even though it was my curse that made Jurij love Elfriede in the first place, it was also my fault he wasn't blindly in love with her anymore. *And even though I once wanted him more than anything, I don't know what I want now.*

But I knew it wasn't this. "What's going on with you two?"

Jurij hugged his knees to his chest. "What's going on with anyone these days?" He continued talking to the ground, like it'd make for a better listener than me. "How is a man supposed to know what love is now?"

I knew the meaning behind his question, and the answer—the real answer—wasn't simple. But I wasn't there to discuss a man's choice to love. I still wasn't used to the idea that a man could *have* a choice. Regardless, I was here to set things right again. "You know what love is. You've experienced it."

"Have I?" Jurij's eyes met mine for the first time since I'd sat down beside him, and I looked away, unable to drink in the darkness without the flame that once danced there. I couldn't respond, so he continued. "The new edict has been a blessing in a way."

His words brought to mind other voices. *"His lordship's edict has been a real blessing."*

"You are not welcome here, Olivière."

I shook my head. No. No, Jurij wouldn't be like them. He had real reasons to love his goddess, not like Sindri and an unReturned love, not like Ailill.

"Yes," I said, interrupting Jurij before he could finish, "because now we know that those who marry truly love each other." I nudged Jurij's upper arm with my own. "And there's no doubt in my mind that you love Elfriede."

"I'm glad one of us has no doubts." Jurij laced his hands together around his knees.

"Jurij, I lived with choice in love my whole life." I took my knees in my arms, just so I could embrace something to stop the wild beating of my heart. "So has every woman. And if you think about it, the fact that Elfriede *chose* to love you is remarkable. It makes her more worthy of your love than many goddesses—*women*—were of their men's love."

My wandering eyes caught Jurij's, and my breath caught in my throat. I'd dreamed of days when he would look at me like that, albeit without the slightly drooping eyelid and the scar that ran over it, a reminder of the first time I kissed him. On his wedding day. His wedding to my sister. I coughed and turned away.

"*You* chose to love me, Noll."

Don't.

"And you knew there was no hope."

I don't want to remember.

"Yet you loved me. You refused the wealthiest, most powerful man in the village because you loved me."

Now hold on, it wasn't just about that.

"You looked for ways to break the curse. Noll, you *broke the curse* because you loved me."

"Stop!" I was on my feet, not even noticing when or how I got there. "Jurij, just *stop*." I held my hands out in front of me as if pushing against a force of air. "Who told you I broke the curse?"

37

Jurij gestured around the cavern like he was pointing out imaginary people. "Everyone! Everyone says it was because of you."

"It wasn't me." I clutched my elbows and stared at the flickering candle at my feet.

"Sure." Jurij didn't sound convinced. "You just happened to be one of the last goddesses to have her man find her, the never-dying, always-watching lord of the village no less, the same lord who now says that all marriages before the break of the curse are invalid, and you have nothing to do with the fact that now every man is as free as a woman to choose who he'll love."

His words bit. Jurij was the last person I expected to be so accusatory. It took a lot to make him angry—to make him feel anything other than love and meekness. "I didn't say I had nothing to do with it." I ran a hand up my arm to my shoulder. "But it wasn't me. It was him."

Jurij shifted on the ground, but I didn't look at him. The drops of distant water punctuated the silence. "Well, I *know* whatever you did played a large role in it."

I said nothing, but I could see Jurij's feet moving at the edge of the candlelight, his legs getting ready to stand.

"And I won't let you tell me it had nothing to do with me."

I'm in trouble. I took a step back, ready to flee, but I dug in my heels. *You're here for a reason.* "Jurij, that's rather egotistical. It's not like you." He was starting to really get on my nerves. *Jurij*—on my nerves. He'd never annoyed me quite like this before.

"How do you know what I'm like? Really? Considering I was obsessed with a woman for years and had no choice in the matter?" His hands clutched both of my shoulders. "Noll, you kissed me. On my wedding day."

I knew it would be easy to slide out of his grip, much easier than it might have been with Ailill, but I was frozen, unable to move. I swallowed. *I won't run from it then. I'll use it.* "I used you." It wasn't what I meant to say, but some part of me wondered if it was true.

Jurij didn't seem hurt or shocked like I'd hoped. If anything, he seemed amused. And I wasn't sure I liked the feelings his amusement stirred in me. "Used me?"

"I didn't like being forced to love the lord. I wanted to make him angry." It was true. I knew that now. I knew a lot of things now that I was too blind to see back then. Before I grew up.

"And making him angry would make him stop loving you?" Jurij didn't believe a word I said. "You are aware that because of the curse we had no choice but to love, so how..."

"He didn't love me. He never did. The curse just forced him to think he did." It hurt to speak the words aloud. I'd buried them so deeply amidst my peaceful day-to-day existence.

"That's what I've been saying. We were all forced, Noll. But you weren't. Not when it came to loving me." He leaned forward, and I had to make myself take a step back out of his reach. If I'd stayed put, I might have been on the receiving end of another kiss.

"My feelings for you made my sister unhappy."

Jurij took a step forward to close the distance between us. "And her loving me, and me loving her, made *you* unhappy."

I moved back in time with his steps, never letting him close the gap entirely, never letting myself enter his embrace. "I caused that injury to your face by kissing you."

"*He* caused my injury."

The tiny blaze of the candles grew dimmer, and the red glow of the distant cavern pool mocked me, warning me to stay away. I retreated into the darkness, knowing the light of day was nearby. "I was selfish, stubborn, focused only on my own desires."

"Sounds like just about everyone else in this village, Noll."

39

I kept retreating until my back slammed against the cavern wall. He grabbed my arms again, this time a little firmer, like he didn't ever want to let me go. I closed my eyes as his face drew nearer to mine. "All right! I loved you!" I said. His grip stiffened, and I opened first one eye and then the other. His face came to a stop near mine, but he was searching my expression, waiting for me to continue. I looked away. "But I don't now. Not like that." *Confused. We're both just confused.* I peeked up at him, waiting to see if my rejection would cause him the pain Elfriede's might have, had he still been in love with her.

Jurij's fingers unhooked from my arms. He turned and headed back to where we left the candles. Instead of blowing them out or picking them up, he sat back down on the ground beside them. I stood watching him for a moment, confused, still reeling from our almost-kiss. "Jurij?"

"Go." He wouldn't look at me as I approached, and I was certain I'd never before seen the shadow of anger on my Jurij's face like I did now. *Not my Jurij.*

"And leave you here?"

Jurij blew out a loud, slow breath. "For a while."

I placed my hands on my hips. "You've been here long enough."

"I can't go home. Not yet."

"To your parents'?"

"She'll find me at either one's. Tell me she hasn't looked for me there already."

"There and at my place."

Jurij laughed, and I saw something of his old, cheerful self dancing across his eyes, but there was no mistaking the bitterness there. "Of course she would assume I was there."

I didn't think she was that wrong in thinking so now, not after the way his eyes drank in mine just moments before. But I didn't think Jurij was in the mood to hear that.

Not if I hoped to steer him through his confusion back to the right path. Back to Elfriede.

"It didn't seem like she'd be back to visit anytime soon." *Or ever.*

Jurij's grin reached his eyes, and I could have sworn I saw the flame flicker there once more. But no, it was just the reflection of the candles. "Looks like I've found a place to stay."

So much for convincing him to join the ever-growing list of people who hate me.

Chapter Five

"**L**ET ME GET THIS STRAIGHT. Jurij expects us to pretend we don't know where he is when Elfriede comes asking, yet somehow we're not supposed to be panicking that he's gone missing? Pass me some more nails, would you?" With one hand, Alvilda balanced two planks of wood for a large chest on which she'd asked me to carve a design. I rifled through her sawdust-covered workbench, found a couple of dusty iron nails, and dropped them into her extended hand.

"I know." It sounded even more ridiculous when someone else pointed out the flaw in the plan. "But if I don't let him stay with me, he'll go back to the cavern."

"You're seventeen, Noll—eighteen in a few months."

"Yeah..." I hadn't stopped to think about it, but come fall, it'd be a year since I moved into the castle. It felt like a lifetime ago.

"So you're a grown woman. And a grown woman has needs. I get that." Alvilda rolled the nails between her fingers. "Are you a coupling then?"

"No! *No!*" I sputtered. "I mean, I know why you might *think* that, but— No, I don't, now that I think about it. Why would you say that?"

"All right, all right. But a man moves in with a woman? What else are people supposed to think?"Alvilda placed one of the nails in her mouth like a piece of chewing straw. She stared me down out of the corner of her eye even as she took a hammer and pounded the first nail into place. "Schounds like..." Alvilda spat out a breath of air as she grabbed the nail from her mouth. "Sounds like he's taking you for a fool." She used her forearm to swat away a stray tendril of dark hair that fell across her face and went back to hammering.

I sat down on the bench beside Alvilda's worktable. My fingers drew circles through the sawdust as I stared across the room at the dining table. I still wasn't used to seeing that table dust-free. Mistress Tailor—no, Mistress *Carver*, or maybe now that I was on my own with my own profession I could start calling her Siofra—had taken over most of Alvilda's house and declared it an actual *home*. "There's work and there's home, and some of us need a little help differentiating between the two," she'd said to me when I first commented on how clean the place looked. "Alvilda can confine her work to the corner. No need to be dragging dust all over where the children are eating and sleeping."

And Alvilda had actually complied without putting up much of a fuss, as far as I knew. I noticed it didn't stop her from letting her work creep just a little bit beyond her "work corner" each and every day. It was why, at Siofra's insistence, building a workshop nearby was on Alvilda's to-do list. "Why not use the commune?" Siofra had suggested. "It's just sitting there, rotting, unused. Tearing down those filthy old shacks would do the village a lot of good."

But somehow, Alvilda had become "so busy" wrestling up projects from customers over the past few weeks that she'd barely done more than knock down the first couple of shacks, which I gladly helped with, feeling some of the painful memories fall away with each wall. Alvilda's lack of attention to the new workspace probably had something to do with the "waste of burning wood for two fires" she kept mumbling about. Not that it was so cold out yet that she'd absolutely need a fire, but she did work late most nights. She'd changed since Siofra moved in. She was gruffer, rougher around the edges. Like she had more annoyances to work out of her system with every swing of her hammer and every twist of a nail than she had back when she'd lived alone.

Alvilda must have noticed I hadn't responded to her remark that I was a fool. I didn't have anything to say; at this point, I probably agreed with it. Alvilda appeared beside me and took a swig from the mug she kept between a pile of filthy rags and a chisel on her worktable. "So how exactly does this living arrangement work?"

"He's sleeping on the floor. On some hay and blankets."

Alvilda peered down at me over the top of her mug. "And... doing what exactly?"

I shrugged. "Nothing. We haven't done anything."

Alvilda raised an eyebrow and put her mug back down. "No, *you* carved this box for me. And probably carved more of your toy animals, too." Alvilda leaned across me to grab a few more nails and went back to her box and hammer. "I want to know if Jurij is doing anything other than moping and trying to get you to make love to him."

"Alvilda! He isn't— We aren't—" I coughed and made a show of covering my mouth so I could hide the blush on my cheeks at the same time. "It's only been a few days."

"A few days becomes a few weeks becomes a few years in time." Alvilda whacked the hammer with probably a little more force than necessary. "Now that men don't need to be told what to do, they seem to need to be told what to do more than ever."

I thought about what she said for a moment, and what initially sounded like nonsense started to make sense. "Elweard still runs the tavern."

"*Vena* still runs the tavern. And Vena being bossy just happened to work out with Elweard looking for someone to boss him around, even without the curse driving him." Alvilda shook the hammer in my direction. "Elweard is about the only good worker left among the lot of them. Well, and Coll." Alvilda's brother—Jurij's father—had both sister and former wife to make sure he didn't slack any just because his whole life was turned upside down.

Alvilda picked up a nail. "Do you know what I had to go through to get an order of these? The blacksmith decided to use his newfound freedom to spend his days *lying in the fields*. Lying in the fields!" She shook her head and positioned the nail, taking a swing at it with her hammer. "I didn't even dare to ask who *with*. His wife—*former* wife— told me he could rot in the fields for all she cared. But I needed my nails, so I made sure to give him a reason or two to get up off his flower-covered ass." She swung the hammer back, resting it over her shoulder, and admired her hammering with a snarl, perhaps either intentionally or subconsciously showing me just how she convinced the man to get back to work. Then she placed the hammer down and snatched her mug up from the table like I might be tempted to steal it out of her hands. "And your father? What was his excuse to pack up shop in the last week? He's retiring?"

I shrugged and looked away. I hadn't been home in weeks. I wasn't really avoiding Father or Mother, but I knew I wouldn't be going home to a happy family reunion. Especially not with how things were with Elfriede.

Alvilda's rant was undeterred by my silence. She swung her arms around the room, sloshing a little of her drink onto the floor. "All this carving to do, and the other master carver in the village has retired?" She shook her head and took a sip. "No. No, I won't have it with my nephews." She slammed the mug down. "And Siofra and Coll won't have it, either."

"Luuk helps Master Tailor and Siofra."

Alvilda nodded. "He helps his father and mother and even me plenty. Nissa, too. They're young. We can still tell

45

them they'd better help out." I didn't ask if youth helped them cope with Luuk's sudden lack of romantic devotion toward his former goddess. I didn't relish whoever was the one to have the discussion with Nissa that her former little love now thought of her as more of a sister. Alvilda pointed directly at me. "Jurij is the problem here."

I crumbled under Alvilda's stare, focusing instead on the circles my fingers keep tracing in the sawdust. I hated to admit what I already knew, that Jurij wasn't *my* Jurij. Even if this probably was the *real* Jurij, the one who'd have existed without the curse. Then again, the curse was the reason for his bitterness, so who knows who he would have been? "I'm working on fixing things."

"*Fixing things*?" I could hear Alvilda scoff. "And what does that entail exactly?"

I met Alvilda's gaze. "Jurij back home with Elfriede. With his wife."

"With his *former* wife." Alvilda sighed and threaded her arms across her chest. "Noll, you're just not getting it. Things aren't the same anymore. You can't influence Jurij now any more than you could when you wanted him to love you."

"That was different."

"Why? Because he *had* to love Elfriede, so there was no hope for you?"

"That's exactly why. Now, his feelings could go either way. Or another way entirely."

"Then wishing *your* will on him seems more hopeless than ever."

I stared, studying Alvilda. "But he can be convinced now."

"You can't shape him like one of your wooden toys, Noll!" Alvilda rolled her eyes. "He has his own feelings, his own desires. Let him figure out how he feels for himself."

"But I don't want him to love me. Not like that. Not now."

Alvilda tilted her head. "And why not?"

"Because." I stared back at my circles, surprised to find that I'd traced a blooming rosebud without meaning to. "It's just easier that way."

"Are you worried about Elfriede?" Alvilda waited for my response before continuing, but I said nothing. "Because she's stronger than you give her credit for, stronger maybe than even she realizes. She's beautiful and sweet, and there are dozens upon dozens of available men out there now. She doesn't need Jurij, even if she thinks she does. She just needs time."

She doesn't need him. And I don't need Ailill. "I need time, too," I said at last.

Alvilda didn't say anything for a moment. Then she picked up her hammer and went back to work. "Well, take it. You could all use a little time to stop obsessing over romance, if you ask me."

"Maybe." I took a deep breath and stood, gathering my tools into my work basket.

Alvilda pointed at me with the hammer again. "You tell Jurij his mother and I expect him here for dinner tomorrow. He's had enough time to mope."

"I don't think I can convince him."

Alvilda laughed and swung the hammer at a nail. "You tell him he can be convinced by you, or he can wait for me to come over and convince him." She gestured at the door with the hammer. "And he might want to spend tomorrow walking through the village, looking for someplace where some other man has slacked off. Because if he's going to relish being free, he's going to find something productive he likes doing. Or if he can't choose, I'll choose for him. He'll take over the tailor work and the carver work both." She slammed the hammer one more time. "And I can find plenty more work that needs doing."

I wouldn't doubt that, not even if the entire village were already carved from wood.

Chapter Six

"**HOW CAN ALVILDA EXPECT ME** to make up my mind in one day?" Jurij had asked that question so many times I was starting to bite my tongue. If he'd spent a little less time asking, he'd have had more time to think about it. The blanket he'd carried for me was slipping out from under his arm, its edges grazing the road to the heart of the village. I shifted the basket of wooden toys onto my arm, scrambled to pick up the blanket hem, and tucked it back tighter beneath Jurij's arm. He didn't seem to notice. "I haven't had time to think about it. I haven't had time to think about anything but..." He stopped speaking and gestured with his free hand. His eyebrows creased, his mouth pursed. "I mean, expecting me to help out with Mother and Father is one thing. When they're busy. I'd even help out Auntie if she *really* needed the help."

I halted at the crossroads, realizing Jurij was still ranting in an entirely different direction. "But that's what I don't get," Jurij was saying by the time I caught up with him again. I grabbed his upper arm to stop him.

"The baker's today, remember?" I tugged him back the way we were meant to turn.

Jurij followed my lead, letting himself be guided, not responding at all to what I'd said. "When I was El—*her* man, no one batted an eye that I went off to do nothing. Nothing

48

but hand her cooking utensils and sweep floors and whatever else she demanded I do, even if it was just to stand there worshipping the ground she walked on."

I winced and readjusted the basket on my arm. Elfriede hadn't been *that* bad, surely. No worse than any other goddess. Probably better than some. Like Jurij's mother.

"No, *worshipping* a woman, doing whatever it took to make her life easier, *that* was a fine occupation of my time. But now that I can do whatever *I* want..."

I dropped the basket onto the ground, hoping the noise it made would snap Jurij out of his tirade. My toys were hardy; they could take the abuse. "We're here." I put my hands on my waist and looked at the little patch of ground in front of the baker's shop like it was something I'd built with my own two hands. Jurij had stopped speaking at least, but he wasn't thinking, either, apparently. "Blanket." I pointed to the bundle under his arm.

Jurij nodded and shook the blanket out, spreading it on the ground in the spot I'd asked Mistress Baker to let me borrow one day a week. She'd been so flustered when I'd asked, elbow-deep in flour and yeast, I wasn't sure she'd heard me. But she hadn't corrected me since, so I was content to keep setting up shop in front of one of the village's most popular stores. Everyone needed bread. And kids almost always tagged along to the baker's, hoping for something sweet.

I sat down on the blanket and opened the basket, setting out the wooden animals I'd brought along. Jurij stood there blankly. "Are you going to walk around the village?" I asked, placing a wooden doe next to the stag whose antlers had taken me half a day to get right. The broken-off one was just part of his appeal. "Look for some kind of work?"

Jurij scrambled to sit next to me, digging into the basket and grabbing a handful of animals. We didn't say anything for a moment. I finished emptying the basket, but

Jurij was still staring at the animals in his hands, utterly unhelpful. He seemed to feel my stare and looked up with a smile. "These are nice, Noll."

I tore away, suddenly forgetting how annoyingly unhelpful he was being and remembering how attractive his face was. That cleft in his chin always had an effect on me. "Thanks." I tucked a little bit of hair behind my ears. It was short, but it still stuck out enough that it could get irritating if I swung my head around quickly.

Jurij put down the cat with the scarred rump and followed it with a dog and her puppy. He arranged and rearranged them until he must have decided they were shown off to their best angles. His hand lingered on the mother dog. "I don't suppose there's a way to get Bow. Tell El—your sister you need some company?"

I laughed, and not kindly. "I don't think she'd have much sympathy. Especially once she discovered I already had some company."

Jurij leaned back, resting his head against the bricks of the baker's shop. "Yeah, I guess that wouldn't work."

I reached into the basket and pulled out the last of its contents, a small wooden sign on which I'd carved "Wooden Playthings, 2 Coppers Each," and placed it in front of the eclectic little herd. "Well, if it's any comfort, she's bound to realize soon enough that you haven't gone off to die, and you'll get your dog back in the chaos that ensues."

Jurij pounded the back of his head against the baker's shop wall once, twice, and a third time. "That's not a comfort at all."

I shrugged. I knew that. But I didn't think he was helping things by hoping it never happened. "Why don't we invite her to your mother and aunt's tonight?"

Jurij tore his head away from the wall and stared at me. "Please tell me you're joking."

I ran a finger in a circle around a squirrel. "You might not find it so bad after all. You might..." *Just go back and make up with your wife already.*

"No." Jurij leaned his head back again and hugged his knees to his chest. He always did that when he was uncomfortable. I wondered if Elfriede knew that about him. Or if she'd ever seen him uncomfortable before the curse was broken.

"You know, Elfriede doesn't..." The giggles of children stopped me from continuing. I smiled at the boy and two girls standing in front of my makeshift shop. "Good day." The girl in the front held two copper coins between her fingers.

"Ask her!" The boy laughed and shoved the girl beside him.

"No, *you* ask her!" The girl he'd shoved dug her heels into the ground and pushed back against the boy's hands in her efforts to resist him, accidentally bumping into the girl with the coins in the exchange.

I pretended to cough and held up the cat. "Do you want to take a closer look? Go ahead. Pick them up."

The well-behaved girl with the coppers took the cat from me and examined it. The boy and girl behind her were undeterred, still pushing against one another. Jurij stared at them, one eyebrow raised. "What's up with those two?" he asked quietly.

I stuck out a hand to stop further inquiries on the subject. It wasn't the first time I'd gotten questions, and it was bound not to be the last. With any luck, they'd both prove too shy to ask, and that would be the end of it.

The little customer put the cat back on the blanket and picked up the squirrel, just as the girl behind her stumbled forward, her battle against the boy's persistence lost. "Um," she said, rubbing a hand over her forearm. "Wanted nolorloolike."

"What?" asked Jurij.

The children burst out laughing, the boy clutching his arms to his stomach, the girl covering her mouth as if she'd said something shameful. She hadn't said anything at all, really, except that I knew exactly what she meant, having heard it a number of times now.

I picked up the puppy figure and held it to the girl in front, who put the squirrel down and took the puppy from me. "They want to know," I answered Jurij, pausing to stop myself from grinding my teeth, "what the lord looks like."

The girl with her hand over her mouth squealed, and the boy stepped forward, practically shoving my customer aside. "Is he real?"

"Is he a person?" added the squealer. "Or a monster?"

"Is he all pale like them?" The boy nodded sideways. I hesitated to look, but out of the corner of my eye, I noticed a specter approaching.

Jurij turned his head to look, and his face soured. He put a finger to his lips. "Guys, calm down."

"This one." It was the first time the girl with the coppers spoke, and I had no idea which animal she'd picked.

I was torn between watching the specter and pretending that my sole focus was my customer. "Okay. Sure. Two coppers then." The cat after all. The one with the rather large rump. I held my hand out for the coppers, my gaze directed as much on the corner of my eye as possible, the giggles of the other children and the buzz of the villagers in the marketplace drowning out any hope of hearing his approaching footsteps.

The coppers landed in my palm. "Thank you." I turned my head just slightly, and for one fleeting second caught the red irises of the specter. It was almost like he was looking at me. But they'd rarely met my eyes before. They'd rarely done anything but fulfill the lord's orders with utmost efficiency.

But it was a fleeting moment. I'd only imagined it was longer. His face *did* so resemble Ailill's, if Ailill had aged to appear much older. His eyes fell, and he opened the door to the baker's shop, vanishing from sight.

"Noll?"

I shook my head to clear it and found Jurij's gaze fixed on me. He nodded sideways, and I followed his gesture to find the three children absolutely still, staring at me.

"She *knows* that servant, I bet!" cried the boy.

"Maybe she *likes* him!" I had no idea how the giggly girl came up with that idea. But then I realized my cheeks were hot, and I pocketed the coppers. I looked down at the array of wooden animals, straightening them back into order.

"Thank you for the purchase." I smiled, remembering what was more important. The girl cradling her wooden cat grinned.

"Oh! That *is* cute." The other girl grabbed the cat from my customer's hands. She seemed reluctant to part with it, but she had little choice in the matter. "I want one!"

"Two coppers," I said, pointing to the sign.

"Never mind." She sighed and handed the cat back to her friend, who gingerly pet it with one finger, like it was a miniature kitten.

The boy peeked his head over the two girls' shoulders, studying the blanket and all of my wares. "They're all right," he said, clearly not impressed. His gaze wandered to the shop window above my head, and I knew he was watching the specter conduct his business in there.

Jurij leaned over and picked up the squirrel. He pretended not to notice as the girl without coppers took in the figure hungrily, and he leaned back against the wall, turning the squirrel over in his lap. "You know, when I wanted coppers as a kid, I asked around to see if anyone had any work that needed doing."

Am I really hearing him say those words directed at someone else?

The girl scuffed her foot on the ground. "Papa used to give me coppers. Now he keeps them."

I didn't want to ask what he used them for. Thinking about how things had changed in the village with so many

53

men refusing to work reminded me of that month no one remembered. When Ailill vanished—when I *made* him vanish—the whole village suffered without his purchases. If one man could make such an impact, albeit one man who spent a large amount in the village, surely dozens, if not hundreds, of men earning and spending less would, too. I grabbed the squirrel out of Jurij's hands and placed it back among the wooden animals. "Well, you earn some of your own, instead of asking your papa for them, and I may give you a discount."

That brought a smile to her face.

The boy was not so easy to appease. "You didn't tell us about the lord." His gaze was still focused on the window above me. "How come he never comes down himself? He must be monstrously ugly."

"He's not." The words were out of my mouth before I could stop myself.

I felt the eyes of all three children and Jurij bearing down on me. "She *likes* him!" whispered that girl again, although not very quietly.

"Then why won't he visit the village?" asked the boy.

"Because then children like you wouldn't have so much fun asking so many questions." Each of the kids responded with a blank stare. "He's more mysterious this way, isn't he? Who'd care about him at all if he wasn't hidden away?"

The door to the baker's shop opened, and I clamped my mouth shut. I busied myself fussing with the nearest row of animals, turning a perfectly fine display into something of a mess. The specter had one of the baker's sons pushing a cart full of bread for him. I had to scoff despite my fear of being noticed. I knew the specters didn't eat anything. What did Ailill always need so much bread for? To make people think the specters were human? I wondered why I'd never seen a room full of rotting, moldy bread, but it could have very well been on the top floor, next to the tower prison. Where he'd kept my mother. And probably Jurij, for that one day he'd stolen him from me.

I shook my head. *From Elfriede.*

The cart stopped. "Oh. It's today."

Darwyn, Baker's son. One of my friends from childhood. A rather annoying friend from childhood. Looking down and clearly expecting me to say something.

"What's today?" I asked, tucking that too-long bit of hair behind my ear.

"Your shop." He let go of the cart handle to gesture at my blanket. "In front of ours."

"Oh. Your mother said it was okay."

Darwyn nodded. "Yeah, sure. I guess we don't mind. But if I knew you'd be here, I'd have..." He stopped, putting his hand back on the cart and turning to go.

I stopped fondling my carvings and stared up at him. "You'd have what?"

"Nothing." Darwyn started pushing the cart again. It carried more bread than would feed one man, but at least it wasn't overflowing like it used to be. Maybe Ailill was trying to be a little less wasteful. But how would such thoughts even occur to him in the middle of a long, brooding day?

The specter stepped out from the shop behind Darwyn, and I *knew* this time that his eyes met mine. I looked away, flustered. It wasn't like Ailill could read minds. Just get a report of all my actions. At least I hoped he couldn't read minds. But even if he could, it didn't matter. He'd already decided I still hated him, so he wouldn't bother reading mine.

The cricketing of the cart faded, the sound drowned out by the movements of villagers going about their business on the road.

"Let's follow him!" whispered the boy.

I looked up, for a foolish moment thinking the invitation included me, the weird lone woman who'd rejected the lord and turned the whole village upside down. But the children were already lost in their own world, giggling and running down the road after Darwyn and the specter. My hand lingered on a wooden horse, thinking of the days when I led a group of boys around the village, always after the mysterious, always looking for adventure. At least, after everything, there were children now at play, children who might have forgotten one another in the days of the goddesses.

"Nothing?" echoed Jurij beside me, sometime after Darwyn had left. He snorted.

I leaned back against the wall beside him. "He probably meant he would have sent his brother."

"So he didn't have to see me?"

I studied Jurij, wondering where he came up with that idea. "Why would he care about seeing you? I was the one who always bothered him when we were kids."

Jurij let out a deep breath and shook his head. "I think everyone bothered him. To tell you the truth, I couldn't even stand the guy until he found his goddess."

I tilted my head and raised an eyebrow. "We barely saw him once he found his goddess."

Jurij shrugged. "Exactly."

I tsked. "So there's something to be said for goddesses after all?"

The laugh I heard from beside me couldn't have been more contemptuous if it had been Ailill's. "And what would that be?"

Jurij and I looked up. Darwyn had returned, the squeaky cart no longer with him to give us a hint of his approaching. I swallowed, wondering how much he'd heard. Not that I'd said anything beyond what he might be expecting. But if there was one thing I didn't miss from the days before my friends had found their goddesses, it was attempting to break up fights between them. *Even if I caused more than a few of them myself.*

"They gave you guys some sense of direction." An idea popped into my head as my gaze drifted between

Darwyn and Jurij. "Say, Darwyn, your brother Sindri, he works in the quarry?"

I didn't have to look at Jurij to feel his accusing glare from beside me, but I purposefully ignored it. "Yeah?" Darwyn said after a moment's pause, clearly not following why I'd asked to begin with.

My eyes traveled to the baker's shop door. "And your mother could use some help these days, right? Since your father..." I cut myself short.

"Moved in with one of the farmer women. Sure. Lots of people doing strange things like that these days." Darwyn tried to state that fact as if it didn't matter, but his voice cracked as he did. He wiped his nose with one finger and crouched beside us, his gaze drifting quickly over my wooden figures and back again. "You looking for work, Noll? The shop, maybe, but I don't know if you have the heft for quarry work."

"I'm set with my woodworking, thank you." I nudged Jurij and looked at him for the first time since I started the conversation. His face seemed dejected, and he wouldn't return my gaze. "But Jurij needs something to do. And maybe it's time he asked some of his *friends* for help."

The look that Jurij gave me made me wonder if I'd finally added him to the list of people who once cared about me but didn't anymore.

Chapter Seven

"AGAIN? WE JUST ATE WITH them last week." Jurij wiped the sweat off his brow with his forearm and placed the pickaxe in its corner by the door. His scarred eyelid drooped heavily. "And where are we going to fit them all?" He shook his head. "Scratch that. You guys can eat here. I'll go to Elweard's with Sindri."

"Ha," I said, pulling open the cupboard and gripping the picnic basket handle on which I'd carved some flowers and thorns. "But is Sindri eating at the tavern? Why don't you invite him, too?"

Jurij regarded me as if I'd just asked him to marry his mother. But I supposed in this strange new life we'd been sharing for about two weeks, everything I asked of him would seem odd and new. I broke the silence. "Tell him he can bring any of his brothers, too."

Jurij glanced around the cottage, his eyes resting on the pork roasting in the fire. "You bought a pig."

I smiled and put my hands on my hips. "I bought a pig." My toys had been selling pretty well as of late—probably because they offered children in the midst of family turmoil a little comfort. Even fathers—or especially fathers—were buying them, despite the fact that they were the ones causing the turmoil in the first place. I wondered if they felt a little better distracting their children with baubles before they went off to the tavern. In any case, I had a sizeable stash of coins now, and it wasn't like I had anything else to save up for. The villagers needed people to spend more, so I wanted to lead by example.

"You knew we were having guests, and you didn't feel fit to tell me until I got home from the quarry." He scowled. "From a long, long day at the quarry."

I skirted the table and put my hands on Jurij's back, twisting him gently and guiding him to the door. "And a big feast will prove just the thing to make you feel better."

"Noll, you invited my parents. My brother. Nissa. *My aunt.*"

I smiled, feeling the sickening sweetness I poured into each muscle responsible for the movement. "Just be glad I didn't invite my family, too." I'd considered it. But since the Tailors had informed Elfriede that her former husband was safe and sound and living exactly where her own sister had sworn he'd never be found, I'd since realized they'd never reunite if Elfriede knew I was involved. "Now, go on. Invite our friends." I opened the cottage door.

"Yes, ma'am," mumbled Jurij. "Are you sure you didn't get a lot of practice being a goddess?"

"What was that?"

"Never mind." Jurij stepped onto the dirt leading to the road between the village and the quarry. "*Friends* is probably the wrong word anyway," he muttered.

He headed down the road toward the mass of men going home from the quarry. My gaze turned to the horizon. *Good. No rain.* The fire popped behind me. "Right. The pig." I rotated the animal on the spit, my mind racing with all of the preparations left to be done.

ຖ ຖ ຖ

"I like this one." Nissa probably meant it, but the extent of her enthusiasm made the comment seem about as genuine as Jurij's love for hard labor. She stroked the wooden rabbit in her lap like it was a live pet. It took a moment of studying her in the flicker of firelight to remember that Luuk had often worn a bunny mask, a hand-me-down from his brother.

I finished chewing my portion of meat. "You can have it." I nudged her. "No charge."

Nissa shook her head, and then, remembering herself, smiled ever so slightly at me. She placed the rabbit gently back into the basket I'd brought outside in order to show everyone gathered around the fire the new additions to my wares. "Let a child have it," she said quietly, failing to recognize that being thirteen hardly made her an adult. She observed the fire, and I noticed a hardness in her heart, maybe even harder than the hardness I'd felt at her age, when I saw the last of my friends leave me behind for my sister. Sure, Jurij had still been my friend, thanks to an unintended command from his goddess, but it wasn't the same. The secret hope I'd been harboring, that Jurij might love me when we grew older, was gone when I was Nissa's age. The way Nissa's eyes kept drifting to Luuk across the fire made me think she felt just as hopeless.

I'm sorry, Nissa. But you don't want a love like that anyway. I tossed the bone onto the fire. *It wasn't real. It didn't last.*

"Nice pig." For a moment, I thought Siofra might be complimenting the wooden pig I'd begun carving before they'd all arrived for dinner, but the block was still too formless for anyone to identify. Siofra was nodding at the tree stump on which I'd placed the roasted pig slices on a large platter and wiping her mouth with a scrap of cloth I'd gotten from the Tailors to serve as a napkin. "Good cut. Good buy. Good cooking."

I tucked the stray bit of hair behind my ear, still not used to compliments from the woman I'd grown up thinking was so surly. "Thanks."

Siofra held her plate out to Master Tailor beside her. "Coll, put another slice on my plate?" It wasn't a command exactly. But she'd already turned her attention to her mug, not even regarding the plate, which she must have assumed Master Tailor would take from her. It fell to the ground with a thunk.

Master Tailor stared at Siofra as he lifted his fork to his mouth and chewed slowly. You could practically hear every movement of his jaw between the crackling of the fire.

Siofra's face darkened as she snatched the plate. "Of course. I can do it myself," she said quietly. "I didn't mean anything by it."

As she stood to refill her plate herself, I cleared my throat, my gaze drifting to the large gaps between us I'd left for Jurij, Sindri, and whatever other Baker boy felt like joining us. My hand dug into Bow's fur. I'd been looking forward to seeing the look on Jurij's face when he saw our surprise canine guest, but now I wanted to grab him by the shoulders and shake him until the whiny, selfish man who'd moved in with me was replaced by the kind and caring boy who'd never spared a thought for himself.

But you were the one who felt it only right to give men their freedom.

"I like this ale," said Master Tailor, taking a swig from the mug I'd served Alvilda's and Siofra's gift in. "Alvilda, did you get this from Vena?"

Alvilda slammed her plate so hard on the ground beside her, I thought for a minute I'd served her meal on glass instead of wood. "All right. We've waited long enough." She bolted upright. "I'm going to search the entire village, I'm going to knock down doors, I'm going to find that lazy, ungrateful—"

"Alvilda!" Both Siofra and her former husband spoke the name at once, one pleading, even angry, the other so surprised, it was a wonder he was able to keep a grip on his mug.

Alvilda whipped around, first to face her wife and then to face her brother. She didn't seem to notice Luuk slinking down beside her as if hoping he could vanish entirely into the ground.

"No. This is ridiculous. I thought last week, when he dined at our house, that his plan to join the quarry workers would snap some sense into him, but that was just at Noll's urging, wasn't it? Leaving this entire meal to Noll, continuing to encroach upon her hospitality."

Despite my own irritation at the man who was the topic of her tirade, I started to feel protective, even defensive in the face of Alvilda's overreaction. "He hasn't been encroaching. He's been going to work every day."

Alvilda's boiling hot gaze fell on me. "Don't tell me he's been doing the minimum of what's expected of him like it's some accomplishment."

"It *is* an accomplishment." I jumped to my feet, staring her down across the fire. "Alvilda, don't you think you're being too hard on him? You didn't say a word against him for doing nothing with his days before the curse broke."

Alvilda thrust her arms across her chest. "Things are different."

"Things *are* different. You can't just expect men to pick up their lives like nothing's changed." My gaze fell on Master Tailor and Luuk. "Tell her," I said, as if my experiences put me in the position of acting like some translator between men and women. "Tell her things are different."

Siofra set her plate on the ground. "She knows that, Noll. She just wants what's best for our sons."

"*Our* sons?" The clatter of the plate on the ground beside me was enough to rival a dozen glass plates smashing. Master Tailor stood, his finger pointed at Alvilda. I'd never seen the man so angry. Granted, I'd never seen his face before the curse had broken, but I never imagined the features behind the owl mask he so often wore could contort so wildly. "Jurij and Luuk are *my* sons. Mine and Siofra's." He patted his chest with his fist. "And the two of you might have tried to forget I existed all of those years—"

Siofra gasped, standing. "We never!"

Alvilda put a hand out to stop her from crossing around the fire to get nearer to him.

"You *always*." Master Tailor's voice grew so deep and troubled, Bow woke from her nap emitting a low growl. Master Tailor paused, the lump on his throat shaking visibly as he swallowed. "It was always the two of you, from the start. I had my uses, but I was nothing to you."

"That's not true." I'd never heard Siofra's voice so unsure.

"No, it *is* true." Master Tailor shook his head. "I may have been too stupid to be hurt by it then, but it hurts thinking about it now." He sighed, his eyes darting between Alvilda and Siofra. Siofra couldn't meet his gaze, but Alvilda stared, daring him to say more. Master Tailor waved a defeated hand, dismissing them. "I don't mean I want Siofra back. I didn't have a choice to love her, you know." He tapped his fingers across his forehead as he paced back and forth before the fire. "But I can remember things. My *own sister*, Siofra, like I wanted to know what was going on between you. Like I was nothing but a messenger without a brain. But I remember what you had me say to her."

I clapped my hands together. "Okay, Nissa, why don't you help me clean up?" I looked across the fire. "Luuk?"

Luuk practically jumped up but stopped himself, his eyes wandering between Nissa, his mother and aunt, and his father, clearly trying to figure out who was least likely to cause him discomfort. And he wasn't having an easy time deciding.

Master Tailor seemed to notice the pause, and his attention drifted between Luuk and Nissa. He grabbed Luuk by the arm and pulled him upright. "No, Luuk's had enough of that. We're leaving." He looked at me. "Thank you for the dinner, Noll. It was great. Thank you for opening your home to Jurij, who is *a grown man* and can do as he damn well pleases." His extra emphasis was clearly not meant for me. "Tell him he can come home to me if he gets tired of the quarry." He looked back at Alvilda and Siofra. "Or of women in general."

I decided to let that last comment slide, given the situation, but some women couldn't.

"Coll!" Some of Siofra's usual stubbornness came through.

"No, let him go." Alvilda slipped an arm around Siofra and pulled her to her chest, roughly, more boldly than I'd ever seen her do before. "Let the man whine and see what good it does when the work still needs doing. Let him see that it's not so easy to think for himself and take on responsibility when someone isn't commanding him."

"So, Nissa," I spoke quietly, turning to see how the poor girl was handling it. She was clinging to Bow and trying to peer around my legs at the path Master Tailor and Luuk were cutting through the grasses, the shortcut that would take them to the Tailor Shop at the edge of the village.

"Oh, for—" Alvilda peered at the northern road to the village, tossing a hand in the air and then cradling her forehead.

Four figures ambled toward us, still some distance away. They were dancing. No, they stumbled every few steps, their arms swinging wildly up and down, their hands clutching mugs. In the quiet, all I heard was the crackling of the fire, Bow's heavy snoring, and the unskilled warbling of the four men.

Alvilda moved around the fire to grab Nissa by the forearm, much as her brother had done to Luuk a moment beforehand. She looked at me. "Thank you for the dinner, Noll. It was great." *Wow, two barely-contained-rage-filled compliments for my cooking.* She peered over her shoulder. "Siofra?"

Siofra looked down the path, worry hidden behind the deep creases in her forehead. "He's drunk."

"He's a fool. And we'll have no part of it." Alvilda tugged Nissa along after her, and Siofra shuffled behind. "Tell him he can come home to us if he gets tired of acting like an idiot," Alvilda called to me over her shoulder. "Or like a man in general."

The three of them passed right by the dancing group, not even turning their heads to greet them.

Chapter Eight

THE YOUNG MAN I WASN'T too familiar with—the one with lips that seemed permanently puckered— poked Sindri in the chest, again and again. "Have I told you about my wife's mornings?" He had his arm around Sindri and was practically dragging him to the ground beside the fire.

"Former—*former* wives," slurred Sindri. His eyes were glazed, his attention focused on the ground.

"Former," repeated puckered-lips. "Every morning, she tooled me—"

"*Told*," interrupted Jurij beside him. He turned to Darwyn and started sniggering.

"Told me, Tayton, make the breakfast. Tayton, clean the house. Tayton, it's cold, chop more wool for the fire."

Darwyn and Jurij burst into laughter. "Wood!" shouted Darwyn.

"Wood." Tayton didn't seem to care that he couldn't get through a sentence without being corrected. He poked Sindri again and flailed his hand around. "Then I had to work in the quarry. And she just lay there, sleeping 'til lunchtime." He reached forward for the mug he'd set down on the ground beside him, completely oblivious to the fact that Sindri was now about a nose's length from the ground beneath Tayton's arm. Tayton let Sindri go and sat back up, taking a swig from his mug. He wiped his mouth. "And *I* had to go home. Make her lunch." He made a spitting sound and widened his eyes, flicking his free hand before his face. "Whatta bibch."

"*Bitch*," said Jurij and Darwyn as one, their arms tight across their abdomens to keep themselves from falling over.

My fingers clutched Bow's fur as I regarded my new set of dinner guests around the fire, not a one of them interested in eating. Bow's head raised at the sound of Sindri's snoring. The baker's son lay there, face down, on the blanket where Tayton had dropped him. He was uncomfortably close to the fire.

I patted Bow to calm her and made my way toward Sindri to pull him back.

"Them's my wife's mornings. A whole lot of nothing." Tayton peered over the top of his mug at me as I rolled Sindri over.

Sindri's eyelids flittered open. "Wha? No, Marden, I'm too tired." He curled his legs against his abdomen and reached a hand out to grab my ankle, snuggling against my feet.

Tayton chuckled and spit back into his mug, swinging it side to side. "He thinks you're his wife."

"*Farmer* wife!" sang Darwyn and Jurij at once—a correction in need of correction—and they found them to be the funniest words ever spoken.

I ignored the cackling and reached down to peel Sindri's fingers from my leg. They proved harder to unfurl than expected, and I hesitated, concerned I might hurt him. In the end, I gave up and used my full strength to tear them away.

Tayton found the sight amusing, but his laughter suddenly stopped. "Hey! I know you."

I looked up only briefly to meet Tayton's eyes and turned back to the task at hand, grabbing Sindri by the upper arms and dragging him back a safe distance from the fire.

"'Course you know her, genius." Darwyn swayed a little where he sat. "She's Noll. Lord's goddess."

"No." Jurij slapped at Darwyn's shoulder lamely. "No goddess."

Darwyn and Jurij exchanged a glance, and they both grinned. *"Farmer goddess."* They snickered. I couldn't guess if they knew what they were saying or not.

Tayton shook his head and brought his mug to his lips. "No. I know that. I know her 'fore that." He stared inside the mug with one eye open and one eye shut, tossing it onto the ground when he found nothing left in there.

I dropped Sindri and exhaled, wiping my brow with my arm. The fire was hot, which made dragging his heft all the more exhausting. I'd managed to get him rolled onto his back, but a terrible thought squeezed at my throat, an image of my father after one of his visits to Vena's, coughing and choking in his sleep.

"The elf queen!" Darwyn and Jurij shouted my *farmer* title, laughing as the sound echoed into the evening sky. They picked up forgotten mugs and toasted them into the air. "To our queen!" They clinked them together and choked down the contents, stopping to giggle between breaths.

Holding Sindri on his side, I grabbed the picnic basket full of rolls I'd brought out for the half-finished feast. I slid it against his back for support. He kept on snoring.

Tayton leaned over to grab his fallen mug, rolling it farther out of reach with his fingertips. At last he grabbed it and lifted it into the air for the "toast," too late, completely forgetting it was empty as he tried to slurp it again. He seemed puzzled as he tore the mug from his lips. "What's the elf queen?"

Darwyn and Jurij found the question hilarious, just like everything else that evening. I stood with a sigh, my hands on my hips. "All right, enough. I guess you can all sleep here tonight." *As long as I don't have to drag all four of them inside by their arms.* I looked at the cottage, calculating how tired I'd get dragging just Sindri over there. It wasn't too cold out. Maybe I could just toss some blankets over the lot of them and put out the fire so none of the idiots rolled into it.

"That's it!" Tayton dropped the mug back onto the ground. This time it rolled until it knocked against Sindri's fingers, but he barely stirred, murmuring something about being tired before drifting back into snoring. "You're the crone!"

Darwyn and Jurij's laughter was not something that should have surprised me, but it made my cheeks burn nonetheless.

"The little one," Tayton added, pointing at me. "The pretty one."

I tore my eyes from him and felt my cheeks grow even hotter. This bumbling drunk's compliment made me about as happy as any of his insults, and I could do without the leering that accompanied it.

I focused instead on those big, puffy lips, reminiscent of a mask I once saw. "Fish Face!"

Cue Jurij and Darwyn, who'd probably never run out of laughter. Tayton cocked his head and studied me, the words slow to reach him. "Fish?"

I pointed to my own face. "Your mask. The day of Elfriede and Jurij's..." My eyes darted to Jurij, but his head was lilting back and forth, not registering what I'd been about to say. "The day Ingrith died."

Tayton laughed, not an entirely appropriate reaction to the death of an old woman, even if he, like the rest of the village, couldn't have cared less about her. He waved his finger at me. "You were so nasty. So nasty." He started slinking backward, losing balance. "She was worse, but you called me unloved. Pointed me to the commune."

I crossed my arms. "You called *me* unloved."

His back slammed against the ground so suddenly I thought I felt the ground shake. I took a step closer to make sure he hadn't hit his head, but he was resting, eyes closed, a smooth rise and fall to his chest. His eyelids fluttered, his puckered lips parted, murmuring, "Unloved." The firelight glistened on a tear that streaked down his cheek.

I swallowed and looked away. Darwyn leaned against Jurij, snoring louder than his brother still curled at my feet. Jurij's eyes were open but glazed. The kind of glazed Father got after too many drinks. I could almost see the fire dancing in his eyes like it once did, could almost see the ghost of who he used to be in the way he stared. I wasn't so sure happy drinking was anything more than painful drinking under the mask of laughter. I wasn't so sure I could stand to watch Jurij wither away like Father had, not when he had so much to live for.

I turned the cuff of one of my sleeves and rolled it up to my forearm. *Okay. I don't need to get Elfriede and Jurij back together. It's probably best for both of them this way.*

I nodded to myself, watching Jurij's eyes flitter. *Screw love. These are my friends. Friends who need me—and each other. Friends who need to learn a thing or two about their own self-worth.*

I picked up the bucket of water I'd kept beside the fire, then watched the flames burn for just a little while longer, relishing its choking cries as it flickered away to its death. The reflection of the flames vanished from Jurij's dark irises before he closed his eyes and fell asleep.

Chapter Nine

POKING AND SHOUTING DIDN'T WORK. I tried to think of how we used to get Father up after Mother supposedly "died," but Elfriede and I just let him be most of the day. After all, what was he expected to do after his goddess was gone? To tell the truth, Elfriede and I kept thinking we'd wake up one day and he'd be gone, too, reduced to just an empty pile of clothes. Jostling him seemed like tempting fate.

Standing over the four sleeping forms, I weighed my options. Jurij was the only one I really had any business waking, even if the other three did fall asleep right outside my cabin. I dragged my bucket from the well, its contents sloshing over the rim.

"Holy goddess!" Jurij sat up so quickly, he nearly toppled over. His hand ran over his face, wiping off the water droplets.

I dropped the bucket on the ground beside him, letting it clang loudly, but it only stirred the slightest of groans from Darwyn. "I'd say you were late for the quarry. Or the bakery. And you are. But I thought today we might do something different anyway."

Jurij guided his palm through his short dark hair, shaking the water out and staring up at me. "We?"

"Yes, *we*. Or did you and your inebriated friends plan to spend the rest of your days drinking?"

Jurij shook his head and stared. "I don't remember you being this bossy."

As if on cue, Darwyn chuckled softly, but he gave no other sign of consciousness.

I crouched beside Jurij. "I was *always* this bossy." I was done making decisions for others, but I could still give them a push in the right direction. I nudged Jurij with my shoulder. "*You*, on the other hand, never used to put up such a fight."

Jurij cradled his forehead, shielding his eyes from the sunlight. "Noll, it's too early for this."

I stood, grabbing the bucket handle. "It's almost lunch time." I glanced between Darwyn, Sindri, and Tayton, choosing my next victim for after a quick trip to the well.

Jurij groaned. "Can you speak a little quieter?"

"You totally messed up my dinner." I glared at him until he opened his eyes. "You owe me." He grabbed my extended hand, and I strained to help him stand. "And you're going to make it up to me today." I shoved the bucket handle into his unsuspecting hand.

ŋ ŋ ŋ

It was warm enough that the four soaking boys—*men*—behind me were practically dried from the air just half an hour later, but you'd think that they were permanently soaked through to the bone from the way they still carried on about it.

"So let me get this straight." I didn't have to look behind me to recognize the sniveling voice of Tayton. "You four used to hang out in the livestock fields. Pretending sheep were monsters. And hitting them with sticks."

"We didn't actually hit them with sticks," I corrected. "That'd be cruel."

"No," snorted Darwyn. "We'd just give the poor things heart attacks by chasing them. Screaming and swinging until they started running."

"And then a few moments later, the farmers down the hill would start screaming and swinging their fists at us until *we* started running," added Sindri.

"Sounds fun." Tayton sounded entirely unconvinced.

"It wasn't just us four." Jurij sounded like he hoped he was making a rational argument to defend us. "Noll led a bunch of boys around the village back then."

Tayton scoffed. "Glad I was too old by then to be under her spell. Like I'd need to be bossed around by *two* women in my lifetime."

I twirled around and clapped my hands together. "We didn't just scare sheep. There's a pond south of the village."

Tayton raised an eyebrow. "You mean the livestock's watering hole."

I chewed my lip, biting back irritation. "Yes. Some of the boys would swim on a warm day. Like today."

"And you're suggesting we do that today?" Tayton pinched his damp jerkin with two fingers and pulled it away from his chest. "Because I'm not already soaked through."

I shrugged and turned back around, cutting through the grass east of the village and walking southward. "You can just sit beside the pond whining if that's more appealing."

"Considering our meat drinks out of that water, it probably is."

I ignored that comment. We'd reached the eastern path, and to my left I could just make out my cottage—my *family's* cottage—at the edge of the woods. Jurij brushed past me without pausing, leading the way southward. He didn't even glance at his father's home, let alone the one he'd shared with his former wife.

73

"Here, girl!" When Jurij turned his head, it was only to beckon Bow from the back of the group, where she'd stopped to sniff the familiar path between her two previous homes.

Bow barked and obeyed immediately, trotting up beside her master and sticking her nose under his hand.

Darwyn laughed. "Looks like *someone's* still under a curse."

"She's a girl," said Jurij, without a hint of teasing in his voice.

"Thus the 'here, *girl*,'" added Sindri.

Jurij paused, confusing Bow, who stopped a few yards ahead of him, whipping her head back to figure out why he'd stopped. "Why weren't animals affected?" asked Jurij. "Why only us?"

Jurij directed the question not at the group, but at me. I swallowed and kept walking.

"Why is it over now? Why anything, Jurij?" Darwyn clapped him on the shoulder. I quickened my steps, eager to put a few more yards between us.

"... probably knows." It was muted, but there was no mistaking Jurij trying to whisper something behind me.

We traveled the rest of the way in silence. When we reached the top of the final hill, I peered down at the sheep grazing amongst the cows, the lilies gone from this field, probably eradicated by endless chewing. Bow didn't hesitate; she barked and charged down the hill.

"Bow! Stop!" Jurij ran past, a look of panic scrunching up his face.

Darwyn and Sindri followed, their faces contorted in laughter.

"Was this part of the game, back when you were smacking sheep with sticks?" Tayton appeared beside me, his hands tucked in his pockets. I nodded, looking up to take in the almost-smile he was fighting to keep from me.

The golden streak plowed toward the herd with three figures jogging after her, Jurij's arms flailing.

74

"Sometimes. I'd forgotten she did that. We didn't always take her along."

Tayton seemed content to watch rather than participate. He nodded as Bow went one way, then zigzagged another, herding sheep and cows to block the men from reaching her. "Until yesterday, the dog was with Jurij's..." He paused, leaving the rest of the sentence unsaid.

"His wife. *Former* wife. My sister."

"I figured." Tayton scratched his chin. "He was complaining about missing her at the quarry the other day. I didn't ask, but I figured there was only one reason why he couldn't get her back."

Jurij managed to dodge a hopping sheep a few feet behind Bow. He held out his hands and took a small step forward. Bow stopped and sat upright, her tongue lolling.

"His parents got the dog back from my sister." I couldn't help but smile as Jurij lunged forward and Bow went flying in the opposite direction. Darwyn and Sindri caught up just in time to keep him from falling. "Since he was too scared to ask for her back himself."

I could feel Tayton's eyes boring into me. "He's not equipped to handle this, Noll. None of us are." He sighed. "I don't know how to explain it, but moving on, figuring out how to keep going forward, it's not simple. I don't know what I want for dinner. I don't know how to decide on what clothes to wear or what shoes to put on in the morning. I don't know when I should buy things or when I'm supposed to go to bed. I've forgotten how to choose."

"Tayton, I'm sorry you guys—"

"I know you are, Noll." He gestured at the sheep, the dog, and the three men running wildly after them. "I know this little trip to the sheep must be your way of distracting us. It's different for you, isn't it?"

I studied Tayton quizzically. "I know, since I'm a woman, that I never really felt what you all felt."

Tayton shook his head. "No, I mean... you're different from the other women." His eyes widened, and I followed his gaze to see Jurij had flung himself around Bow's torso and was rolling with her in the grass. He jumped up, unscathed, rubbing Bow's belly hard. I was so lost in the moment, so full of joy at seeing Jurij smile so freely, that it startled me when Tayton began speaking again. "Maybe it doesn't bother you as much. You don't have to see your former husband. And you never loved him."

"He wasn't my husband," I snapped. I lifted my skirt, some age-old instruction not to get my hem too dirty drilled into my mind, and started walking toward the flock. I should have said more—I *wanted* to say more—but I wasn't in the mood to discuss the details of my heart with Fish Face, whom I hardly even knew.

After half a minute, Tayton jogged down the hill beside me. "I'm sorry if I—"

"Never mind." I swallowed and tried to smile. "Let's just enjoy today, okay?" I let go of my skirt and ran, stumbling down the rest of the hill, frightening the nearest sheep who'd only just recently come to a rest.

Sindri's and Darwyn's brows sparkled with sweat in the brightness of the sun, and Darwyn was bent forward, clutching his thighs for support. "This... was a lot easier... as a kid," he sputtered between breaths.

Sindri patted Darwyn's back. "Life was much easier, little brother." He looked up, cupped his hands around his lips, and shouted, "Woo!" for no reason whatsoever.

The nearest sheep was probably four house lengths away by now, but it likely felt much too close to this noisy band of too-old warriors. It bleated in protest and skipped a few steps farther. Everyone's eyes met, one after the other, and we all laughed. My eyes held Jurij's for a beat longer, until I had to look away. I collapsed onto the ground beside him, rubbing Bow's belly as she rolled over.

I caught Jurij's eyes again for just a moment. Long enough to remember the feeling I used to get when I imagined the eyes behind his mask, or when I first saw the flames that danced there.

"Noll, do you remember—" His head turned, his attention drawn behind me. Bow flipped over, her head cocked. A dog's bark slipped into the silence between us.

"Uh-oh." Darwyn shielded his face from the sun with his palm. "Tell me that's not some farmer's dog, come to chase us away from his sheep."

Bow jumped to her feet and barked back.

Sindri smirked. "What would a journey to the livestock fields be without being told to go away?"

"I was just hoping we could spend more than a minute here before it came to that," Darwyn replied.

Tayton craned his neck forward, as if the additional inch it gave him would make the barking dog coming over the top of the hill easier to see. "That's no sheepdog, it's—"

Bow barked and bolted, sending the sheep scattering once more. She whipped past one bleating sheep without so much as halting to round the bend, ruffling the sheep's wool with her tail.

Tayton shrugged. "I was gonna say it was a gold dog, like Bow, but I guess she figured that much out for herself."

Jurij stiffened on the grass beside me, his arm bending slightly to lower himself further down among the blades. I crawled up to get a better look at the commotion.

"The dog's with someone," said Tayton, his hands around his eyes to get a better look. "Two people."

Maybe it's Mother and Father. Or at least, if it's her, she's with Mother or Father. Might be a bit less awkward.

Sindri laughed so loud, I jumped. "It's Jaron!" He slapped Darwyn on the back, and they both followed after Bow. Tayton lifted a foot and then paused, looking at me and Jurij, who was now completely flat against the ground. "Did I miss something?"

I felt my cheeks crack as I forced a smile. "No. It's nothing. Jaron. I haven't seen him in a while. It'll be good to say hello. I just didn't know he'd gotten a dog."

"Ha, that man!" Tayton's attention was drawn back

to the hill. "A different lady on his arm every time I see him!" He jogged after Sindri and Darwyn.

My mouth dried, and a surge of panic hit my stomach. *Mother?*

"It's Elfriede," spoke the grass at my feet, Jurij's head not so much as lifting up to confirm for certain.

Chapter Ten

"NOW, THE BLACK ONES, THEIR wool is harder to dye, so it doesn't go for as much." Jaron pointed at one of the black sheep with a fried leg of lamb, probably not realizing the irony. Elfriede had cooked all of the food Jaron pulled out of Father's carved picnic basket, I was sure of it. Jaron took a bite and gave himself half a minute to chew. "But the black ones have their uses."

"I can see that." Sindri laughed, staring at the voracious way Jaron attacked the leg of lamb. For a little while, it felt good to see him eating. He never ate much in the commune. True, I hadn't seen his face in those days, but he was a friend of sorts. And I could tell he was skinny—too skinny. He'd filled out rather nicely since, for an older man.

I blushed, my gaze accidentally catching Elfriede's as I looked away. *I can't exactly fault her for dating a man almost twenty years older.* I gripped a handful of grass, ripping it free of the dirt with such force, the roots popped out. The lord wasn't *my* man. But he was a thousand years old, thanks to me.

Darwyn extended his chin toward the towering black castle some distance behind me. I still always made a point of sitting with my back toward the east. Old habits. "He'll take black wool, won't he?" Darwyn posed the question to Jurij specifically.

Jurij shrugged, his expression the same stony look he had the moment Jaron and Elfriede joined us. He rubbed his hand over Arrow's head lazily. "Out of the tailoring business," he muttered under his breath.

Like he'd have forgotten the answer to that question just because he hadn't helped his mother and father for a few weeks. I let the blades of grass tumble from my fingers.

Jaron put down the remains of his lamb leg, scouring the picnic basket. "You're sure you're not hungry?" he asked. "We may not have enough for seven, but Friede packed plenty of rolls. She made them herself, and they're some of the best I've ever—"

"You work with livestock now?" I asked. The grass left a greenish stain on my palm that I rubbed with my fingers. "Did you do that before? Uh, that is..." I stopped, suddenly aware of Elfriede's pale eyes on my face.

Jaron didn't seem to mind. He laughed as he tossed a roll at Sindri, who caught it and started eating as if he wasn't sitting in a circle fraught with unspoken tension.

"I can barely remember what I did, Noll." Jaron shrugged. "Seriously. Maybe if I asked someone who knew me then. Life in the commune is pretty much all a useless blur in my mind. For the most part. There are a few things I remember, but..." He tossed another roll, this one to Darwyn, who fumbled but caught it before it fell on the ground. Too bad for Arrow, who seemed to be watching with interest.

"What about your parents?" Darwyn asked, too curious to start eating.

"Gone. Probably." Jaron passed a roll to Tayton and offered one to me. "Noll?"

I shook my head. "No, thank you."

Elfriede stopped glaring at me and dug into the basket, unwrapping a wedge of cheese she didn't offer to share with anyone. Jaron bit into the roll, pointedly forgetting Jurij.

Sindri spoke with his mouth still half full of bread.

"What do you mean *probably*?"

Jaron cocked his head, as if Sindri was the one making the strange statement. "They were farmers, I think. I forget which kind. I didn't get any social calls from them when I wound up in the commune. I kind of forgot what they looked like after all that bleakness."

Tayton chewed his roll slowly. "But surely they would remember you? If your father didn't care, then your mother?"

I flinched with guilt at the idea that a man could be so enamored with his goddess he barely cared about his own children. *It's not always true. Remember Master Tailor. Your own father. Sort of.*

Jaron raised a hand to stop him. "I really couldn't tell you." He popped the rest of the roll into his mouth and waited to finish chewing. "Maybe she did visit me early on. Maybe she commanded my father to do so, too. I wouldn't have been able to focus on anyone in the commune, especially not with *her* living so close."

Without being asked, Elfriede uncorked the bottle she'd carried along with the basket and filled Jaron's wooden cup with ale. There were no cups for the rest of us. They'd clearly planned a picnic for two.

"Thank you, dear," said Jaron as he took the mug from her. The "dear" sent a shiver down my spine, and Elfriede seemed to notice. She smiled at me—actually *smiled*—perversely as she placed the bottle back on the grass beside her. *Bet you didn't know that Mother used to love that same man beside you, did you?* I smiled back at her. I felt dirty doing it. But still. Of all the men she could have used to taunt Jurij and show she was moving on, why Jaron? Why a man so much older, someone who spent years pining for Jurij's aunt? Unless that was exactly why. Someone who'd moved on from Jurij's family, just as she would. Someone older because she used to be embarrassed her man was a little younger.

I grabbed another handful of grass. Not *her* man any

longer.

Jaron nudged Tayton with his elbow before taking a sip from his mug. "So why is it the one time I see you young men at the tavern, you get so drunk you can hardly stand straight?" He leaned his head back and swallowed the rest of his mug's contents. "You scared all the young ladies away. Not a great impression, if you're looking for companions."

Elfriede's eyes widened, and her head whipped immediately toward Jurij, but Jurij didn't so much as flinch. He continued his slow, methodical stroking of Arrow's head, his focus on the grass in front of him.

Tayton stuffed the rest of his roll into his mouth. "Who faid we were wooking for wommm?"

"No one *said* anything." Jaron extended his mug out to Elfriede, who uncorked the bottle and poured more without a word. Jaron had had little experience serving a goddess himself, so he might not have thought anything of it, but it still felt strange to see a woman serve a man. The liquid sloshed as Elfriede's eyes darted back to Jurij every few seconds. Jaron pulled the mug back to his chest, not seeming to notice that Elfriede was still pouring. "Thank you, dear." He turned back to Tayton. "But a man knows. You're all young, hardly with your goddesses before—well, *before*." He took a sip as Elfriede hastily corked the bottle, her eyes darting to the wasted liquid on the ground. Knowing her, she was probably considering ripping off her apron and sponging the spill, even though it was on the dirt and grass. "Love is so different without being forced into it, lads. It's fun."

"I wouldn't have guessed that, from your behavior." Darwyn's words were coated in sarcasm, and he and Sindri both burst into muffled giggles as they probably imagined Jaron seen each night in town with some different woman on his arm. I wondered if this was Elfriede's first chance to be so honored, and if so, what were the chances of the two of them deciding on a picnic the same day I decided to take the guys out for a day of relaxing in the fields.

Jaron was undeterred. If anything, he seemed flattered as he took a sip from his mug. "Women are beautiful, lads, kind and lovely, if you let them be. If you can just put everything else behind you—"

"I think we've had enough of women." It was the first thing Jurij had said in ages, and everyone in the circle stopped to stare at him. "At least *I* have."

Jaron set his mug down on the ground beside the basket. "And that explains why the first place you ran to after the lord's decree was into the arms of his own lovely goddess." He raised his eyebrows at me.

I swallowed and focused on the grass in my hand, squeezing the blades so hard they bled wet green juice into my palm.

"I didn't *run into* Noll's arms."

"Really? Could have fooled me, and half the village while you were at it." Jaron's hands were intertwined, his weight against his elbow as he leaned a little too casually against the grass. "I'm surprised the black carriage doesn't ride up to the door of that shack the two of you share and give you another puffed eye to go with the first one."

"Jaron!" I dropped the blades of grass, and some of them stuck to the wetness on my hand. I'd forgotten Jaron, a shade of the man sitting before me, had been there to witness that debacle.

Darwyn gasped. "A bit harsh, my good man. Jurij is just as much a victim as any of us."

Jaron stared at the ground. "If you count breaking not one but two sisters' hearts over the course of his young life, then fine."

It wasn't like that, I wanted to say. If Jaron thought my time at the commune was because of Jurij, he was mistaken. I looked between him and Elfriede for any sign of shame at what he'd just said, but I found none. Her eyes were on the ground, as if pretending we weren't there would somehow make it a reality.

Jurij stood up, walking past me with both Bow and

Arrow trailing after him. Jurij's lips trembled into a semblance of a smile. He rubbed behind Arrow's ears. "Stay, boy. Just your mama and me are going."

"Take him, too."

Elfriede hadn't said a word since she came down the hill. It had been so long since I'd heard that delicate voice, and it'd been even longer since I heard it approaching anything near composed and refined.

It was enough to finally get Jurij to look at her.

She didn't return the favor. "Take the dog," she said, her nose scrunched up and her gaze locked on Jurij's knees. "He's too much work. And he was just something from *you* anyway."

Jurij scoffed. Then he did something really strange. He bowed toward Elfriede. "Goddess forbid you have *too much work* to do by yourself, Elfriede. Fine. *Thank you.* He was the last thing I regretted leaving behind." He turned on his heel and pushed past Tayton and Jaron, weaving through sheep, with Bow at his heels. "Here, boy!" he called, turning back just once to wave Arrow toward him.

Jumping to my feet, my cheeks burning with anger, I opened my mouth to say something, then snapped it shut. Elfriede's lips trembled, and a glossy shine enveloped her eyes.

Chapter Eleven

I COULD HARDLY MAKE OUT his silhouette in the darkness beside me. The fire long extinguished, the two of us settling in earlier and earlier each night. "To sleep," I'd said. "Exhausted," he'd told me. Since encountering Jaron and Elfriede at the livestock fields, Jurij had done nothing but work and sleep, eat and think.

I couldn't see him clearly in the pile of hay and blankets we'd used to fashion a mattress on the floor, but I could hear his breathing, the wavering inhale and exhale just barely audible beneath the dogs' snoring.

I couldn't sleep. I never could sleep that early. If I'd been alone, I'd have stayed up later, carving another animal. If I'd been at my former home, Mother would have found something for me to do. The only time I could remember closing my eyes and wishing for sleep to come this early was during that silent time in the castle. The time when I had no one and nothing to keep me company. Nothing but thoughts that hurt and festered, and no promise that the next day would be any better.

If I had known then what I know now, would those days have been different?

If I had apologized for dooming him to that fate from the start, would he have ever been cold and cruel? He was kind during our first meeting.

The memory of him tending to my hand in the darkness brought a raging heat to my face. I wasn't angry at him—I had no cause to be angry at him then.

What if I'd tended to that kindness and learned to love him before my seventeenth birthday?

What if I'd been able to push Jurij out of my heart back then? At least Jurij and Elfriede would have been happier. Ailill would have been happier—if he'd never gotten to know that stubborn side of me. I would have been...

"What shall we do for dinner this evening?" Ailill's knight would have snagged my rook when I wasn't paying attention. I'd have been focused instead on those pale brown eyes.

"Mother invited us to dine with her and Father. Friede wants to ask my opinion about her gown for her wedding."

"A lovely idea! We shall invite them here. It is far roomier." Ailill would have signaled to a specter at that and relayed his instructions. He would have grinned as his attention turned back toward me and I moved my queen diagonally across the board. "Perhaps you should put on the gown you wore for our wedding for the occasion."

"It's just a dinner, not the wedding. Besides, it's not our wedding day. We already had that with the Returning." I would have been blushing then—I could feel the heat in my cheeks even now. Ailill would have caught my queen with a pawn. I wouldn't be able to believe how distracted I was, how I couldn't have seen the danger I'd just put the poor piece in. "Thank you again, for saving my mother..." I would have to say something sobering, otherwise I would never have been able to tear my eyes from him. "I still wonder, at that miracle."

"You need not thank me." Ailill would have leaned over the board, his elbows knocking over the pieces, neither of us caring. "I would do anything for you." His face would have been mere inches from mine, his breath like a surge of fire across my cheek. "Thank you, for loving me. That is the true

wonder..."

This is ridiculous. My fantasies couldn't capture Ailill properly. He was cold, not warm. He was stubborn, not agreeable. The whole thing rang false. My dreams could never capture happiness—whatever that was like.

Of course, if I'd been happy, I'd have had no reason to leave, voices calling me or not. I'd have had no reason to cause Ailill to break the curse. But then I'd also have had no reason to create the curse to begin with, and Ailill wouldn't have loved me, and Jurij wouldn't have loved Elfriede, and Elfriede wouldn't have loved Jurij.

It was all so confusing. I couldn't lay there a moment longer, lost in my thoughts.

I flung back the blankets and swung my legs over the side of the bed, my toes scuffing the rough wood floor. In the dark, I could just make out Arrow's head lifting. "Shh," I whispered, wrapping my cloak around my shoulders. It was still summer, but the season was waning and the nights had grown colder. I slid on my boots and tiptoed to the door. Arrow clopped toward the moonlight, his toenails scuffing the floor with each step.

I patted his head. "Stay." He nudged his nose past my hand, determined to fit his entire body under my arm and out the door. He never did respond to me that well. I let him go and followed. As I shut the door behind me, I spared one last glance at the pile of hay. Dog and master were blissfully breathing, lost in the respite of their dreams.

"Arrow!" I shout-whispered. "Here! Don't go too far!"

Arrow clearly hadn't insisted on coming out to do his business. Or if he had, he'd forgotten the task entirely and taken to frolicking in the fields of flowers like it was the perfectly natural thing to do when the rest of the village was sleeping. "Arrow!" But he took off even farther.

I'd planned to get a taste of fresh air. Maybe take a moment away from the man I'd once loved—perhaps still loved—sleeping there in the shack beside me. To remind myself that I was finally free to walk away from my problems, to push aside the anger in my head. Regardless, it was clear I was following Arrow's plan now.

"Arrow! Come!" My voice grew louder farther from the cottage, where I wasn't concerned about waking Jurij and having him interrupt my escape. "Arrow!" But he wasn't listening. He ran straight through the fields as if chasing something only he could see.

The moonlight was just bright enough that I could make my way after him. He was heading home—to Mother and Father's home, to Elfriede. If I could just grab him before he whined too loud outside their door, I could go back without them ever being any wiser.

But damn, that dog was fast.

I gave up on calling after him and headed for the eastern path, not because I cared about getting my dress and cloak stained with the dew forming on the grass, but because I thought I had a better shot of running fast on the dirt path. It worked, but there was still no hope for catching up to him before he got there. By the time I came over the last hill, he was already there panting outside my parents' door. The slightly *cracked* door.

I froze. Elfriede seemed to be smiling as she rubbed her hands over his head. I wondered if I should turn back, leave it to her to give Arrow back or to keep him, pretend I never knew he'd run off. But Arrow gave me away, and Elfriede saw me.

I swallowed and pulled the cloak tighter at my neck. "He ran off," I said, taking a few careful steps closer.

Elfriede's lips soured, and she wiped her cheeks with the palm of one hand, the other still digging in behind Arrow's ear, which made him melt in joy beside her. She looked back over her shoulder—a fire was still going, albeit a dying one—and shut the door behind her. "Take him." She glared down at Arrow, as if he were the one she was talking to.

I stepped closer, running a hand atop Arrow's head. He looked back up at his former mistress, his tail wagging

88

like he had no sense that he wasn't wanted. But I didn't feel that from her, either. "You can keep him if you want."

Elfriede sniffled. "No."

"He's *your* dog." I patted Arrow's head. "He's always been your dog. It doesn't matter if he was born from Bow."

"It matters to me." Elfriede inhaled a long, tortured sniff, fighting the mucous her pinched tears wanted to let loose from her nose. "Mother and Father are asleep already. I don't want him waking them up. Go."

"Sure." I turned, laying pressure on Arrow's neck to guide him away, but he wouldn't budge. I pinched my lips together as Elfriede stared at Arrow. Her eyes sparkled too fiercely in the moonlight. "Why were you with Jaron?" I'd meant to think it, but I was asking it, even though I had an idea of what kind of answer was in store for me.

Elfriede's eyebrows arched slightly, and she used the back of her hand to wipe furiously at each eye. "I don't see how that's any of your business."

I nodded. "Maybe not. But he's not exactly known for his faithfulness these days."

Elfriede glowered at me. "Maybe I don't expect faithfulness from men anymore. Aren't you the one insisting women need to start treating men differently?"

"Where did you hear that?" Arrow slid down, throwing his front legs over my feet, as if deciding he and I were going to be standing there indefinitely. "Before today, you hadn't said a word to me in weeks!"

Elfriede took another ragged breath, too proud and dainty to blow her nose into her sleeve in front of me. "I don't need to speak to you. Everyone knows you're going around with all the young men these days, giving them ideas about how they're finally free from women."

"What are you talking about?"

Elfriede jutted her chin out, either to appear standoffish or to keep the snot from flowing. "I *saw* you with four men."

I flung my hands up in the air. "I wasn't *courting*

them!"

Elfriede seemed as oblivious to my words as she was to common sense. "Not only my husband, no. You couldn't just keep it in the family. But Marden's and Roslyn's, too!"

Of course. Her friends. The ones I wouldn't touch with a three-foot stick, although as a child I did swat at them with Elgar, which was basically the same thing. "And you're spending time with Jurij's *aunt's* former man."

She seemed to hear *that*. "It's not the same." She squeezed her arms tightly across her chest. "Alvilda never had the slightest interest in Jaron, and you *know* it."

"Maybe not, but Mother did!"

Elfriede stopped speaking, but her jaw hung open a moment before she snapped it shut. "That's a lie!"

"No, it's not!" I pointed to the door behind her. "Ask her!"

Elfriede threw her arms into the air and sniffed loudly. "Sure, let me wake both Mother *and* Father and ask if Father wasn't the only man Mother ever—"

The door opened behind Elfriede. A cold sweat formed on my forehead, and my cheeks flushed. I hadn't spoken to my parents in so long. It was Father, looking every bit as disheveled and empty as when he was first parted from Mother. "What is going on—Noll? Is something wrong?"

I stared into my father's bloodshot eyes, a haze of fatigue over his face that seemed to have no hope of lifting. I swallowed. I'd barely seen him the past few weeks—no, months now. I'd run from the castle, but I'd also run from everything else. I'd tried to put it all behind me, thinking things would get better in my absence. "No," I said, too late, after a moment of staring. "No, Arrow just ran away, and I came back to get him."

Father grunted and turned his attention to the dog at my feet. A flicker of a smile lit up his face and even made his tired eyes brighter. "Aw, there he is! Missed you, boy!" He crouched and ruffled Arrow playfully behind the ears.

Arrow lapped up the affection, rolling over onto his back.

I raised an eyebrow. Elfriede's lips were pinched as she turned to go back in. "If you like him so much, Father, he can stay." She glared at me. "But I better not see you here tomorrow, demanding I let you take him back."

I scoffed. "Wouldn't dream of it. But if I do miss him, I'll just send *one of my men* along to pick him up."

Elfriede went inside without another word.

Father murmured in an infantile voice from my feet. "Good boy. Good boy, that's a sweet little boy!" He finally seemed to notice I was still standing there and looked up, his eyes hopeful. "So the dog is staying?"

"If that's what Elfriede wants," I said. "I don't really have a say in anything anymore."

Father patted Arrow absentmindedly, looking back into the open cottage door behind him. "I have a feeling nobody does, Noll. Not anymore."

I searched for the moon, wincing as I realized just what it hovered over in the eastern sky. "If we ever did." Was he watching now, the lord who was "always watching"? I tore my gaze from the silhouette of the castle in the night and nodded at Father. "Good night, Father."

He didn't look up from Arrow, but his patting of the dog's stomach slowed. "Good night, Noll."

Arrow flipped over and turned toward a sound in the woods beside us that only he could hear.

But then I heard it, too. The turning of the wheels enveloped me with the feelings of nostalgia and dread I'd experienced when I'd heard them every day for months after I refused to visit the lord. My eyes fixed on the path to the woods, my body aflutter with anticipation and revulsion, my mind spinning and as conflicted as ever.

The black carriage emerged from the edge of the woods, the moonlight glistening off its roof. My heart beat so fast, I could barely make out the pounding of the horses' hooves. Not quickly, no, never quickly with him. He had nowhere to be in such a hurry. But then again, I couldn't be sure. Not with the way the moment slowed down impossibly so, cutting me off from everything else, from all my other senses.

White seemed to shine as bright as the sun in the dark carriage window. I thought of his paleness, how his brown hair framed his face, so lacking in color. But my eyes caught his—just for a moment, but a moment that lasted—and they were red. Of course. One of the specters. An Ailill. Him but not him at all.

The specter turned his head and looked forward. I felt dismissed, ignored. Nothing to a ghost of a man. Time resumed its normal pace, and the carriage fled west down the dirt road, fading into dust and darkness.

"What are they up to so late?" I'd almost forgotten Father was still behind me.

I clutched my forearm. "I don't know." I shivered from the cool breeze. "But it's none of my business."

And it wouldn't be ever again.

Chapter Twelve

"**Y**OU THOUGHT WE WERE *WHAT*?" Darwyn rolled a wooden wolf in his palm, dropping a few crumbs from the bread he was chewing atop the wolf's nose.

I yanked the wolf from his hand so he could devote himself to properly eating and flicked it to send the crumbs onto the blanket. Annoyed with the way the yellow crumbs stood out amongst my forest of animals, I slapped the wolf down next to a doe and picked the crumbs up between my fingers. "Courting women. At the tavern."

Darwyn laughed and stuffed another bite of the roll into his mouth, oblivious to the spray of crumbs flying from his open jaw. "Just how many women do you think visit the tavern?" The question was partially muffled by the bread, but his tone made it all rather clear.

"I don't know. Dozens?"

Darwyn swallowed and shook his head. "Most women are pretty angry about the whole former-husbands-leaving-them thing."

I dropped the crumbs to the side of the blanket, resisting the urge to brush the rest of them from where they'd settled across Darwyn's tunic and trousers. "Then what *have* you been doing since we met with Jaron?"

Darwyn shrugged as a woman dragging her young son behind her entered the bakery door beside us.

"Working. Sleeping. Eating."

"Eating *at the tavern*."

Darwyn raised an eyebrow and popped the last of his roll into his mouth. He chewed a few times before speaking. "You must really be interested in what goes on at this tavern." He swallowed. "I'd love to visit this place you've invented. Sounds like the women fawn all over you there. Might be interesting to see how it feels the other way around." He stared off into the passing crowd contemplatively, but I could see the mischievous glint in his eye.

I hugged my knees to my chest, not bothering to fix the skirt that bunched up as I did. "If you're not courting women, then why hasn't Jurij gone off with you?"

Darwyn studied me. "Probably because I haven't been up to much lately. I mean, I've gone to the tavern a few times."

"I knew it!"

"For drinks." He coughed, and his cheeks darkened slightly. "With friends."

"Have you seen Jaron there?"

"Yeah, sure. I guess *he's* courting women. But there haven't really been that many there to court. If you care about that sort of thing." He genuinely seemed like he didn't. "You think Jurij is avoiding Jaron?"

"Of course he is!"

"Even though he left his goddess—his former wife—of his own free will?"

I buried my nose in my knees. "It's complicated." I knew full well it was possible to feel disgust and affection at the same time.

Darwyn nudged my arm with his elbow. "It's only as complicated as you make it, Noll."

His gaze traveled from one passing villager to the next, a grin lightly touching his lips. He seemed happy. Happier than I'd ever seen him, though I couldn't recall ever seeing his face, even after his Returning. I was otherwise occupied at the time, being trapped in the castle.

The door to the bakery swung open, and Darwyn's mother stuck out her head. "Darwyn, how long does it take you to eat?" She had flour mixed between her black and gray tresses, and more than one lock of hair had fallen out of her bun. The flour reminded me of Alvilda's sawdust, but I'd never seen so flustered an expression on the woodcarver's face.

"Yeah. I'm coming." He rolled his eyes at me as he stood. And he was certainly taking his time to stand.

"Just as useless as your father," mumbled Darwyn's mother as she turned to go back into the bakery. "I wish you hadn't chased Roslyn away." The rest of her rant went unheard as the door shut behind her.

Darwyn winced at his former wife's name. The bit of happiness I'd seen was gone, replaced with as much seriousness as Jurij usually wore these days. He wove his fingers together and stared at them. "Roslyn was good at baking," he said, answering a question I didn't ask. "Me? Not so much. Even if I was raised by bakers. That's why I get stuck with the delivering most of the time."

"She lived here?" I hadn't known. Maybe Elfriede or someone had said it, but I hadn't paid attention to my friends' love lives after they found their goddesses. Most goddesses wanted their men to move in with them. To help their parents with their professions, or just because it was what they were used to, and men would have no complaints.

Darwyn nodded. "Mother asked her. She'd only had sons, and they were all leaving. Roslyn's parents already had Marden and Sindri to help with the tanning."

Oh, right. Roslyn and Marden. Darwyn and Sindri. Two sisters paired with two brothers.

Darwyn loosed his fingers and ran one hand over his hair. "She liked it, so she said that was fine. She wasn't here long. We'd only been married a short while before... well, *before.*"

I studied him, cupping a hand over my eyes to shield them from the bits of sunlight that trickled across the tops of the buildings. "You don't hate her."

Darwyn blinked. "Why would I?"

I blinked back tears from the sun. "She bossed you around? You resented being forced to love her in the first place?"

Darwyn cleared his throat. "Well, sure, maybe. But she wasn't so bad. And it wasn't her fault."

The door to the bakery opened and Darwyn flinched, but it wasn't his mother. Two customers, the mother and son. The child's arms were wrapped around a basket full of bread, but he stared at my carvings as he passed. His mother, oblivious to his slowed pace, put a hand on his back, guiding him in front of her.

"Darwyn! Now!" Mistress Baker's voice made him flinch again, but the door closed and his shoulders loosened.

He grabbed the wolf he'd been playing with and tossed two coppers on the blanket beside me. Holding his purchase out in front of him, he turned the wolf this way and that. "This is good work, Noll. I like it. Reminds me of my favorite mask."

I tucked that too-long bit of hair behind my ear and grabbed the coppers. I could feel my face flushing as I thought about all the fighting I did with the boy in that wolf mask. "Thanks. You didn't have to."

Darwyn gazed over the wolf he rolled between his hands to meet my eyes. "I don't hate Roslyn. I don't even dislike her."

"You're not at all the Darwyn I remember. I'd have thought you'd be, I don't know—"

"More agitated?" He grinned, and I wondered if that was the grin he wore as a child, if this was the boy who was once my friend and annoying rival. He glanced back at his wolf before tucking it into his pocket. "I just don't have feelings for her. Not like that. Staying with her wouldn't be fair, don't you think?"

I chewed my lip. "But how can you be sure you won't fall in love with her again? What if all you needed was to spend more time with her, to learn to love her?" I sounded like the villagers back when they used to say the same things to me. Only now I felt like I knew what they meant.

"I would do anything for you."

Now I was remembering my daydreams as if they were real memories.

Darwyn coughed. "Are you really counseling couplings to get back together now? Or are you wishing they'd stay apart? I'm not entirely clear on that."

"I'm not *counseling* anything. It's not really my business."

"Right. But since you're curious, I'm sure." He laughed. "I'm *very* sure."

Certainty was written all over his face, and I flinched, remembering something similar on Ailill's face the last time I saw him.

Darwyn crouched beside me, balancing on the balls of his feet. "This thing with you and Jurij and your sister, it's not really my business. But I think you were right to get Jurij out in the fields, get his mind off things."

Two little girls squealed with excitement as they pattered up to my blanket, one bouncing up and down, her hand clutching something tightly. "Looks like you've got customers." Darwyn stood and reached for the door as the girls crouched before my display of animals. "Get him to the tavern, Noll. You come too. Keep them both from drowning in ale and sorrows." He saluted me and went inside.

Both?

"You have another squirrel! She has another squirrel!"

One of the girls shoved the squirrel in my face, interrupting my thoughts on what Darwyn might have meant. "Can I have him?"

"Sure. Two coppers." It was the girl from a month or

so ago, the one who'd wanted to buy something when her friend did, that same friend now digging through her pocket to hold up a wooden cat.

My new customer grinned sheepishly and held out her other hand, the one she'd clutched into a fist. "Can I pay with this?"

In her hand she held a yellow coin. *Golden*. Like the bangle Elric wore and the rings that held up the veiled curtain.

Metal a color I'd only seen with the lord and his brother.

My blood ran cold, and I swallowed, unable to speak, my heartbeat thundering in my head. I wrapped my fingers around the coin she held out to me and nodded.

Chapter Thirteen

"YOU AND ME." JURIJ POINTED at me and then himself. "You want to go with me to Elweard's tavern." Buried beneath the exhaustion of a long day at the quarry, the look on his face was pained disbelief.

I rolled the golden coin between my fingers and the table. I didn't make supper, or even start a fire. I was hoping that might be enough to convince him. "Fine. Let's not go, then. There's some bread in the cupboard. It'll have to do for supper."

Jurij patted Bow's head and climbed over her to reach the table. He pulled the chair out and sat down beside me. "No, it's fine. It's just... why?"

"Why what?"

"Why the sudden invitation to the tavern? The tavern you've yet to set foot in since you went through all of that with your father." He took a deep breath, and the skin between his eyebrows furrowed. "Is *she* going to be there?"

"What?" My thoughts were so far from Elfriede, it actually took me a moment to figure out who he was talking about. But there could be no other. Jurij might not have known the pain of the commune, but his watered-down version of those men's torture centered pretty clearly on my sister, the woman who supposedly *used to* have a hold over him. I tapped the coin on the table. "I doubt it."

"But you don't *know*."

"Do you want me to ask her?"

"No!" He eyed me suspiciously. "But you didn't tell her we'd be there at the livestock fields that day, did you? You didn't tell her we'd be at the tavern tonight?"

"Of course not!" The accusations stung, but I knew he was thinking about how I tried to convince him to go home when I found him in the cavern. "Jurij, are you going to live your whole life in hiding? Or are you going to learn to put this awkwardness behind you?" The coin slipped between my index and middle fingers, and the last of the day's sunlight streaming through the window caused the coin to sparkle. "You're not the only one who feels awkward, you know."

Jurij snorted and slapped a palm on the table. "I don't think Sindri or Darwyn or Tayton seem to run into their former wives as much as I run into mine."

"You've seen her *one time* since you left."

"And that was more than enough. She teased me about Arrow and then stole him back right after."

I leaned back in my chair, tapping the coin on the table. "You act like your feelings are her fault."

"Of course they're not. But they're not exactly my fault, either." His gaze wandered across the table, catching sight of the coin I rolled beneath my fingers. "What's that?"

My hand froze, my mind racing over the possibilities. A part of me wanted to keep it secret, as well as what it might mean. But the other part of me was rolling it on the table in plain sight, and I could hardly pretend I didn't know what he was talking about. I slid the coin across the table to him. "I got this as payment today for one of my carvings."

Jurij took the coin between his fingers and held it up to the last rays of sunlight. "It's not copper."

I leaned over and snatched it back from him. "I know that."

"But what is it? It's hard like copper."

I examined the coin again. Whenever I moved it, the fiery glint of the sun sparkled. "Golden copper."

Jurij looked as skeptical as he did when I first invited him to the tavern. "Who gave that to you?"

"A little girl. I don't know whose daughter."

"And you didn't think to ask where she'd gotten it?" Jurij dragged the coin across the table for a closer look.

"I *did* ask," I corrected him. "She said she found it in the village, on the ground. But I might know where it really came from."

"There's a golden copper source, and you're keeping it a secret."

"Not a *source* exactly."

"The cavern?" Jurij picked up the coin, examining its smooth, unadorned surface.

"No."

Jurij froze, and the coin slipped from his fingers and bounced onto the floor, rolling away.

"*Jurij!*" I jumped to my feet, stepping over Bow to stop it just before it disappeared beneath the cupboard.

"You mean it's from *him*, don't you?"

I held up the coin to get a look in the dying light for dents or scratches. But the coin was flawless, except for a speck of dust. "How would a random village girl find a coin from the lord?"

Jurij scoffed. "Why don't you ask him?"

I rubbed the coin against my sleeve, buffing away the dirt and restoring the impeccable surface. "Maybe I don't really want to know," I mumbled quietly.

"You don't want to know anything."

I gripped the coin in my fist. "And what's that supposed to mean?"

Jurij pushed his chair back and pointed east. "There's a man there who, if rumors be true, has lived since before our parents were born. Before *their* parents were born."

I said nothing as I clutched my fist to my chest, my

focus on Bow, who'd put her head down, satisfied what I held was nothing she wanted.

"The village exists one way for generation after generation. No one was complaining," he continued. "Well, practically no one." We shared a pointed look. "And then one day, for no discernible reason, it just stops. Everything we know, our entire way of life just... stops."

"And you're upset about that?" I asked. "I thought you were happy to finally have your freedom."

"This isn't about me being happy or unhappy." He stared at me like he was waiting to study my reaction. "This is about you." He pointed to the wall again. "And him. Isn't it?"

I couldn't look at him. I opened my fist and rubbed the coin with my fingers.

"Noll, do you know why the curse broke?"

I didn't answer.

"Do you know how the lord was able to heal your mother?"

I still said nothing.

Jurij sighed, and I heard him push his chair back. "All right. Keep your secrets. Keep your weird golden copper and your weird former husband."

"We never got married."

"Right." He grabbed his cloak from the stand Alvilda and I made together. "You're right. It's a nice night for the tavern."

He slammed the door behind him, waking Bow from her nap. She stood and looked at me, the door, and back again.

I closed my fist over the golden coin until it dug into my palm. *A nice night for the tavern?* "I know, girl," I said to Bow. "I'm going."

But I'm not walking there with him. Let him stew a bit.

I thought I'd gotten used to the stares. In a village where nobody seemed to care about anyone other than their goddess or their man, it had taken a lot to be noticed. But between the kinds of trouble my friends and I would get into, being so long without a man, and the lord finding the goddess in me, I'd managed it. And then there was the fact that my father, who'd somehow managed to live while his goddess was "dead," had practically moved into the tavern, and on more than one occasion, I'd had to go collect the man before he drank our last copper. I'd walked this path down the village many times before, feeling all the stares.

But I thought those days were behind me. Everyone else had their own problems now. I wasn't just a thorn in their sides, disrupting their blissful couplings with my oddness. We were all odd now. So why did I swear every head turned my way as I passed by?

I stopped in front of Vena's tavern door and took a deep breath. No, I was imagining it. I sold my own carvings now, and no one batted an eye. I bought bread and cheeses. Delivered Alvilda's carvings. I thought I'd finally earned the right to disappear into the crowd. Even if it was past sunset and the crowd had significantly dwindled.

The door opened, and the laughter from inside spilled out into the alleyway. The man who stepped out was grinning from one ear to the next, a dark flush over his cheeks. He barely noticed me as he passed, and for once, I felt validated. I was just imagining the prying eyes. The sound of laughter grew muffled as the door swung shut behind him.

I could do this. I put my hand on the door handle and pulled.

No one looked up as I entered, even with the bells on the door chiming to signal my arrival. I pulled the hood of my cloak back and scanned the tavern for familiar faces in the muted light of the fire. The place was bustling, far more packed than I'd ever seen it when I'd come to get Father. There wasn't a free table in sight, and there were only a couple of small spaces at the counter if you felt like wedging shoulder to shoulder with men on either side. And almost every table was full of men. I recognized one young woman, maybe one of Elfriede's friends, on the lap of a man at the table nearest the fire, and I nearly choked in surprise. No. That couldn't possibly be one of Elfriede's friends. Those girls were always too reserved. They were all supposedly devastated by their husbands' departures. Not exactly the type of woman I expected to sit with her arms around a man's neck, her lips brushing the tips of his ears.

"Oop. Careful now!"

I stepped back just in time to avoid the slosh of ale that escaped one of the mugs Vena held in a single hand. Her other hand held a platter of meat arranged hastily with some wilting parsley leaves for garnish. She put it all down at a table several paces away, her intrusion not even noticed among the men doubled over in laughter. Rubbing her face with the back of her wrist, she smiled. "Haven't seen you here in ages! You looking for your father, dear?"

She passed by me again, slipped into a small opening between two men at the counter, and tapped the countertop. "Two more, honey!"

I could just make out tall Elweard on the other side of the counter over the heads of the men in front of him. "Sure thing!"

"Hey, there, sweetheart!" A man from a nearby table sloshed his mug toward me. "I know who you are!" He raised his mug higher. "To your man. No. To the lord!"

"To the lord!" said the two others at his table. They clinked their mugs together and took large gulps, laughing as they slammed their mugs down.

One of the men winked at me. "Nice of you to drive him mad enough to decide he'd had enough of all this goddess business."

"She can't have been any worse than my wife," scoffed his tablemate. He eyed me over the rim of his mug. "She's a fair sight better to look at, too."

I stared at a grain in the wood on the counter, determined to ignore him. The look in his eyes reminded me painfully of the men from the past who'd set me down the path I'd regretted to begin with.

"All right, all right," said Vena. "You leave Noll here alone."

"Aw, Vena, you're no fun!" said one. He raised his mug. "One more!"

"Not for you! I'm not stupid. I've learned my lesson: You show the coppers you have for the night upfront. You only had enough for three mugs. You want more? You bring more coppers."

The man and his nearest tablemate started snickering. One quietly said something like, "... can mine some more tomorrow," but Vena didn't notice. Was Ailill keeping watch over the quarry workers? Along with the stone for buildings, the workers used to mine copper not just for use for all of our metals, but for coins on occasion, too, which the blacksmith made and the specters collected for... Quarry worker wages? I'd never thought about it before, and it would have never occurred to those men to make coppers for themselves back then. But I just realized I was staring at two quarry workers and the rarely working blacksmith, and it didn't seem so impossible anymore.

Vena leaned her elbows atop the counter and sized me up. "Don't mind them. They've been doing that for weeks. Toasting the lord for, well, their newfound freedom, I guess you'd call it. But you don't care about that." I think I was starting to. Who was running this village if Ailill allowed the men to spend their days doing nothing? Toasting him indeed.

"Your father hasn't been here since..." Vena looked at the ceiling and took her time thinking, so I answered for her.

"Many months ago."

"Two nights ago," finished Vena at the same time. She turned back to grab the mugs Elweard plopped down behind her. "Don't think he's been here tonight."

She brushed past me, again holding the mugs in the air as she squeezed through the small walkway between me and the parade of men walking back and forth from the counter. *The both of them.* I stepped up behind Vena. "My father still drinks here?"

Vena jumped slightly but tapped my shoulder as she managed to squeeze back past me. "Honey, *everyone* drinks here. Every man anyway." She gazed around her crowded tavern and put her hands on her hips, something approaching pride on her face. I could almost hear the gratitude for the freedom of men on the tip of her tongue, but maybe considering her man didn't use it as an excuse to leave her, she knew better than to be grateful for something that few other women would count as a blessing.

Vena pulled a wrinkled rag off of her shoulder and dashed across the room. I followed, my gaze darting from one smiling man to the next, not recognizing anyone I'd come for. Vena stopped at a table that had just emptied, her rag a flurry of action across the tabletop.

"I'm looking for—" I stepped back to let one of the table's recent occupants pass, the stench of alcohol foul in the air as he let out a belch. "I'm looking for Jurij."

Vena's hands didn't stop moving, one dragging the rag around, the other stacking the mugs and plates together. Her eyes, though, moved up to meet mine, and the firelight sparkled off of them mischievously. "Is it true what they say then? You and the tailor's son living together?"

I gripped my cloak with one hand. "It's not like that."

"Uh-huh." Vena paused to wipe her forehead with her wrist again. "I haven't seen him, but it's hard to keep track with all the business. His father and brother are upstairs, if you want to ask them."

"His *brother*?"

Vena swung her rag over her shoulder and gathered all of the dishes. "Let me know if you want to order anything," she said, passing by with a tune on her lips.

I spotted a staircase at the back corner, a dozen or so men milling about between me and it. Sighing, I made my way through. "Excuse me," I mumbled, but I couldn't tear the men—and women entwined between the men as if carved from their bodies—away from each other for more than a moment. I had to squeeze myself through some uncomfortably tight spaces, and when I made it to the corner, I practically somersaulted forward as I broke free from the crowd. My hand rested on the wall as I caught my breath. Candlelight flickered at the top of the stairs. I'd never been up there, and I wasn't sure what to expect, nor how Vena was expected to serve a second crowd equal in number up top.

Only there wasn't a crowd at the top at all. The noise from below was audible but faded. Lit torches hung from the wall every few feet, but it was still dim. There were rooms, maybe nine or ten of them, with closed doors on either side of the curving hallway. Of course. I'd heard Vena had the idea of making extra rooms out of her and Elweard's living quarters on the second floor. Alvilda had even carved doors for rooms they must have previously left open. "Lodgings," Vena had called it. Some men didn't have a home to go back to if they weren't staying with their wives any longer. The commune men never had a home to begin with. Vena's new "lodgings" wouldn't come close to providing enough space for all of them. It made me wonder where the rest of those men were now hiding. *With new loves? In the fields? In the commune?*

But Master Tailor wasn't one of those men. He had his own home. His former wife had been the one to move out. So why would he need a room?

As I approached the nearest door, I heard the

murmur of voices. The reddish glow of fire protruded from beneath the door. I knocked loud enough to be heard over all of the voices. Then I realized this wasn't the room they were coming from. And I heard *groaning.*

I took a few steps back and tried to disappear down the darkened stairs, but the door opened before I could get there. A man emerged, his shirt missing, his dark chest slick with sweat that shined in the dim firelight. He covered his bottom half with a sheet. I tore my face away. "I'm sorry, I was looking—"

"Noll? Is that you?"

I looked back up despite myself. It was Darwyn, running his hand through his hair. Darwyn's half-naked body was covered in sweat. My cheeks burned. *I'm very sure.* I didn't dare peek to see who lay in the room behind him.

"I didn't think you'd actually come!" He reached back awkwardly to close the door with one hand, the other clutching the sheet in front of his lower body. "I'm sorry. I didn't expect you."

I stepped back as he stepped forward, until my boot hit the wall behind me. "No, I wasn't... I didn't mean to bother you."

Darwyn laughed and turned away, beckoning me to follow him down the hallway. He took small, careful steps so as not to send the thin sheet wrapped around his waist falling. "Let me show you where Jaron's been staying."

My foot froze mid-step. "Vena told me the Tailors were up here."

Darwyn nodded. "They're with Jaron. It's better when it's a private party." He pointed to a door around the corner. "But you probably don't want to go knocking on all of the doors around here." I blushed as I caught up to him, the murmur of voices—the muffled *noises*—growing louder.

"I'll be there in a minute." He smirked and pulled his sheet a little higher. "Just need to freshen up a bit."

I stood still, cringing as his shuffling footsteps faded behind me. I wasn't sure I could look him in the face again so soon after that. *Then you better get inside so you don't have to walk in with him. Or with whoever he's got with him.*

I straightened my shoulders, tucked the too-long piece of hair behind my ear, and raised my fist, ready to knock.

The door spilled open, and my fist hung suspended over the chest of a specter.

Chapter Fourteen

"AILILL?" IT FELT LIKE SOMEONE else was speaking. I didn't realize the name had passed my tongue until the thunder of my heartbeat quieted.

"Need something else, my good man?" Someone from behind the specter spoke. I didn't know who. My senses were dulled, and I couldn't stop myself from staring up into those red, unblinking eyes. Like all the life had been drained out of him.

I cursed under my breath and looked away. *Since when have you called them by that name?* But this one was younger than many of the rest. He looked so like him, I'd nearly forgotten I didn't care anymore. I stepped back to let him pass, watching as his white, shiny shoes scuffed the wooden floor and disappeared into the darkness of the hall.

The ghost of a past life. But how does it work? Does he die, become a shell, and then appear out of thin air as a baby? The thought of a castle of specters silently attending an infant not yet knowing he was fated to join them sent a chill down my back. I thought of Ailill, the *real* Ailill, the young boy I'd known who became the first shade. He'd had no one. No one at all for years and years after I'd left him.

And now, after a thousand years, there was the man who'd been mine at the castle. Ailill but not Ailill. Some muted copy, twisted and unused to company that didn't do everything he wanted.

"Noll? I'll be!"

In the firelight, Jaron, Sindri, Jurij, and a young woman I barely knew were gathered around a table, mugs and half-empty plates scattered across its surface. Each gazed at me expectantly.

Jurij was the only one less curious to see me and more flabbergasted. Like he couldn't believe I had the gall to show my face.

Jaron didn't seem to share the same sentiment. "Did you come to join us? A bit late for dinner, I'm afraid." He pointed to an empty chair beside Jurij. "Have a seat. Next time Vena comes up, we'll order another round."

"I'm not sure Vena will ever have a spare moment." I shuffled to the chair, taking in the room. Beside the fireplace was a small bed in the corner, but nothing else of note. A single window looked out into the night, the pointed roofs of the homes and shops across the way just barely visible. The silhouette of the tall spires of the castle beneath the mountain was but a conspicuous fleck in the background.

Jaron chuckled. "Well, it probably doesn't help that we've been keeping Roslyn so long." He patted the shoulder of the woman beside him gently. "Thanks for wasting your short break with this old man, darling."

The corner of Roslyn's lips twitched, but she settled into an easy smile. "No waste at all." Her dark eyes roved over the table, meeting mine. I flushed, thinking of Darwyn in the room down the hall. "Besides, you have Noll now. You won't have to be alone."

Jaron sniffed and leaned back in his chair. He failed to contain his smirk. "Now don't you go spreading rumors, sweetheart."

"I wouldn't dream of it." Roslyn's smile grew uneasy as she passed behind Sindri to the open door.

Jaron leaned over the table. "You have to excuse her, Noll. There's this rumor that I'm just about the only man in town who welcomes the company of women these days. That I can't be seen without one." He took a sip of his drink, and I watched what impact his words had on his companions. Jurij stared down at the table blankly, but Sindri hardly seemed to be paying attention. His eyes followed Roslyn hungrily.

"Oh!" Roslyn jumped as (a fully clothed) Darwyn appeared out of the darkness of the hallway. She clutched her chest as if to keep her heart from beating right out of it.

Darwyn nodded and tried to speak, but his voice caught. I noticed the lump bobbing at his throat. "Roslyn," he said at last.

Tayton stepped up behind Darwyn, giving Roslyn someone else to look at. Her gaze fell to the ground, and she pushed past them both, careful not to brush against them.

Darwyn took a deep breath and smiled at me. "I see you found your way, Your Majesty."

Tayton grimaced and stepped around Darwyn to sit in the open chair beside me. "Is this another one of those things from your childhood I don't get to know about?"

Darwyn nudged Tayton's shoulder playfully with his fist and tugged on the back of his brother's chair. "The elf queen, remember? I told you about that."

Sindri got up from his chair and sat in the one Roslyn had vacated so Darwyn could slip in beside Tayton.

"Oh. Right," muttered Tayton. He did his best to stay grumpy, but I thought I saw his pouted fishy lips almost straighten into a smile.

"Did he leave out the part where he found the whole elf queen thing obnoxious?" I asked.

Tayton shook his head. "Nope. Got that part pretty clear. He probably fancied himself someone who'd eventually usurp you."

I appreciated the conversation, if only because I was still shaking from my encounter with the specter. "A retainer usurp the queen? He had no chance. Not when love proved such an easy distraction for him." I regretted the word *love* as soon as I said it. "Or passion. Whatever you'd call it. At least he's over that."

"Hmm? Over love and passion?" Tayton rubbed his fingers under his chin as if pretending to think hard and then exchanged a sly glance with Darwyn. "I'm not sure. So I doubt he'll ever get a chance to usurp you."

Now I felt like the one being left out of something that seemed to make perfect sense to those around me.

"All right, all right." Jaron clinked his finger against his mug. "Nobody came here to discuss what goes on betwixt the bed sheets, right?" Jaron pointed at me. "Have anything to tell us?"

I looked from one face to the next, surprised to see all but Jurij staring expectantly. "What are we talking about?"

Jaron tapped Jurij's shoulder. "What was it? A golden copper?"

My head whipped instantly to Jurij. "You told them?"

Jurij shrugged. "Was it a secret?"

"No, but..." I reached into the band at my waist in which I'd tucked the golden copper. "I don't see why it should matter."

Jaron reached out his hand, and I hesitated, running my fingers over the golden surface. He seemed undeterred, so I dropped it into his palm. He held it out above him, a little bit of the firelight flickering off of its surface. "Well, I'll be. It *is* yellow."

"Let me see." Sindri snagged the coin from Jaron's loosened fingers and held it out just as he had. His face soured. "What is this?"

Darwyn grabbed it from him and leaned over to show Tayton. Their fingers brushed each other's lightly as they stroked the surface. "It feels like copper." Tayton took it in his fist and shook his hand up and down. "Maybe a little heavier."

He opened his fist, and I snatched it back before the coin kept passing from man to man indefinitely. "Okay. So I have a golden copper. Care to let me know why you all seem so interested? Or why one of the lord's servants came out of this room before I did, for that matter?"

If I hadn't been so flustered, or so determined to convince everyone—and myself—that I wasn't bothered, it would have been the first thing out of my mouth as soon as the specter had left. Instead, I posed the question now, ready to know why they hadn't thought fit to bring it up earlier. *Push me, and I'll push back.*

Sindri's eyes immediately fell downward, and if I'd hoped Jurij was going to start looking at me now, I was mistaken. Darwyn and Tayton seemed puzzled, curious— but it wasn't to me that they turned their attention. It was to Jaron, who leaned back in his chair with a sigh. "What do you think of us, Noll?"

Jaron stared relentlessly, and I had to stop myself from turning away. "What do I think?"

Jaron ran a hand over his face. "Are we the men you knew before? Is any man?"

I studied each of my friends in turn, but none would return my gaze. "What's this about?"

"It's not enough for some of us, just to move on." Jaron scratched the stubble under his chin. I wondered briefly if when he wore his mask in the commune, he'd grown a thick beard beneath. "It's not enough for most of us."

"What do you mean, not enough?"

Jaron opened his mouth, but Jurij snapped to attention, cutting him off. "We want to know why, Noll. Why things changed. Why they were ever the way they were. Don't you?"

I felt the weight of the golden coin in my palm.

"She *does* know something!" Sindri pounded his palms the table. "You told us she did, but I wasn't sure."

"Who's *sure* I know anything?" I glared at Jurij, finding none of the easy demeanor that used to dominate his features. "Jurij, what have you told them?"

He shrugged. "That you might have broken the curse."

"Me?" I swallowed, glancing out of the corner of my eye to see if anyone was reading the guilt flushed all over my face. "But how—"

"You love him, don't you?"

The words were like Elgar slashed across my chest. The real Elgar.

Jurij didn't seem to notice. Or maybe he did and didn't care. "You Returned to the lord of the village, and then everything changed."

"If I Returned to him, why am I here and not with him? Why would my Returning be any different than any other woman's?"

"Maybe he didn't love you back." The harsh tone in Darwyn's voice was enough to stop my assault. He fumbled with his hands on his lap, like he was trying to pretend he wasn't the one who'd spoken.

I threw my hands up in the air. "If he didn't love me, why did he find the goddess in me in the first place?"

"That wasn't love." Tayton put a hand on Darwyn's shoulder. "Maybe once you Returned to him, he broke free from the spell. Maybe we all did."

I dropped the golden copper on the middle of the table, crossing my arms against my chest as the coin wobbled slowly into silence. "I wasn't aware that you'd been conferring with the lord of the village about his opinion on love."

"We don't have to," started Sindri. "We know from *our* experiences."

"Your experiences don't come close to that man's." I tilted my chin at Jaron, surprised at my own defensiveness. "Answer my questions, and I may answer yours." I tapped the coin with my finger. "What did you want from one of the lord's servants?"

The corner of Jaron's lips twisted just slightly. "You know, you may not be asking the right question."

"What do you expect me to do? Walk up to the castle gates, invite myself in, and ask if oh, maybe, the gold copper a child gave me was his indirect way of saying we need to talk?" I slid the golden copper off of the table, tucking it back into the band around my waist. "If he wanted to talk to me, he could come himself."

Jurij scoffed. "You claim the lord won't explain what happened to us, but asking him directly isn't exactly what we had in mind."

Jaron got on his hands and knees, reached beneath the bed, and pulled out a small, carved keepsake box. I recognized it as one Father had made—old and a bit worn, probably not without a previous owner or two—and wondered if Jaron had made a point of avoiding Alvilda's carvings. He returned to his seat, shoving aside his mug to put the box on the table. He opened it. "He'd come himself if he wanted to talk?" He pulled out the single item inside the box, a yellowed piece of paper that crinkled at his touch. It was a drawing of a room much like this one, with a man in the bed and a child in a chair beside him, focusing on something in his hands. There was a single jagged edge to the parchment, as if it'd been torn from bindings. "Think you could make him want to come see you? It might give us the time we need to explore where he keeps more of these."

Jaron nodded, and Darwyn got up from the table. He knocked on the wall and leaned against it, then, seeing my gaze on him, pointed to Jaron.

"Me and the man staying next door do each other favors on occasion," explained Jaron, and I wondered briefly if it was rented to one of the other men from the commune. "He's downstairs enjoying the raucous company, so I asked some friends to stay in his room, out of sight, until the lord's servant left." Jaron held the paper closer toward me. The boy had gotten up, leaving a shirt and a needle on the chair where he'd sat. He leaned over the form of the sleeping man and shook him awake.

The drawing. Shook the man awake. On the paper.

The man sat up. And somehow, even though he was drawn in plain black ink, I saw it clearly: Master Tailor in the bed, little Luuk beside him. Both moving on paper.

Jaron tapped a finger on the paper. "So what you should have asked is, what did one of the lord's servants want from us?"

The door to the room opened, and in stepped Master Tailor and Luuk.

Chapter Fifteen

"WHERE DID YOU GET THIS?" I asked. "*How* did you get this? And why, if the specter wanted it, do you still have it?"

Jaron flipped the paper over, and there was writing on the back:

We have no need for so much bread. Send enough for one. The payment will remain the same. Distribute the food or pocket the payment as you see fit.

I scoffed, turning to Darwyn. "The specter gave your mother a note. On the back of a moving piece of paper?"

Darwyn shrugged. "Mother is so harried, she didn't bother to flip it over. But I did, when she was scrambling in the kitchen. I didn't know what to do with it, who to tell. It wasn't until after we met Jaron that day that I wound up spending time here and unloading the burden. I gave it to Jaron—and now that pale man keeps dogging him, probably wanting it back." He shuddered at the "pale man."

Jaron flipped the paper over. The image had changed to the very table at which we sat, down to the detail of Jaron holding a piece of paper over the mugs and plates on the table. My drawing self stared at the paper in Jaron's hands, my hair longer and thicker in the back than I pictured. I was afraid to move. Afraid to see the change in the picture.

"It follows Luuk." The drawing of Jurij turned to the drawing of me. And as if to prove his point, Luuk walked to the fire, grabbing the poker to turn over the log. My drawing disappeared from view as just Jaron at the edge of the table remained in focus, the image echoing Luuk's steps across the room.

I gripped the golden copper through the band at my waist. "Why is the lord watching Luuk?"

No one had an answer.

ŋ ŋ ŋ

Jurij didn't come home—didn't come back to *my* home—that night. Or the night after. For the second morning in a row, I carved at the table in my shack, my blade moving too fast without my attention. I sliced the tip of my finger, cursing as I dropped the half-formed wooden cow on the table. Rushing to the basin, I tipped a bit of the water out of the nearby bucket to wash the blood away. My finger stung as I washed it clean of the blood, only for it to ooze out in red again seconds later.

Blood on the chest of Elric, the man who so looked like Ailill. There was nothing, and then there was a pool of blood.

I grabbed a rag and twisted it around my finger, pulling it tight and wincing at the pain. I clearly had no idea how to fix this. Ingrith once told me, right here in this room, about a man who'd been a "healer." Only she didn't mean "healer" like the men from Ailill's village, who had a power I still couldn't explain. She meant someone who fixed your wounds and tended to your illnesses, but without the violet glow. Without the assistance of something I didn't understand pouring out from his fingers.

Little Ailill cradling my face to remove the bruise from the slap. Little Ailill taking my pain away after the stocks.

119

When I was so cold to him during my first night in the castle, what was going through that same person's head?

"This will be your room." He nodded toward the nearest specter, who seemed to read his intent as he went to the window and pulled back the drapes. I expected to see dust flying, but it was annoyingly pristine. *"You may let the light in as you please."*

Thank you for the instruction on how to push aside drapes. *I scoffed loudly. But I was determined not to speak to him.*

Ailill stiffened just slightly, but I was too concerned with seeing the prison hidden beneath the extravagantly plush bed and the shimmering baubles before the mirror. A mirror. I'd even have my own mirror! I squashed that feeling of gratitude and wonder as soon as I felt it.

He took you from your home. Against your will. Isn't he supposed to do what you want him to do? He refused to help your mother when you needed help the most.

I pushed past the specters and back into the hallway.

"Are you hungry?" Ailill asked, appearing at my side. "I have instructed a meal to be ready as soon as we have finished our tour."

I stopped in my tracks, not sure what would be worse, dining with him or continuing on this tour of his extravagances. Probably the former. I'd never eaten with a masked man before, let alone one who was so good at getting my blood boiling. Besides, I wasn't hungry. I couldn't imagine being hungry ever again. I shrugged.

Ailill joined his hands behind his back. "This castle... displeases you?"

You displease me, not the castle. *I didn't say it, but it was almost like he'd heard me anyway. He flinched. I didn't say anything.*

"Is there anything I can do... to make you more comfortable?"

I clenched my jaw, knowing I couldn't ask him to let me go. Knowing everyone expected me to just accept him.

Just live forever with this man I didn't even know. With this man who'd done nothing to help my mother!

The tour continued after that in near silence, and the disastrous meal together—followed by the truth about my mother. *No, not the truth. Not the whole truth. Just enough for me to despise him even more without realizing...*

Without realizing it was that scared little boy beneath it all. He'd been so eager to please me. He'd pushed down all the anger he'd felt about what I'd done to him, and he'd tried to be friends again. He'd hoped I was the "Olivière" he'd gotten to know as a child. He'd hoped I'd come to free him, that I would reward his efforts with, at the very least, a tender smile.

It's no wonder he treated you cruelly after that. I leaned against the table with my good hand, drumming my fingers across the surface. Two days I'd been alone. Two days I'd finally been back to the solitude I'd enjoyed at the start of the summer, and peace was still unattainable. My mind clouded freely with thoughts and images I'd done such a good job of suppressing until now.

"Doesn't everyone in the village say the lord is always watching?"

"Watching, perhaps, when it strikes his fancy."

Ailill had been so smug, then, as if daring me to guess what exactly in the village might have captured his interest.

I felt my chest tighten at the memory and almost lost my balance. I'd clutched the injured hand to my breast but reached out to steady myself, wincing at the pressure. The rag was dyed red, the blood dripping out onto the table.

What was it Mother had taught me? What kind of leaves would make a poultice? My head swam, flashes of memories searing into my mind. I ran back to the basin, leaning over, almost sure I was going to throw up. Darkness danced at the edges of my sight as I stared at the puddle of water dyed red.

So Luuk had "struck his fancy." A child would have

been my last guess. He was Jurij's brother, and Ailill was sensitive about how I'd once felt about Jurij. But why Luuk, then, and not Jurij himself? Of course, this was me seeking a message in every coded action, a message meant for myself when I knew he was no longer in love with me. If he ever truly was.

What was I supposed to tell Jaron and the others? I'd never seen moving pictures on a page and could only guess that was how Ailill was "always watching." But I'd seen things—I'd *lived* things—that couldn't be explained. That would turn everything upside down far more than their piece of paper.

I dry-heaved over the red-dyed basin. My blood soaked through the rag, dropping one crimson pearl after the other onto the water's surface.

I thought of the time I'd spent in the castle. Of how Ailill had taken Jurij after his wedding, held my mother in a room to which I had no access. I'd worried then that he'd have his revenge on everyone I cared about, no matter how thin the connection. Luuk and Nissa. The Tailors. Alvilda. Father and Elfriede. And I was right to worry. He *was* watching them. He was watching us. He was *still* watching us. He had to be. If he had paper like this, then it only made sense.

But what made little sense was why he'd send the paper. He wouldn't have *accidentally* written the note on an enchanted piece of paper and ordered it to be given to one of my friends.

I fumbled at my sash for the golden copper with my good hand. *But then why all the indirect messages? Why bother me now, after he told me to leave him alone?*

My finger stung, and I felt the pressure of tears stirring under my eyelids, the pounding of the crying I refused to do weighing on my head. *What was the poultice Mother used for cuts?* I wondered again. *Why am I so helpless? Why won't my thoughts leave me alone?*

I took a deep breath, rubbing my good hand across

my cheekbone and trying to soak up the moisture that had escaped against my will. *Alone. Alone.* Even when I wasn't alone, I felt alone. There was no one who could even begin to understand. No one but Ailill. And I wasn't in the mood for any of his games.

After staring at the blood pooling on the rag over my finger, I straightened my back and grabbed my cloak, swinging it awkwardly over my shoulder with one hand. *You lost her for well over a year. You thought you'd never get her back again. Why haven't you gone to her?*

I may not have been able to tell her everything. But I sure as rain could ask Mother for help.

ŋ ŋ ŋ

When Elfriede opened the door, I almost turned right around and walked away without a word. *It's not like you didn't expect to find her here. Seeing as how her new man has plenty of other women to share his time with.*

Elfriede's lips soured just slightly, but she didn't study me long. Arrow barked from behind her. I could just make out the swish of his golden tail.

"Shh, Arrow. It's fine." She looked at me. "Have you been *crying*?"

I rubbed my cheek again with my good hand, clutching the injured hand tighter against my chest. "No." I tried peering over her shoulder. "Is Mother in?"

Elfriede chewed her lip, as if considering refusing to answer me. Her gaze fell on the wrapped hand against my chest, and a flicker of something, maybe pity, passed across her pale eyes. She nodded. "Out back." Then she slammed the door in my face.

I took a deep breath and stepped around the house to the small yard we—they—kept behind the cottage. It's where we grew our potatoes and other vegetables, just to save a few coppers on the stuff we had to buy from the market. We got most of our daily eggs from the chicken coop. *Their daily eggs.* With how long Father had been not working—since before the rest of the men lost interest in their work, thanks to Mother's illness—I was certain Mother and Elfriede had been relying on their own crops as much as possible. I wasn't sure what they would do now that summer was winding to a close.

As I passed the window over the basin, I heard laughter. Elfriede's delicate peals punctuated by a gaggle of hens. She had company. There was so much work to be done in the village, and Elfriede and her brood had nothing better to do than monopolize my family's home and whisper about her outcast of a sister with the bloody hand.

"Mother?" I called. I felt lightheaded. Warm, sticky blood crawled down my forearm from beneath the rag.

Mother appeared from around the chicken coop, wiping her hands on her apron. "Noll?" She smiled and reached her arms out for an embrace. "Why haven't you come by earlier?" She stopped, her face and arms falling. "What happened to your hand?"

I winced as I unwrapped the blood-soaked rag. "I cut it while carving. It won't stop bleeding." The rag fell to the ground, soaked and useless.

Mother examined my hand. My finger stung as she turned it over, dyeing her own palms red. "It's bad, but not too deep. We need a poultice." She tugged on my elbow and led me back toward the cottage.

I froze, thinking of the women in there.

Mother stopped. "What is it?"

"Elfriede has company."

Mother nodded. "I invited the girls for dinner. We do that a lot now. Pool our coppers to afford a cut of meat once a week or so. Although I wonder if more of us should follow Roslyn's example and look for work in the village. There's plenty of it to be had now."

I hadn't thought about how quickly Mother and

Father's savings might deplete, considering how we'd spent so much of it even before the curse broke. And at least back then, Jurij was so concerned with Elfriede's health and happiness that he gave her all of his earnings from the Tailor Shop so we could afford more food. Now, with neither Father nor Mother nor Elfriede working...

"I'm sorry I haven't been more help." Guilt squeezed at my chest. "I haven't been drowning in riches, but my work is paying off. There's still enough for me to buy bread and vegetables." It helped that both were cheaper than they had been in years, to attract more customers, since everyone I knew seemed to be economizing. Every woman, anyway. "I should have brought something."

"Nonsense. You have your own hearth to heat." She paused. "But today, you should stay, once we've gotten this taken care of."

"No, I ought to get back."

"Noll, you live a short walk from here, but I haven't seen you in months. I've tried giving you your space. I just assumed, at some point, you'd finally have enough of it. You're staying."

I swallowed, nodding. Even if I was unwelcome, the hostility might prove a distraction.

Mother guided me gently to the door and opened it. "Friede, grind some yarrow."

Elfriede picked up a bowl from the counter on which she prepared the roast. She pulled a pestle out of the bowl and walked across the room toward us, Arrow's eyes on her the whole time. "I've already prepared it, Mother."

Mother smiled, and I could almost hear the "what a perfect, helpful daughter" oozing out from between her lips. "Thank you, dear." She took the bowl and continued dragging me along, only letting me go long enough to pour some water from the bucket into the basin before dunking my hand into it.

Mother added a little water to the bowl and picked up the pestle. I waited, unmoving. Even though I couldn't see them, I could feel the eyes burning at my back. I'd only spared the women the briefest of glances before being dragged over to the basin. If I knew Elfriede, Marden had to be among their number. I couldn't for the life of me think of any of her friends I hoped would be there. Somehow, all of Elfriede's good friends seemed to have been paired with mine. I supposed it only made sense. Most goddesses weren't a thousand years younger than their men, after all.

Mother spread the poultice over my wound. It stung, but she grabbed harder so I wouldn't have a chance to pull away.

Someone cleared her throat from the table behind me. "Perhaps we should get back."

Mother patted my hand dry with her apron, taking care not to touch the goopy mixture at my fingertip. "Marden, dear," she said without looking up. "You told me you'd stay for dinner."

I took in the women at the table out of the corner of my eye. Marden twirled her fingers through a curly, dark tendril. "I don't think we should impose. I didn't realize you'd have company."

"It's just my daughter, dear. My husband's out for the evening, so there's plenty of space." Mother smiled and let the apron fall, patting my hand gently. "It'll be just us women." She squeezed my hand as if to emphasize I belonged with the group.

"Roslyn's got an early shift tomorrow."

"I can stay."

I turned to face the table and saw the beauty who'd been with Jaron and the other men at the tavern a few days before. The one who'd left almost the moment I sat down to join them. She struggled to smile at me when I caught her eye. But she seemed to put in the effort—so much so, I felt compelled to smile back. Just a little.

"Wonderful." Mother clasped her hands together and crossed the room to the cupboard, pulling out the plates. "How's the roast, dear?"

I hadn't noticed Elfriede standing beside the fire, turning over a hunk of well-charred meat. "It's ready," she said, reaching out for a set of tongs behind her.

I grabbed a handful of skirt in my good hand and shuffled my feet, trying to decide whether it was better to run for the door or remain standing beneath the assault of the Tanner daughters' gazes.

"Noll, for goddess's sake, help me set the table."

I jumped at the word "goddess," immediately shuffling over to where Mother held out the wooden plates.

"Let me," said Roslyn, standing. "Noll is injured." She smiled tightly again. "Why don't you have a seat?"

I took one look at the thin, hard line of Marden's lips and immediately cut my own struggling smile short.

Chapter Sixteen

"DOES ALVILDA STILL GIVE YOU her surplus of work?" Mother put her fork down beside her plate. She hadn't taken very big portions, and she'd barely touched what little she'd taken.

I coughed, feeling the silence hanging over the table, remembering the day we'd first brought home the stool on which I sat. The day Elfriede first invited Jurij for dinner. "She does. I mean, she *did*. I haven't seen her much the past few weeks."

Marden snorted and stabbed a chunk of meat with her fork. "Why doesn't that surprise me?"

Elfriede stifled a laugh, making a great show of getting up from the table to bring over another pitcher of water.

I tapped my plate with my fork. "She's not upset with me, if that's what you think. Things have just been... awkward. All around."

Roslyn watched me carefully over her forkful of potato. Even while Elfriede and Marden had spoken to one another and to Mother, Roslyn had yet to say a word since we'd started eating.

"Awkward," Marden spat as Elfriede filled her mug and sat down beside her. "That's a mild way of putting it."

Mother seemed about to say something but instead

took a sip from her mug. I wanted to ask if Father was at the tavern—if Father was *frequently* at the tavern—but I didn't think it right to ask the question in front of an audience ready to jump down my throat.

"Some people seem to have adjusted." I picked at a potato on my plate. I didn't mean for my eyes to flit accusingly toward Elfriede and Roslyn, but they did. Roslyn hadn't done anything to make me unwelcome, and I'd already sort of hashed things out with Friede. I quickly turned to Mother. "Jaron is about as happy as I've ever seen any man."

Mother's shoulders stiffened at the name, and I couldn't help but watch for Elfriede's reaction. She cupped her hand in front of her face and whispered something to Marden that caused both of them to dissolve into stifled laughter. Not what I'd expected.

Roslyn set down her fork. "I think you'd have to be a man to be happy with how things are now."

I shoved a too-large piece of potato into my mouth in an attempt to stop the feelings that threatened to swell up through my chest.

Mother stroked her mug with her finger. "Women like Alvilda." A corner of her lips turned up. "Siofra. They're probably happier than anyone."

Marden raised her eyebrows. "Because they each fell in love with another woman?"

"Because they no longer have the burden of what to do with the love of men." Mother reached across the table to grab Elfriede's pitcher of water and poured herself a glass. "Men whose love they never wanted anyway."

I lowered my fork. There was something about her tone that made the rest of the food on my plate suddenly unappetizing.

"I'm glad you've all been trying to move on." Mother cradled her mug, not overly concerned with drinking from it. "Girls, it's time we stopped feeling sorry for ourselves. It's time we stopped waiting around for men to worship us. It's not going to happen anymore."

"Mother, is there something wrong with you and—"

She held out a hand to stop me, lowering her mug without even having a sip. "Things with your father are right where we both want them to be."

"But you never got remarried."

Mother snorted. "Who needs a piece of paper?" She grimaced. "We're... working through some things. We both need some space. Time to reevaluate who we are. And there's no room for bitterness in this. Things are different. We just have to accept that."

Roslyn burst into tears. She sobbed so hard her shoulders shook. Marden wrapped an arm around her and pulled her into an embrace. Elfriede jumped up to stand behind her, tucking Roslyn's hair behind her shoulders. Mother touched her elbow. I froze.

"It's just..." Roslyn pulled away from her sister and wiped her cheeks with the heel of her hand. "I lost *everything*. Not just Darwyn, but my way of life. The feeling that someone was there for me, no matter what happened. Knowing I meant everything to someone, even if I meant nothing to anyone else. The things that got me through the day, the reasons I woke up in the morning."

Elfriede stroked her hair. "*We're* here for you, Roslyn. We feel the same way."

"And you're not *nothing* to us, Lyn. We're family," Marden added, her own eyes glistening.

"I know. I know." Roslyn hiccupped as she took a deep breath. "It's not that I'm not grateful to have the job at the tavern. Or to be back home. But the tavern work is so different, nothing like the bakery, and things are so tense between Mother and Father at the tannery. And you're just as miserable as I am, Mar."

Marden snorted. "I'm *over* being miserable. Sindri can take a jump off the mountainside for all I care."

"*Marden*. You don't mean that." Elfriede was crying, too. She let go of Roslyn's shoulder just for a moment to wipe a tear from her own eye. Then she and Marden stared at one another and laughed, choking on hiccups.

"No, I *do* mean it." Marden threw her shoulders back and tossed her dark hair over her shoulder. "I mean, I wouldn't be *happy* if he jumped off the mountainside."

Roslyn's voice was quieter. "But what if there was never any hope of you getting back with Sindri?" She craned her head up to look behind her. "Or Jurij?"

Elfriede's smile vanished, and she patted Roslyn's shoulder lightly. "There *isn't* any hope."

I grabbed my mug of water with a shaking hand and brought it to my lips, dying for a way to occupy myself.

Marden shook her head. "It's not a matter of hope. I'm not hoping for that." She leaned back in her chair. "Why would I want this man I hardly know back? He's not the man who worshipped me. He's not *my* Sindri. That man's gone."

Roslyn wiped her nose on her sleeve. "But my Darwyn really *is* gone." She heaved a great sob and buried her head in her arms on the table. Mother carefully leaned forward to pull the plate out of her way. "He's in love with another *man*!"

I spit out my water, immediately drawing the attention of every other person in the room—and the dog for that matter.

Marden rolled her eyes. "Don't tell me *you* didn't know. I thought you were *one of the boys*."

I nearly tipped the mug over as I clumsily put it back on the table. "I've seen them a few times. I don't know *everything* they've been up to." Darwyn wrapped in a sheet, walking into the room a few minutes later with Tayton, the looks and light touches that passed between them that night—all of a sudden everything took on a very different meaning. I wiped my mouth with the back of my sleeve.

Roslyn was only fleetingly deterred by my outburst. "And they meet *at the tavern*! I'm working tables and practically passing out from exhaustion, and he's upstairs with that big-lipped, obtuse fool that Rosalba never really liked in the first place." She burst into louder sobs and slammed her head against her arms once more.

I opened my mouth, ready to defend Tayton. Not that we were really good friends. Or that I'd forgotten how he'd acted toward me and Ingrith a few years back. I was at least a little amused by the fact that I wasn't the only one who'd noticed his resemblance to a fish, even with the wooden fish mask removed. But Elfriede seemed to read my mind, and the glare that she gave me before I could move my tongue was enough to shut my mouth again.

Mother grabbed a fresh rag from the basin, dipping it in the clean bucket of water before wringing it out. She slid back into her chair and patted Roslyn's elbow gently, rousing her and offering the cloth. "It's good to let it out sometimes, dear." She nodded as Roslyn took the rag and began tapping it against her cheeks. "So long as you know that tears won't change anything."

Roslyn nodded sullenly, and even Marden let out a great sigh. The fire seemed to have left her, if just for a moment. Roslyn held the damp cloth in both hands, staring at it. "It's not that I'm jealous." She grinned as Marden nudged her. "Okay, I'm a *little* jealous. But like Marden said, I miss *my* Darwyn. I don't care what *this* Darwyn does. I just miss what we once had." She gently put the rag down on the table. "I hate working at the tavern."

"Mother and Father could use your help with the tanning," said Marden.

Roslyn interrupted her. "No. I was so glad to be done with that the first time."

Marden shrugged. "It's not *that* bad. I guess. A little tiresome now that I have to do it without Sindri..." She smiled sheepishly. "*Okay*, without him to boss around. I said it. I miss bossing my husband around."

Roslyn laughed and rubbed some of the moisture off of her face with the back of her hand. "*You* would."

Marden grinned. "What did we need a man for, if

not for someone to support us?" She looked at her sister, Elfriede, and Mother in turn. "I'm serious! What do you miss so badly?"

Roslyn tried her faltering smile. "The bakery."

Mother tossed her head back. "His arms around me."

Elfriede pinched her lips. "His eyes. And the flame within them. It seemed to light up the world around us, like it burned just for the two of us, and the love we shared."

The four of them fell into silence. Even Marden lost some of her fire.

I cleared my throat, bringing their drifting attention back to the fact that there was someone else left in the room. "I think I can help at least one of you." I nodded at Roslyn. "Darwyn's mother really misses you. Why can't you keep working at the bakery?"

Roslyn seemed to light up for just a moment, but a shadow fell quickly back over her face. "I can't."

"Why not?" I reached for the golden copper I kept tucked in the band at my waist, finding comfort in the solid shape. "I get it. I get it more than any of you might believe. It's not a great feeling when your entire world is ripped out from underneath you."

Marden's nose crinkled. "I thought *you* were happy with the way things turned out. Since it freed your sister's husband to move in with you."

"Oh, but consider how much she lost, too!" Roslyn covered her mouth at the outburst, clearly embarrassed. "I just meant... the castle. You could have been not just his wife, but his *lady*. Lady of the entire village."

"I'm not cut out to be anybody's wife. And I'm nobody's lady."

I glanced at Elfriede to see what she thought of the comment. Her usually plush lips were thin, unmoving. "Imagine what it's like for the men," I said. "They went from knowing exactly what they wanted—from knowing *all* they'd ever want, experiencing bliss or despair because of it—to suddenly having the freedom we've had all along.

How can you expect them to trust their own hearts, after years of their hearts misleading them?"

I let go of the coin and put my hand flat against my leg, willing myself to forget Ailill. "The power we had over men was dangerous. But at least if we loved the men back, everyone knew that love to be true." I locked eyes with Elfriede. "The love the men gave us—it was never true. It was never their choice."

I stood up from the table. "But that doesn't mean we have to just curl up in the corner and wait for the men to sort out their messes. We have our own lives. We should be finding what *we* can do to make ourselves happy, instead of lamenting that there isn't a man who's a slave to our whims anymore." I threw back my shoulders. "I'll go with you, Roslyn. Let's get your job back. Darwyn's mother said you were good. It'd be a shame to waste your talent."

Roslyn regarded her sister for a moment, and Marden simply shrugged and looked pointedly away. "But I can't deal with Darwyn," said Roslyn. "He hates me."

"He doesn't hate you. I promise you." I moved around the table and held my hand out to Roslyn. "But if you want someone to hate, hate the first goddess, not him. She caused all this to happen in the first place. She didn't really think things through."

Roslyn studied me, and I wondered what kind of pain was written on my face. Perhaps some part of me wanted to give it all away, to tell them who I was really blaming. But then Roslyn took my hand and stood up slowly. "If you really think they'll take me back."

Mother smiled and nodded, encouraging me to continue.

"I *know* they will," I said, squeezing Roslyn's hand. "And if working there makes *you* happy, the rest will follow."

Roslyn smiled and squeezed back.

Chapter Seventeen

$\mathfrak{I}$T WAS GETTING DARK BY the time Roslyn and I reached the middle of the village, and people were shuffling out of their shops to light the torches that illuminated their doorways. Roslyn looked happier than any woman had ever looked on her Returning day. She looked happier than I'd ever seen her with Darwyn—although, to tell the truth, I'd hardly paid attention in those days. Darwyn's mother burst into tears and embraced Roslyn the moment the request to move back in and keep working at the bakery was out of her mouth.

"My sweet girl, you dearest!" Darwyn's mother kissed her atop her head over and over. "You'll always be a daughter to me. You don't even have to ask."

The next half hour was filled with both women laughing and crying, and Mistress Baker assuring Roslyn she was doing her the greater favor, and Roslyn insisting the opposite. Finally they both just agreed to disagree and continue to think they owed each other everything. If it weren't for what I wanted to ask Roslyn, I might have left, leaving the two women to have their endless moment.

Now all that was left was for Roslyn to work one last shift at the tavern and tell Vena and Elweard she was moving on. And to tell Darwyn she was moving in. Just not into the room they'd shared.

"You really don't think Darwyn will mind?" Roslyn's ecstasy was interrupted every few moments with a wrinkled brow as she kept asking the same question over and over.

"No, I don't."

"I mean, it'll be awkward for me regardless. But I *know* he's moved on. And baking will keep me busy." She cocked her head. "It might actually go smoother without having to tell him to do one task after another. I always thought he kind of got underfoot when he was my husband. I'm not like some women. I don't need kisses every few seconds to keep me going." She nodded and kept walking, jauntily placing one foot in front of the other. I decided not to let my curiosity about which women she might have meant distract me.

I grabbed her arm gently. "Roslyn."

She hugged me before I could stop her. "Oh, *thank you*, Olivière!"

I felt my cheeks burn and my throat grow dry, both at the hug and the sound of the name only one person still called me. "Noll," I corrected. I patted her gently on the back, not used to embracing other women my age. Other than Elfriede, that is, and we were out of practice.

Roslyn laughed and pulled back. "Of course! I know. Sorry. I just think your full name is so pretty. And it's a very pretty evening, isn't it?" She turned on her heel and started walking back toward the tavern.

"Wait!" I called, jogging a few steps to catch up to her. "Before you go in, can I ask you something?"

Roslyn still seemed to be floating in her bliss, her smile only faltering slightly when a man's shoulder shoved against her back as he went ahead to enter the tavern. "Is this about Friede?"

"No." I opened my mouth to speak again, only to feel a lump forming in my throat at the way Roslyn's face fell. "Is there something I should know about Elfriede?"

Roslyn threaded her fingers together. "She's not happy."

"I know that." I took a deep breath. "She's far from the only one."

This time it was my turn to be jostled from behind as another group of men found their way into the tavern. "Hello, sweetheart!" one called out to Roslyn. His smile and wink reminded me distastefully of the men who'd spurred me to start this whole mess long ago.

Roslyn waved halfheartedly and tucked a strand of hair behind her ear, shrugging at me. "I definitely won't miss all the attention from the tavern."

I nodded. I wasn't going to be distracted again. "The other night, when I visited Jaron's room—"

"He's just a friend. I don't like him the way the other girls do. I wasn't seeing him or anything."

I gripped the coin in my sash with my poultice-free hand, resisting the temptation to cut her off with my hand over her lips. "I just want to know what happened between them and the spec—the lord's servant."

Roslyn cocked her head, her joy completely erased by bewilderment. "The lord's servant? He usually sends one or two a night to collect ale and wine."

I wondered what a man who'd reduced his bread intake to skip the appearances of feeding a hundred still had to do with daily shipments of alcohol. And ale as well as wine. I shook my head. "But why was one in Jaron's room then?"

Roslyn hugged her arm against her side. "I don't know. They don't speak, you know?"

"I know."

She looked over her shoulder at the tavern door, as if eager to step away from the conversation. Instead, she turned back and kept her voice low. "But Jaron seemed to know he wanted something. He teased him and told him to join them for some food and ale, but the lord's servant didn't budge from right inside the doorway." She covered her mouth and sneezed, and I just about shouted out in frustration at the delay. She sniffed. "He stood there for a quarter of an hour. It made for an awkward meal. Then Jaron told the servant he could either take 'it' himself or stand there all night, but he wasn't about to hand 'it' over 'just because some wide-eyed vacant man stood there staring at him.' And then the servant left."

So Roslyn didn't know anything about the page with the moving drawing. "Does the servant often stop by Jaron's room when he comes to the tavern?"

"I don't know. I don't spend all my breaks up there, but Vena said it'd be quieter than it was on the ground floor, so I kind of got used to it." She looked over her shoulder again. "I should really go tell Vena this will be my last night." She turned on her heel and then stopped. "Do you mind breaking the news to Darwyn for me?"

I let go of the coin in my sash. "That you're moving back in?"

Roslyn nodded.

"I can go with you to tell him if you like, but it really should come from you."

Roslyn put her hand on my shoulder. "Great, thank you! I'll be upstairs after I talk with Vena. You can just ease him into it."

She was gone inside the tavern before I could say anything more. I squeezed my fists together, almost forgetting about the slight jab of pain it would cause in my poultice-covered fingertip. *She's given you an excuse to talk to them again. Just take it.*

I pulled open the door. The tavern was as crowded as it had been the other night, and I wondered why setting men free from the curse of love meant they all felt the need to gravitate toward more ale than was good for them. *Don't any of them eat at home with their wives anymore? Do any of them have wives anymore?*

I caught sight of Roslyn leaning over the counter, talking to Vena and Elweard as they scrambled to fill up mugs. Vena's mouth was slightly puckered, and Elweard nodded solemnly. I hoped Roslyn left my name out of it.

I slid between two tables to reach the staircase, stretching my hand out to grab hold of the railing like it was the ledge of a cliff in the suffocating noise and warmth of the crowded tavern.

"Noll?"

If I hadn't been half expecting to see another specter or a half-naked friend, I might have jumped more at the sound of someone calling my name. As it was, it wasn't the presence that startled me, but the identity of the person who'd spoken. "Father?"

His eyes were glazed, his cheeks slightly darker than they ought to have been. But then again, my memories of him anything but flushed with ale were starting to fade. I'd been home so seldom after Mother returned, and it didn't look like being reunited with her was improving his health, now that there was nothing left to tie them together but history and two daughters.

Father stumbled a little and on reflex, I reached out to catch him. He threw a hand out to stop me and caught himself on the rail, slapping his feet down the last two stairs. "They say you won't help."

I pulled my arms back. "Won't help?"

"Jaron said he and the others might be close to getting some answers, but they need your help." He brushed his face with his forearm as if to clear his eyes of the cloudiness. "But you wouldn't help them. Just like you wouldn't help me."

The laughter in the tavern grew louder, buzzing in my ears. "Help you? I did nothing but help you in all the time Mother was at the castle."

Father let go of the railing and pointed at me. "You and that castle. You won't have anything to do with that castle. No matter how many people must suffer for it."

He was wrong. I'd *gone* there. Even though I hadn't wanted to, I'd done it for him and Mother and Elfriede. But it wasn't enough for him. It never was. I backed up as much as I could to get out of the way of his trembling finger, but there wasn't enough space to move. "What's this about, Father?"

There were tears welling around his dark, lifeless irises. "I don't love her anymore." He wiped his nose with his wrist and hiccupped. "And I don't like it."

Although I half expected it, my stomach clenched at his admission. "If you don't like it, then change it. *Choose* to love Mother." I reached back to grab the railing, tapping my fingers atop it.

"I don't know how." Father took a deep breath and clutched his shirt. "I don't know how to deal with these feelings. Like wanting to be alone, but feeling anger at the idea of her with someone else. Like having this *hole* in my chest and not knowing how to fill it." He stared at me accusingly. "But *he* might have the answers. And you won't get them from him."

He hobbled off, almost tumbling against a man seated at a nearby table. The man laughed. "Little too much to drink, hey, Master Carver?" He turned back to his companions, chuckling away. Father kept walking, undisturbed, vanishing into a crowd of men and mugs and plates.

I watched him pityingly, then squared my shoulders and walked up the stairs. I had enough to think about without Father blaming me for his problems. That wasn't anything new anyway.

I paused in front of the door to Jaron's room, about to knock. I couldn't think of what I wanted to say, if I should go in on the pretense of speaking with Darwyn, or if I should just come out and ask what they wanted from me.

The door creaked open at my knock. I poked my head in, but there was no fire roaring, no man in sight.

"Hello? Jaron? Darwyn? Sindri?"

The room was a mess, with plates scattered on the ground and clothing and bed sheets tossed about like someone had been looking for something in a hurry. I noticed the box in which Jaron kept the page open and upside down atop the bed.

"Hello?" *Maybe someone found something in a hurry.*

I took a step into the room and felt a pair of arms embrace me from behind, pulling me roughly backward into the hallway.

Chapter Eighteen

MY ASSAILANT WANTED TO DRAG me into the neighboring room, but I reached out for the doorframe and pulled hard, kicking back at his shins. "Let me—"

A hand covered my mouth, even as he muttered, "Ow. Noll, it's me. Be quiet and come in here."

I let go of the doorframe and stomped my foot. Jurij tugged me inside by the elbow and closed the door behind us. The room resembled Jaron's, only there was a fire roaring and the room wasn't torn to pieces. I tapped my foot. "Well?"

Jurij put a finger in front of his lips as he shook one of his legs. Probably the one I'd kicked. He walked over to the table and pointed to a piece of paper. *The* piece of paper. My good hand trembled as I stepped forward, leaning on the table for support. The drawings were moving, little Luuk walking in place—or that's what it seemed at first. The trees in the background kept disappearing off the edge, and I realized he was walking forward.

Trees. "He's in the woods."

Jurij placed a hand on my shoulder, stopping me. "One of *them* is in the next room over," he whispered.

I frowned. "One of the lord's servants? Jaron's room was empty. Ransacked, but empty."

Jurij's lips twitched. He pointed to the wall. Not the wall bordering Jaron's, the other one.

I studied Jurij's face but realized I was about as likely to get him to explain what was going on as I was to find Ailill himself in the next room. I looked back at the piece of paper and watched Luuk walk down the path that ran through the woods. His lips were drawn in a tight line. He shivered. The sun had set, and the nights were getting cooler.

"What's he *doing*?" Lowering my voice seemed to be the only thing that would make Jurij willing to talk. I wasn't in the mood to explain the volume of our voices probably didn't make any difference. It wasn't like someone had *stolen* the piece of paper. Ailill had clearly wanted us to have it.

Jurij ignored my question. "What if he has pages for all of us?"

I thought about that. Paper Luuk flinched and crouched, only to see a rabbit burst out of the line of trees in front of him. He breathed easier, stood, and kept on his way. "Maybe he does," I admitted.

Jurij tapped the paper. "Well, he at least doesn't have Luuk's anymore."

"What are you saying?"

I didn't think it was possible, but Jurij lowered his voice even further. "Then Luuk's the only one he won't see coming."

"You sent a child to the castle alone?"

Jurij shushed me again. This was beginning to feel a bit ridiculous.

"*Okay*," I whispered, pointing at the paper. "What is he going to do?"

Jurij shrugged. "Just look around a little."

I crossed my arms, not caring that I scraped off some of the hardened poultice as I did. "Luuk. The kid whose hand Nissa had to hold every time they strayed too far in the cavern."

"You wouldn't help us."

"So I keep hearing." Luuk arrived at the castle gates. At least they were bound to stop this foolish plan, since I doubted they'd open. "Does your father know? Or your mother?"

"Father does." Jurij pulled the paper closer to him. Luuk was pushing on the gates to no avail. "We haven't spoken to Mother in days. It's not really easy between Father and Mother at the moment."

"Of course." I imagined Siofra or Alvilda would have tried to knock some sense into them. Maybe literally. Luuk was running his hand over the wall now. Looking for a secret entrance? "So why is a spec—*servant* in the room next door? Is he looking for this?" I pointed to the paper and gasped when I saw Luuk grab onto a protruding stone and haul himself up. He dangled on the wall, his feet a short distance from the ground.

"We think we convinced him it was stolen. Maybe." Jurij seemed unconcerned with the little drawing of his brother, who swung his arm out a few times until he finally found another stone to grab. "We ransacked Jaron's room ourselves before the servant got here."

"He's going to hurt himself." My face snapped up from the paper. "*You* guys did that? Why?"

Jurij stepped closer, one finger in front of his lips to quiet me, the other reaching out to touch my shoulder. "The servant in the room next door can hear you."

I tore my eyes away from Jurij to make sure Luuk was okay. He'd reached the top of the wall. "How is he going to get down?" I whispered. Luuk answered my question for me by swinging his legs over to the other side and dangling from the top. He slipped, falling the few feet straight to the ground. I flinched, but Luuk stood up and brushed off his pants.

I let out a breath I didn't realize I was holding as Luuk slinked away from the wall. I tapped the paper. "You think *he* has pages like this to watch everyone?"

Jurij nodded.

"So he could be watching us watching Luuk right now."

Jurij nodded again.

"So what was the point of the ransacking if he can see us looking at the paper?"

"We just wanted to make sure we kept the servant nearby. Jaron and the others are explaining that it was stolen."

"What's the point of keeping one servant nearby? There are at least a hundred servants at the castle! Where you sent Luuk!"

"We know. We just figured that if the lord's watching, he'll be watching the servant in the village. The one with us."

I touched my forehead with my fingertips, shaking my head and not caring about the tiny prick of pain in my sore finger. "I wish I *had* offered to help you. I could have told you that the man's not as stupid as you seem to think."

Jurij reached for the hand that was tapping my forehead, tugging it gently downward. "What happened to you?" He cradled my hand, running a fingertip across my skin so lightly I couldn't help but picture a flower petal swaying gently across the back of my hand. Lying down in the warm grass. Jurij at my side. Right there, yet so out of reach. *Ailill.* Of all the people to think about now, I had to think about Ailill, holding my hand just like this the night I first met him. *Were they so different, now that I knew Jurij capable of anger, and Ailill capable of compassion? Was it the curse that made them seem so different to me at first, or was it... Ailill had been alone for so long. Jurij didn't understand how fortunate he'd been, having a family to love him. Having Elfriede accept and love him.*

"A small cut." I pulled my hand away and forced my breathing to slow. "Jurij, you need to tell me what's going on, or I'm about to march to that castle to find Luuk." The drawing of Luuk paused. There were no windows on the ground floor at the front of the castle. He gave the door a tug with both hands. I whipped my head back to Jurij. "What is the point of all of this? If he gets caught, he could—"

Jurij grabbed hold of both of my shoulders and pulled me toward him, his lips pressing hard against mine.

I don't know how long we stayed like that. I don't even remember if I had adequate time to step back and didn't—out of shock, maybe. Or because some part of me wanted the kiss.

Fool.

Our door burst open, and I finally came to my senses. I was just about to release his lips and pull back, when Jurij took charge and ended the kiss for me. "You must have felt us calling for you," he said, smiling. It was a hollow echo of the smile he used to give Elfriede at one of her kisses.

A specter stared at us—stared at *me*. Behind him, the firelight just barely flickered over the forms of Jaron, Master Tailor, Sindri, Darwyn, and Tayton in the hallway.

Jurij grabbed my hand, threading his fingers through mine. He brushed against the poultice, and the skin beneath it stung. I watched him warily out of the corner of my eye, but he looked straight ahead, facing the specter.

He grinned. "Noll and I would like to get married."

Chapter Nineteen

HE SPECTER STOOD PERFECTLY STILL. I lost my sense of time, only awakening when I noticed the group gathered in the hall disappearing into the darkness of the stairway.

Jurij squeezed my hand, and I studied him. The lump in his throat wobbled, but he still looked straight ahead. "Don't you need to bring out a piece of paper for us to sign?"

At the word "paper," Jurij seemed to remember what he'd left clear as day on the table. He guided me by the hand to block the view, his free hand extended toward the specter as if expecting him to produce one of those marriage certificates from his pocket.

The specter didn't respond, his red irises locked on me. Then he reached into his pocket and pulled out an ink well, quill, and piece of paper.

I tugged on Jurij's hand and whispered, "What. Are. You. Doing?"

The specter crossed to the table in a few strides. Jurij reached back and grabbed Luuk's paper, crumpling it into a ball in his fist. I almost gasped, wondering if such a thing could be broken.

"Jurij," I whispered. I didn't know whether to expose Jurij's audacity in full view of one of the lord's servants. This had to be a distraction so Luuk—and the others now too?—could explore the castle unimpeded. They'd wanted me to summon Ailill out of the castle, and I'd refused, but they'd gone ahead and figured out a way they just might do it on their own. Only it still relied on me, and without my consent. I ground my teeth together. "*Darling*," I said, in my best impression of Elfriede at her finest. Jurij's hand twitched at the word, his palm moist and sweaty against mine. "I know we've discussed marriage, but perhaps we should wait until our parents can attend."

"Marriage is just a piece of paper now," he snapped. "And I've had enough overdone ceremonies to last me a lifetime."

The specter dipped the quill in the open ink well and began writing.

"We've discussed this, too. *You've* had ceremonies. I never loved anyone else enough to even have a Returning."

The specter's arm stiffened, halting his writing. Then he dipped his pen again and wrote even more furiously.

"Yes, but it has to be tonight, sweetheart." Jurij squeezed my hand hard, as if to emphasize his point. I squeezed back to emphasize that I was going to slap him for using me this way the moment it was all over. I didn't think he got my message. "You agreed, just moments ago. We can't keep living a lie. It's time we were husband and wife."

"Noll? Darwyn—oh, sorry. Am I interrupting?" Roslyn poked her head in through the open door. She glanced at the specter hunched over the table and took him in from head to foot. She didn't comment, just pointed behind her. "I tried the room that Tayton stays in. And I was about to try Jaron's when I saw this door open." She shook her head. "Never mind, I'll just tell him later."

"No!" The volume of my voice made Jurij jump. His grip slackened, and I pulled my hand away, wiping it on the front of my skirt. I'd worn the poultice down and felt my skin rip a little again. I rushed across the room and slid my arm through Roslyn's. She cocked her head as if to ask what had come over me, but I pulled her toward Jurij and the specter as if it were only natural, as if Roslyn and I had been friendly for years instead of just the past few hours. I patted her arm. She was going to be my excuse to stop this whole mess without admitting in front of the specter that my friends were idiots. "Seeing Roslyn reminds me, Jurij. I'd really prefer we had some witnesses. It will be tonight, of course, but you have to do this for me. It's my first and only time, after all. *Please.*"

Jurij's eyes darted from the hunched over specter, to Roslyn, to me. The specter didn't react at all. I frowned. Had anyone ever seen a specter write anything? All the notes I assumed came from Ailill himself, written ahead of time. The marriage certificates for Vena and Elweard or Alvilda and Siofra were already written, without names, when the specters brought them out of their pockets. They just required signatures. No one had ever gotten one of these silent spirits to respond in any way—no one besides Ailill, in any case. The only way we knew they could understand us was because they acted differently when we spoke to them.

I could feel Roslyn shrink back just a little in my grip. "Are you two getting *married*?" She pointed at the specter. "Right now?"

"*Yes—*" started Jurij.

"No!" I shook my head and swallowed, feeling Jurij's expectations boring through me along with his pointed gaze. "I mean, not right *now*, we were just discussing that."

Roslyn pulled her arm out from mine and, although I expected her to flee or get angry, considering her relationship with my sister, she took my hand in both of hers. "Noll, it's really none of my business. I won't try to stop you from getting married. If you're both happy, I have no reason to stop you."

Jurij and I exchanged a glance as Roslyn dropped one hand and guided me gently toward him. She placed my hand atop his, shackling me back to the man I once loved—maybe *still* loved—who'd just tried to force me to marry

149

him because of a stupid plan. He hadn't even asked if I was willing to participate. I felt the crinkle of paper in Jurij's fist and slipped it out into my hand, hopefully without either Roslyn or the specter noticing. But the specter wasn't looking. He stood straight now and put the stopper back on the ink. Jurij gripped my wrist before I could pull my hand away.

Roslyn's lips quivered. "It's just—Elfriede's awfully unhappy."

Jurij's face soured. "Things aren't the same as they were."

"I know! Believe me, I know." Roslyn spoke quietly as she broke into a shy smile. "And things being different doesn't mean they have to be unhappy."

I tried returning her smile, but my focus was drawn to the specter. He tapped the quill on the jar of ink to shake out the remaining droplets and laid it down beside the certificate, straightening his jacket.

"I just think—I mean, Noll and Friede are sisters. They may not have a lot in common, but they love each other, right?" Roslyn's voice quivered at the end of the sentence, perhaps not as sure about her statement as she pretended to be.

I hesitated but nodded. "Yes, but—"

Roslyn held out a hand to stop me. "I understand things between the three of you are complicated. But I do think Elfriede can be happy without Jurij. I *know* it. Only..."

Jurij's hand on my wrist slackened at the same time his back stiffened. "Then what's the problem?"

Roslyn tilted her head toward me, as if waiting for me to speak. The specter stepped around Jurij and walked toward the doorway, the ink well, quill, and certificate left behind on the table. I leaned around Jurij, trying to get a better look at the certificate. "I think Roslyn is saying we need to make peace with Elfriede."

Roslyn clapped her hands. "Yes!" She reached forward and wrapped her arms around my shoulders for a hug. "I told Friede she just needed to talk to you!" She pulled back to look me in the eyes. "That there's no way her sister could be doing anything to hurt her on purpose!"

Jurij had let my wrist go in the confusion, and I patted Roslyn's back awkwardly. Even with the paper in my fist, I figured it was better than to pat her with my hand that had started bleeding again. "Roslyn's right," I said, glaring at Jurij pointedly. "We shouldn't say we're getting married before *discussing it* with the people most affected."

Jurij furrowed his brow and refused to return my look. I followed his eyes to the doorway and noticed the specter had left us. Before we'd had a chance to sign anything.

Roslyn noticed now too and pulled away from me, covering her mouth with one hand. "Oh! Sorry. Did I make you reconsider?"

I scowled. Agreeing to talk to Elfriede first wasn't the same as telling the specter we'd changed our minds. "What do you mean?"

Roslyn stood on her toes and tried to peer over Jurij's and my shoulders at the table behind us. "Well, they're not supposed to pull out a marriage certificate unless they know both parties want to get married, right?"

I felt a twitch at the pit of my stomach. She was probably right. But I'd been taken aback. I'd tried to play along, but was that the same as accepting the marriage? How did the specters judge that anyway? The piece of paper showing Luuk felt heavy in my hand, and I tucked it into my sash beside the golden copper.

"So I figured if he left before you signed it, he must be waiting for you to make peace first." She smiled.

I gave her a faltering smile in return. "You're right." Jurij turned and peered over the table. Roslyn seemed eager to get a look, too, so I grabbed her hand gently and led her to the door. "Thank you," I cooed, trying again to sound like Elfriede. "You've given us a lot to talk over. Um..."

"I'll give you some privacy," said Roslyn. I almost

laughed at that, considering what we'd discovered about moving drawings on pages. She squeezed my hand. "And thank *you*, Noll." She pulled the door shut behind her.

I had a feeling that might be the last time I'd hear those words from anyone for quite a while.

"Noll, Luuk's page! Quickly!"

I was across the room with my hand digging into my sash for the crumpled wad before I could think about how embarrassed and angry I was. He sounded *that* worried. Jurij peered over my shoulder as I unfurled the paper.

It took me a moment to orient myself to the drawing. But Luuk was crying, tears clearly visible on his ink face. His hands gripped iron bars, and he shook them. His mouth was open, and I could almost hear the cry for help passing across his silent lips.

"Damn it." I shoved the paper at Jurij's chest. He caught it with trembling hands. "I could have told you there was no way he'd get away with it. What were you thinking?"

Jurij pulled the page away from his chest and examined it. "They're on their way. They'll find some way to help him. And *you* wouldn't help us."

"Well, you pretty much forced me to help anyway, didn't you? You might have told me what you were planning."

Jurij paused. "We thought he might be watching you too closely."

I threw my hands up in the air. "Well, in that case, he would have already seen me meeting the lot of you and being shown this page."

"That's why we stalled the one servant. To keep his attention on him."

I exhaled a deep breath. "Do you think the man's an idiot?"

The lump at Jurij's throat bobbed, and he laid Luuk's page on the table, absently smoothing it with one hand. "I don't know anything about the man. Other than he changed you."

"He changed *me*?" I crossed my arms. "Don't talk to me about change. I haven't changed. *You* have!"

"You *have* changed," Jurij said. "The Noll I love *loved* me. The only thing I can think of that might have changed your mind is him!"

I snorted. "Not falling in love with my sister, having a Returning with her, flaunting your sickeningly sweet affection in front of me day after day, and marrying her?"

"You loved me even so. You kissed me on my wedding day."

He had a point. I'd assumed that hadn't meant anything to him because he didn't have a will of his own. "It wasn't him who changed me."

Jurij let out a breath. "Then what did?"

I almost told him. He'd probably swear I imagined the whole thing or call me a liar. Yes, this new and changed Jurij would probably never believe me, but staring into his eyes and remembering the flames I once saw there, I felt the tension release from my neck and shoulders. I wanted to burst out crying. I wanted to hug him, to tell him everything. I took a step forward. But the marriage certificate on the table caught my eye.

If you think I am about to give my blessing to your happiness...

This is what the specter had written while we'd been trying to distract him. He hadn't been distracted at all.

If you think I am about to give my blessing to your happiness, you are mistaken. I cannot stop you from spending your nights beside the former husband of your own sister, but I am lord of this village, and under my new law, only my Ailills give permission to wed. There is no will of the first goddess in this village now. She foolishly gave me permission to crush her power into dust.

But it does not matter. I cannot hear you when not around my retainers, but I can see you, as I assume you and your cohorts might have learned. I allowed you this knowledge. I do not understand why they seem to think they can enter my castle unseen when they know what I can do. But I must forgive them for being foolish; they are quite new to the freedom of will that you and the other women have so long enjoyed.

This proposed marriage is a falsehood, a distraction meant to send me running to you. I have seen you. You push away this boy for whom you once risked everything because now he has free will. You do not like men with free will. You never have. You may stumble over your feelings for him now, but you will never commit to marrying him, or any other. Men are no longer docile enough for you.

Nothing you could do would make me come running. If your cohorts want answers, they should have asked you. You played a larger role in all of this than I ever could. As it is, they trespass without permission in my castle, and here they will stay.

Perhaps you will bring my pages back to me when you stop by for a visit, as I no doubt expect you to soon.

I flipped the paper over, dreading what I might see on the other side. A drawing burst to life of Master Tailor in a cell, his legs crossed on the stone floor. Beside him sat Sindri, his shoulder against the iron bars, and Darwyn and Tayton, who held hands even as Darwyn seemed to be shouting something and gripping his hair in anger. A pair of legs paced on and off the page, boots I guessed belonged to Jaron.

"He got them all," I said. Since it hadn't been that long since the men had left the tavern, I could only imagine Ailill had sent out his specters and a carriage to bring the rest of them to his cells that much quicker.

Jurij growled and began pacing back and forth across the room in echo of Jaron. "Now what?"

I folded the second moving drawing and tucked it in my sash. "Now we walk in through the front gates."

Chapter Twenty

WE DIDN'T SPEAK UNTIL WE'D reached the outskirts of the village, past the Tailor Shop. Seeing the empty, darkened windows emphasized where we were going like a punch to the stomach. I spared a moment's regret for not racing to tell Siofra and Alvilda. But then we'd be headed to the castle trailing behind a raging, screaming woman who probably wouldn't make it past the first set of specters.

"What did he mean, you played a larger role? And that we should have asked you?"

I was so distracted by my thoughts I flinched at hearing Jurij speak beside me. The timid smile that had formed at the thought of Alvilda in a rage faded, replaced by the cold hardness of the reality I'd created by going through the cavern pool.

The moon was bright, but I kept my eyes fixed on the path. I shivered as we neared my childhood home. Not just because of the cold nip in the air, or even due to the sister who slept behind closed doors. But because of the memories of another night I ventured down this path, cold and damp, determined to free the man who now walked beside me, the one I now pushed away.

He sighed and ran a hand through his hair. "Of course you wouldn't answer." He gave the home in which his former wife lived the briefest of glances and led the way into the woods. "How about this then: What did he mean, the Ailills?"

"That's his name. The lord's, I mean. Ailill."

A twig snapped loudly beneath Jurij's foot. "Huh. I guess no one ever bothered to ask his name before."

I tucked the pesky too-long piece of hair behind my ear, feeling guilty for so long not caring to know his name. "No one cared about anything outside of their men and goddesses before." *Or, in my case at least, other people's men.*

Jurij pushed aside a branch hanging across the path. "So the Ailills? Plural?"

"It's what he calls the specters."

"The what?"

"His servants."

"Why?"

"Long story."

"I'd like to know."

"I'm not sure we have time." The beaten shrubbery ahead marked the path to the cavern.

We were quiet then, but soon Jurij interrupted the silence. "You know, you never asked."

"Asked what?"

Jurij nodded toward the path ahead. "What it felt like the last time I was here. What it felt like to have my wedding day turned upside down."

I stopped. We didn't talk much about *my* time there. I didn't even think to ask about his. "You remember?"

"Not much. My whole life until things changed seems like a haze." He paused beside me. "But I remember... the shaking. Then waking in a strange place. The blur of white figures, the dark void at my bedside."

"The servants. And Ailill," I said. "Wearing his veil."

"I asked for Elfriede." Jurij traced the line of the scar on his cheek. "I remember the pain on my face, I remember how much it hurt, but it was nothing compared to how I felt being apart from Elfriede."

And he was parted from her because of me.

"But that was stupid of me," he said, his fist tightening around the paper in his hand. "I know that now."

Neither of us said anything for a moment, a moment we shouldn't have wasted just then.

"I was so consumed with thoughts of Elfriede," said Jurij, breaking the silence, "I didn't stop to think about it at first, but the lord, he was... a mess. He was wet. His veil and hat were uneven."

That was after he saved me from the pond. I shuddered thinking about what happened then, and how we'd fought in the cavern—how I'd almost killed him then and would go on to "kill" him for a time shortly thereafter. In the time between then, we'd parted as soon as the carriage door opened. Before he'd joined me in the dining room, he'd stormed upstairs—probably to treat Jurij. Although not to the "best of his ability," as I remembered asking.

"He took his gloves off, and I remember thinking how *pale* he was. How ghastly pale. Like one of his servants dressed in black."

"He's not quite so pale as that," I said, realizing Jurij had never seen Ailill without his mask. "But yes, he's fair."

Jurij didn't comment on it. I was glad. I didn't want to explain how I came to know Ailill's face so well.

"There was warmth on my face, then," continued Jurij, "and for a moment... I saw things with a clarity I'd never felt before then. The pain on my face lifted. The pain in my heart eased. I wasn't thinking of Elfriede. I wasn't thinking about anything."

He did try to heal him with his magic.

"Then it all stopped. The lord pulled his hand away and tugged on his glove roughly, like he'd burnt his hand. He said, 'I suppose you felt nothing then. When my goddess's lips touched yours.'"

My goddess? I'd forgotten he would call me that

from time to time. I knew I was his goddess once, but I'd bristled every time he said it. Now...

"I was so confused. I remembered you kissed me." He chanced a glance my way. "But it meant nothing to me when it happened. It wasn't the first thing on my mind even until he asked, but as that warmth faded away, I saw it clearly. Just for a moment. I *felt* something for you. Something greater than I'd ever felt for you, something like what I'd thought I could only feel for Elfriede."

Did his healing powers "heal" the curse right off a man? Could he have freed him when I asked and he chose not to, or did Ailill himself remain unaware of that fact? I never even thought about it!

"But it was just a moment. I remember... the lord said something more, something quieter then. 'If only you knew what you took from me. It was not even your fault. But I confess I cannot help myself even still.' As the pain rolled back over me, so did my longing for Elfriede. I was growing delirious, blind to everything about me. I asked for help, for some explanation, but they ignored me. I don't really remember what happened after that. I don't remember what happened for a *long* time after that."

"It wasn't just you, Jurij. Ailill didn't make you forget the next month. That was the month that no one seems to remember."

"But you do, don't you?"

I picked up my skirts. "We should go."

Jurij crumpled the paper in his hand, then seemed to notice what he was doing and smoothed it out. "The two of you keep so many secrets from the rest of us. And you wonder why I was so reluctant to ask you to play your role in this plan." Jurij held the paper showing Luuk up above him, trying to get the filtering effects of the moonlight to show him his brother. "What would he lock them up for?"

I rolled my eyes. "Breaking into his castle against his edict might have had something to do with it." I clutched Master Tailor's page in my hand, the paper with the message written so coldly for me on its reverse side. Some of the men in the image stood, and others sat. There wasn't much change. "We'll get it straightened out. He won't hurt them."

Jurij laughed, but there wasn't any joy in the sound. "You mean like how he didn't hurt me?" He pointed to his scarred eye.

"I don't think he meant to do that."

Jurij stuffed Luuk's paper into his pocket. "Well, I'm glad you don't *think* he meant to slice a gash down my face. Or take me captive thereafter."

"It was the earthquake!" I grabbed Jurij's hand, and he stopped, stiffening. "Before the curse broke, Ailill was doomed to cause the ground to shake if he left the castle. And he was trying to treat you when you woke up."

Jurij's features softened. I could just make out a glint in his irises in the silver light that trickled through the leaves above us. "So he didn't cause the earthquake on purpose?"

"No. Yes." I shook my head. "Whenever he left the castle back then, he'd cause an earthquake. He knew that, but he didn't control the tool that cut you."

"Why just him? The rest of us may have been cursed, but I don't recall any other man making the ground shake just because a woman looked at his home. Or because he stepped out of it."

"To protect him."

Jurij's gaze drifted over my head. The cavern lay behind me. I wondered if for some reason it was calling him too. "I have a feeling you know more, but you won't tell me if I ask."

I dropped Jurij's hand and moved forward, pushing the call of the cavern away with each step. "You wouldn't believe me if I told you."

"Tell me anyway." Jurij's hand gripped my shoulder, pulling me back to face him.

I faltered a moment. The castle gates were there, just

in sight at the edge of the path. The cavern still called me in some way I couldn't explain. I could run away to either of them to avoid answering him, to avoid thinking about my past—but both were the places I was most likely to remember. "I'm the first goddess."

Jurij's hand slackened. "What?" He was almost laughing.

I drew a deep breath. "The one from the legend. The one who balanced inequality and cursed the men."

"Huh." Jurij dropped his hand from my shoulder. He looked about to say something more, and then he shut his mouth again. "Are you sure he wasn't deceiving you?"

I sighed and kept marching forward, crumpling my message tighter in my fist. "Never mind."

"I'm serious!" Jurij said. "What if he gave you visions while you were with him? Why else did I feel those things I felt while in his castle?"

"Visions?" I repeated. We'd reached the castle gates, and I didn't even blink when they drew open. I'd yet to approach the castle walls and find them slammed shut. To me, anyway.

Jurij stepped between me and the open gate, suddenly forgetting his haste to rescue his friends and family. "If you go in there, will you see visions again?"

I clenched my fists at my sides. "Jurij! I'm not seeing, nor have I ever seen, visions!" I thought about my experiences in the pool and shook my head. No need to explain the things the pool showed me. I pointed back down the path. "You know the cavern?"

"The cavern?"

"*Our* cavern! The one with the glowing pool."

"The one you almost drowned in."

"Yes." *The one where you rejected me, then tried to force me into your arms.* "I traveled to... well, I guess I traveled to the past there."

"In the cavern." Jurij looked at me as if worried I was unwell. I remembered too vividly his looks in that alternate time he didn't remember, the time when the lord never was, and my parents were gone.

"Through the pool," I corrected. He stared at me blankly, and I threw up my hands. "Ugh! Never mind! I knew you wouldn't believe me."

Jurij glanced over his shoulder and held his hands out as if to stop me. "All right, all right. Let's say I believe you."

"Sure. *Let's say.*"

"How did *you* have the power to curse all of the men?"

"I just used the power I was born with."

"Which was?"

"Being able to control any man who found the goddess in me."

I could tell Jurij desperately wanted to check over his shoulder again, but he also didn't want to let me out of his sight. A bead of sweat trickled down his forehead. "So in *the past*, and we're talking a long time ago, the lord was there?"

This was hardly the time or place to get into this. "Yes. But I didn't mean he was the one who found the goddess in me. Not *just* him anyway." Jurij let me lower his arm without resistance, and I walked past him.

"There's only *one* man for every woman," Jurij said as he stepped beside me. "At least before..." His gaze fell over the darkened room, and his jaw opened. "What happened here?"

I'd spent so long thinking of the castle as some sort of prison for just me, the lord, and the specters, I'd forgotten that Jurij had been here a few times himself to deliver clothing.

The place was a mess. The door to the inner garden was open and swinging in time with a gentle breeze, slamming against the wall every other moment. Moonlight illuminated the rest of the room, even if the torches went unlit. There were barrels lying on their sides throughout the foyer, small puddles of liquid seeping out through a number of them. A pile of rumpled black clothing lay scattered between the entranceway and the stairway, boot prints clearly visible on the fabric, like someone had kicked and stomped on them rather than picking them up and moving them out of the way. I could see why the specters had asked for less bread to be delivered. There was a stack of green, rotting bread near the foot of the stairs, knocked over like a mountain after a landslide.

What has that man been up to?

"So where is he?" asked Jurij. "Hello?"

"Shh!" I put a finger to my lips, not even sure why. He was here, obviously. Our friends were here. But the place was too quiet, and I was reluctant to make a sound. I reached for the slip of paper in my sash. "Let's just get the guys and go," I whispered, not at all convinced it was going to be that easy. "If they're where my Mother was being kept—"

"What is *that*?"

I turned around. "Jurij?" He was walking toward the dining hall. "Jurij, it's not that way." But he went into the room without a moment's pause. Satisfied the men remained holed up in their pen, I stuffed Master Tailor's page back into my sash and followed. "Jurij?" There wasn't much light in the room. It was almost like he'd vanished.

"What are these?"

I walked toward the noise and knocked into Jurij as he stood up, his hand gripping something he'd picked off the floor.

I blinked. "A bangle. It used to keep a veil up over the table."

"A veil?"

I bent down to grab another bangle that glistened in the dark. My fingers brushed the fallen veil. Had it laid there since that day he'd vanished?

"Did you used to dine together? Before he could remove his mask?" Jurij cleared his throat. "I mean, his veil?"

"Yes. Sometimes." I reached into my sash and pulled out my gold coin. It also glistened in the slivers of moonlight.

"The gold in the castle, like you told us about."

The gold on Elric's arm. The bangle he wore that glistened in the firelight.

"Where'd he get it?" Jurij asked.

"I don't know." I swallowed and tucked the gold coin and bangle into my sash. I grabbed Jurij's arm. "The prison cells are upstairs. On the third floor."

Jurij wrenched his arm away, like he thought I would grab for his bangle. For the first time in this conversation, his voice didn't sound incredulous. "If you're the first goddess, why did you curse the men?"

I clutched at my chest, unable to contain the pain I felt there. "I was trying to save the women. I meant to punish *some* men. The men who deserved it."

"How would men *deserve* it? For loving the wrong women? For not obeying their goddesses quickly enough?"

"You think I'd punish helpless men over something so trivial as that?"

"I don't know what I think. You—"

"They hurt women." That caused Jurij to shut his jaw quickly. "Really *hurt* them. I don't know if you've ever even thought about it, but men are physically stronger than women for the most part, and these men... Their actions..."

The door to the foyer slammed shut, and the air hissed with the scrape of steel on firestone.

"And you made the innocent men suffer for it."

The wood in the dining hall's fireplace roared to life.

Ailill stood gazing at the flames, his forearm pressed against the mantel.

163

Chapter Twenty-One

"**D**ID YOU COME FOR YOUR marriage certificate?" Ailill stood back from the flickering fireplace and gave Jurij and me a faltering smile. "I suppose it is unfair that I denied you one when asked. But then, I could not be sure you both felt ready."

Jurij, all fire and flame when he first sprung the marriage announcement on me, took a step backward, fading into the darkness.

I straightened my shoulders and took a step toward the firelight, my rapid heartbeat be damned. "How do you know when someone is ready?" I pulled Master Tailor's crumpled page out of my sash. "Would this have something to do with it?"

Ailill laughed. "I see you got my message."

I shook the paper in the air. "You see a lot of things."

"Yes, well, since there is no sound, I have to imagine the rest of the story."

I tore my eyes from Ailill's face, not sure if the gaunt features were a trick of the dim firelight or a sign of poor nutrition. If it was the latter, he had no one to blame but himself. The specters did all the cooking and cleaning, so—

Where were the specters?

"Our friends. Are they in the prison cells?"

Ailill nodded toward the paper. "What does it look

like?"

"*Why* have you imprisoned them?" Behind Ailill, a speck of light danced among the shadows. The glistening of Jurij's golden bangle.

If Ailill heard the door to the entryway cracking open behind him, he didn't show a sign of it. Only, I didn't believe he was that stupid. "I said that no one was to set foot in my home, and I have had half a dozen visitors tonight already. Would you really blame me for enforcing my edicts?"

I lowered my hand and bent the paper slightly, keeping it out of Ailill's sight so he wouldn't notice me checking it for signs of a specter near Master Tailor. Or a foolish Jurij. But it was too soon for that. "Your home is a mess."

Ailill raised an eyebrow and stood straighter, dropping his elbow off the mantelpiece. "Am I to believe these boys are on a cleaning mission?"

"*Boys?*"

He crossed his arms and shrugged. "They are all boys to me."

Then am I nothing but a little girl to you? "What happened to the spec—the Ailills?"

"You just saw one tonight."

"Why haven't they cleaned up after you?" I looked him over, head to foot, noticing the way his usually tight clothing seemed to bunch and hang loose here and there. It was dirty, too, no longer the sharp, dark black he once wore. "Or cleaned *you?*"

Ailill tossed his head back and started pacing the room, taking a step away from the fireplace and me. "I am grateful, as ever, for your apparent concern."

I scoffed. "I'm sorry I asked. If you want to rot away in this castle when you're finally free to go where you please, that's your business. But my friends—"

"Free to go where I please?" Ailill stopped pacing, his back to the door and the sliver of moonlight let in when

Jurij had opened it. He scuffed a boot against the floor. "And where would I go, pray tell? To the tavern to fill myself with drink? To the fields to whack sheep with sticks?" He shook his head. "No. I am quite trapped in this place. Same as you, or any other of the oblivious people here, but it feels worse when you know just how trapped we all are."

I pretended to pay attention as I cautiously flipped the page open just enough to see a new set of feet in front of the bars. Master Tailor stood, shaking Jaron beside him. I tucked the paper quickly into my sash and made a show of tossing the too-long bit of hair over my shoulder, even though it swung right back into place. "A little company might do you some good. Even if it is just some sheep."

"I have tried company," Ailill sneered as he looked away. "I did not find it worth the trouble. And I do not think you have found company much worth the trouble, either."

I resisted the urge to cross my arms and instead pulled the coin out of my sash, leaving the gold bangle tucked in beside it. I tossed the coin onto the table, kicking up a small cloud of dust. "Did you send this to me?"

Ailill seemed hesitant to move, but he looked back over his shoulder, keen to see what I'd tossed on the table. It glistened in the dark, just like his veiled curtain's rings. He frowned and dropped his arms, crossing the room to step beside me before I could blink. "Where did you get this?" he asked, holding it up to the firelight.

"From you, I thought."

Ailill pinched his lips into a thin line, his eyes mesmerized by the flicker of flame over the golden coin. "Is this the coin you have been playing with? The one you got from that girl and showed to your consorts?"

I snatched the coin from his fingers, a shiver running down my back as his leather-coated fingertips scuffed against mine. My wounded finger stung. "You've been watching me. On that paper."

Ailill's gaze darted down to my hand, to the coin that glistened there. "Yes. It gets rather boring."

I tucked the coin back into my sash, not sure I wanted to part with it now if it wasn't some part of his scheme. "So why are you surprised I have it?"

"Because I do not see the goings-on in full color, now do I?" He reached forward, and I stepped back, determined not to let him touch my hand. But he was after the paper tucked in my sash. I felt almost faint from embarrassment, thinking he'd noticed my injured fingertip and wanted to fix it, like he did that first time we met. Or the first time *I* met *him*. He unfolded the paper and examined it thoughtfully. "I wondered why you paid such close attention to the coin, but I did not dream it was anything but a copper."

I tried pulling the paper from his hands—*Jurij*—but Ailill lifted the paper higher, out of my reach, still examining it. "No. No color." I paused in my attempt to grab the paper, my heart stilling. *Of course. Jurij would have had to find a key to unlock the cells. They're probably still in there, waiting.* "See?"

Ailill held the paper up so I could see the moving drawing. Master Tailor was no longer in his cell. He and the rest of the men—even Luuk—were in a place I didn't recognize at first. A sparse room on the third floor that contained the lord's throne. It hadn't had a hole in the back wall when I'd last seen it.

Ailill turned the paper back around and studied it, his face hardly registering any surprise. *He's not that stupid. He* planned *to let Jurij free them.* "Ah," he said at last, his eyebrows raised. "You were wondering about the Ailills? Here they come. Just in time to stop them." He turned the paper back to the other side, and I saw Master Tailor jolt as a score of specters circled around him. The men drew near each other, back to back, and Jaron's fists went up like he expected a fight. Several specters pushed the throne back over the hole, sliding it perfectly in place beneath the sole decoration on the wall, a blade hanging downward, its tip pointed to whoever dared sit in the chair below it.

Elgar. Back above the throne. But how?

Ailill nodded and crumpled the paper, tossing it into the flame beside him. I jumped as the fire sparked outward. "Well, that is that," he said, putting his hands on his waist, his elbows akimbo. "A night in my cells for trespassing just became a lifetime sentence."

"What?"

"I do not make all the laws, Olivière." He raised a finger to stop me from speaking. "I do not wish to hear it, considering the laws you passed yourself. Just be content I had the Ailills stop them from proceeding. A step into that hole carries the penalty of death." He turned and walked out of the room.

Chapter Twenty-Two

EVEN THOUGH I RUSHED AFTER him, Ailill was nowhere to be found. "Ailill!" I hadn't addressed him by his name in perhaps a thousand years. "Ailill! I'm not done with you."

A blast of cold air flew into the entryway through the open garden door. I had to hold my skirt down. "Ailill?" He wasn't to be found in the garden. "Ailill!"

Forget it. Ailill had an annoying habit of making himself vanish or appear whenever you wanted the exact opposite. I stood on my tiptoes to grab one of the unused torches from the wall. If the entryway was an example, I'd have to expect the rest of the castle to be equally dark. The fire from the dining hall breathed life into the torch. I stared at it, remembering the fire in the men's eyes before I'd uttered my curse. *The men may have explored the castle in darkness. But I'm not concealing my presence here.*

Let him come.

Ailill clearly had no intention of stopping me, as not a single specter appeared to block my path. I climbed first one set of stairs and then the next to the third floor. The disarray continued as I climbed. Open doors creaking in the cold dampness of the hallway were the only obstacles in my path.

He won't frighten me. It was as much a message to

myself as it was to him. *If he does mean to frighten me.* There was more to this darkness, this disarray, than Ailill let on. It was almost like he'd lost all fire, all fight—all reason to carry on and live.

I stopped as I reached the third floor. Elgar was there, just a few steps away. How? It should have been gone, lost to time. How did Ailill... ? I shook my head. It wasn't the time. My friends were at the end of the hallway.

No sense in going in unarmed. The blade is more mine than his.

I strode into the darkened throne room. A blast of absolutely frigid air turned my breath into puffs of white smoke. I resisted the urge to shiver and held the torch higher.

The faintest violet light glowed from behind the throne, now that I knew to look for it. I wasn't sure if the shiver that ran down my back was due to the cold or the familiar glow.

Pushing aside the throne got my friends sentenced to his dungeon for life. But whose life? Theirs or his? What if he died first?

I shook my head. *You're not going to hurt him again. You've seen what fighting can do.* I swallowed, too embarrassed to dwell on my thoughts any further.

I strode up the patched carpet to the throne, my hand already outstretched for the blade, when I heard a rustle beside me. I swung the torch in that direction. There was nothing. Nothing but that book on the stand Ailill kept, open and yellowed.

The book. I strode over to the stand. It was open to the page I'd so recently held, the wrinkled page Ailill had tossed into the fire. Impossibly, it was there in that book, bound within it, showing Master Tailor back in the cell. The writing was still there on the back. I shivered and flipped forward more pages, each with a drawing of a person. My eyes quickly darted from one to the next until I found an ink silhouette of my sister, lying in bed, her eyes wide open.

Almost as if she knew I was watching her.

I jumped back. So this was the source of the pages. The lord who was "always watching." *Where did he get this book?*

I felt a burning at my waist, and I reached inside my sash, withdrawing the golden bangle. The coin grew hot as well, but I left it there. Once I held the golden bangle over the book, the metal burned my hand, and I cried out, dropping it. I bent over, about to pick it up.

"You ought to have kept hold of that. It could have saved you from prison." Ailill, the ever-watching lord, stepped out from the shadows. He snatched the bangle up from the floor before I could grab it. "But as you are so keen to find your friends, I would be glad to let you join them."

He waved a hand at the doorway, and a dozen specters entered the throne room. He turned his attention to the bangle in his hand, dismissing me as a dozen pale hands reached out to take hold of me.

η η η

"He expects us to stay here for life?" Tayton paced back and forth, back and forth, his footsteps on the cold stone floor echoing miserably in my head. "And he doesn't have the guts to tell us that? Just pass a message along through you, and we just accept that?" He gripped the bars of our shared cell and did his best to shake them. They barely moved, but they made a terrible clatter.

I cradled my forehead. "Tayton. Stop that. Please."

"Ugh!" screamed Tayton. He kicked the bars, causing more of a racket. The specter guarding us didn't even flinch. Tayton had already tried sticking his hand through to grab him, but of course, he was just out of reach.

"Tayton, you're not helping." Jaron's voice was recognizable from the cell beside ours, even if I couldn't see anything more than his arm sticking through the bars. I found out he'd been locked up with Luuk and Darwyn, and that the specters had to pry Darwyn and Tayton apart. "Quiet down. Some of us are trying to think."

Tayton kicked the bars one more time for good measure before plopping down on the pile of hay beside me. He scowled, as if daring me to comment on the last kick.

Jaron cleared his throat. "Thank you. Noll, please explain again. Without outbursts from the audience this time."

I threw my hands up in the air. "I don't *know*. He's being stubborn. And secretive. And frustrating. As he *often* is. He knew you were coming. He knew Jurij had left to go free you. He let it all happen so he could catch you in his throne room."

Jurij's frustrated snort came from the other side of my cell's wall, where he, Sindri, and Master Tailor were imprisoned together. "For what?"

I crawled closer to the bars to make my voice carry more clearly. "You tell me. You somehow knew to move the throne." I eyed the specter in front of my cell as I spoke, but he continued to stare straight ahead, oblivious to the prisoners in front of him. Some of Ailill's contempt was etched deeply into his wrinkled face.

"That book." Jurij's hand appeared out from his cell, as if to confirm I was speaking with him. "We found the source of those moving pages."

"I saw." I didn't mention I'd seen Elfriede. "It looks like everyone in the village has his or her own page."

"Yeah, well, we flipped through it. We found what must have been one of our pages because we saw ourselves there in the throne room, looking at the book."

Another hand appeared out of the cell with Jurij's. "Only, on the page, there was something strange about the throne in the throne room." Sindri. "There was a hole in the wall behind it. We could see it on the page, clear as day."

"And what about that... it was a sword, wasn't it?"

asked Tayton. "Above the throne? I didn't think those things were real."

I wondered if Jaron remembered giving me the same blade, in a time that did and didn't exist.

"It was all suspicious," added Darwyn. "So I thought we should see if the hole was really there behind the throne. Some of his servants were waiting behind it." He laughed miserably. "I didn't think... that is, I'm sorry if that's why we're here."

Tayton plastered himself against the opposite wall, holding out his hand toward Darwyn's cell. "It's not your fault! You couldn't have known." Another hand appeared in place of Jaron's. After stretching and bending awkwardly, their fingers grazed one another's.

"It's my fault!" The trembling wail from Darwyn's and Jaron's cell reminded me that Luuk was still half a child, even if he'd grown taller and spoke deeper. "I shouldn't have come alone. I knew I'd mess it up." Despite his physical differences, Luuk really seemed the least changed by the curse's breaking.

"Enough!" thundered Jaron. "We all agreed to this risk. Let's just figure out why the lord let us get as far as we did, and what exactly we did to get thrown in here."

"You mean besides entering his castle against his edict?" Master Tailor asked.

I shook my head, even if he couldn't see it. "That wasn't going to be a lifelong offense. He purposely baited you to the throne room."

"Not because of the book," added Sindri. "I mean, he gave us pages from it. That can't have been something he'd jail us for."

"Then the throne. And the hole," said Jurij.

I gripped the nearest bar. I'd seen the hole, and he hadn't stepped out of the shadows until I'd read the book. No, until I'd dropped the golden bangle. I patted my sash, looking for my golden coin. I panicked. There was nothing there. I shot up and removed my sash, shaking it out.

"What are you doing?" Tayton twisted away from his attempted handhold with Darwyn to stare at me. "Is there a mouse in your clothing?"

"What's she doing?" Jurij's voice sounded panicked. "Is she undressing?" I can't say if he was panicked or angry about that.

"*No.*" I kept shaking the sash. "My golden coin is gone."

Jurij sighed. Definitely anger this time. "Oh, no. How will we be able to buy anything now? Oh, wait. We'll never need to buy anything again because we're never leaving this castle."

"What if he doesn't feed us?" Luuk's voice shook.

"We'll be noticed! The women won't stand for us suddenly disappearing." Jaron spoke with calm confidence.

Master Tailor snapped. "Speak for yourself! My former wife and sister aren't speaking to me. Even Luuk's former goddess won't help."

"Coll," interrupted Jaron, "we'll be fine. You know that. We didn't come here without realizing the risk."

"Elfriede! Or Nissa!" I stomped my foot. "Luuk, Nissa isn't angry with you."

"But my mother and Auntie are, and she's with them."

"I know, but Nissa feels different." I stared at Tayton. "And maybe not all of the wives care, but Roslyn does, Darwyn. They'll notice we're missing. They'll come."

"Sure. If we're not dead before then." Sindri coughed.

"Why did you mention Elfriede?" Jurij's question was quiet under all the comments, but I heard it clearly.

"I saw her in the book. She was wide awake in bed. Almost like she knew something was wrong."

"How would she know?" interrupted Sindri.

Master Tailor spoke next. "Does it matter? If there's a chance someone knows we're here—"

"How is a woman who happens to be awake at night

a sign that she knows we're here?" Darwyn dropped Tayton's hand. His voice had a little edge of that gruffness I expected from him as a child. "Does it surprise you a woman would be so upset about things she'd be unable—"

"Enough!" Jaron spat. "Okay, everyone? Enough." The dungeons fell silent, but for the crackling of the torches. "We haven't even spent a full night here. No need to panic. People will notice we're missing."

"And know to look for us in the lord's castle?" Tayton ran a hand through the short, thick hair atop his forehead. "It's hopeless. Why did we even come here?"

"We wanted answers!" Something clanged in Jaron's cell, and I just made out the sole of a boot kicking against the bars. "And goddess help me, we at least deserve that!"

My eyes flicked guiltily to the ground, even though only Tayton was there to witness it.

Jaron continued unabated. "A lifetime in this prison? After the commune? He hopes to threaten *me* with a lifetime in this prison?" He scoffed, and I could practically hear him spit. "With my friends here? With someone to talk to? With endless things to want and wish for, with something else to think of other than the bitch who sent me to my torment?"

"Jaron," Master Tailor's voice wavered.

Jaron seemed to catch himself. "Coll, I'm sorry. I don't blame Alvilda. Now I know how she feels. I'm not in love with her. Not in the slightest. If someone asked me to be with her now, I'd be just as repulsed at the idea as she was." He paused. "No. You know what? She gets just a *tiny* bit of blame. Maybe a whole lot of blame. She could have just ordered me to sit in the corner, and I'd have been fine. She could have carved me a little hovel outside of her door and told me to lay in it like a dog, and I'd have felt better than I did in that commune."

Darwyn must have seen something on Jaron's face that the rest of us weren't privy to. He sounded alarmed. "Jaron, please. This isn't helping."

"This isn't *helping*? It's helping me just fine!" I heard Jaron's boots pound over the cell floor. "So she loved someone else. I get that. Oh, boy, do I understand what it's like to love someone you can't have." He paused again for a few paces. "But it wasn't the same for her, was it? The one she loved also loved her back. And she could go more than a breath without thinking about her."

"Jaron. Stop." Master Tailor's voice was firm. Louder than I'd ever heard him speak before. "You think it would have been better being at her side with that feeling she'd never love you back? It wasn't."

A lump at Tayton's throat bobbed noticeably. He seemed to be straining to contain himself.

"Ha!" Jaron's laugh was anything but genuine. "You had a roof over your head without holes in it. You had warm food in your belly. Sons to call your own." Jaron's voice wavered so, I could almost see the tears forming in his eyes. "You had someone to love you."

"But that someone wasn't her." Master Tailor sighed. "Now I know just how important my sons' love was. But it didn't matter then. Everything was so messed up for us. The important things didn't matter."

"Jaron." It was my voice that called his name. "You weren't unloved. I know someone who didn't forget you."

I had no idea if Jaron could even guess at my mother's affections, if his childhood memories were wiped out after years of suffering for Alvilda.

Jaron's voice came closer, and I saw his hands wrap around the bars of his cell. "Noll! Goddess, Noll. How could I have forgotten? You spent a time in the commune with me."

Tayton's head shot up, his eyes wide with wonder.

Jaron's voice drifted, like he was searching his memory. "I remembered thinking you were nice. You talked, unlike the other men..." He stopped. "Why? Why would I think you were there with me?"

I stared at Tayton. "I was. For a month before the

curse broke. I just didn't think you'd be able to remember."

"That month that no one can clearly remember." It was Master Taylor who spoke. "What happened then?"

"You wanted answers?" It'd been so long since he'd participated in the conversation, I'd almost forgotten that Jurij was in the cell behind the wall I leaned on. "Then you should have asked Noll."

It was time I shared what they needed to know. It was time I shared everything.

"I'm the first goddess."

Chapter Twenty-Three

EVERYTHING WAS SILENT IN THE cells on either side of me. Tayton stared. Even Luuk had stopped sniffling.

Jaron was the first to respond. "The *first* goddess?"

"Yes," I admitted. "I placed the curse on men."

"How?" asked Tayton. "Why?"

I felt my heart thumping hard against my ribs. "I think it had to do with my powers as a woman. I don't know why or how exactly, but I was there. In the past."

"You're making this up!" Darwyn sounded angry, angrier than I'd heard him in years. "Noll, this isn't helping."

"She's not making it up." Jurij seemed strangely confident for someone who'd just been arguing the opposite a few hours before. "Why else would our curse suddenly be broken? Why is everyone unclear on what exactly happened the month before?"

Darwyn wasn't deterred. "Because *Noll* is the first goddess? The woman from the tales at the Returnings? The one who cursed men long before we were born?" He snorted. "Yeah."

"He has a point," added Sindri. "How is that even possible?"

Luuk piped up. "Noll said she was the elf queen!"

Darwyn laughed, and it wasn't very nice. "Don't tell

me you actually believed that."

"Hey!" I jumped to my feet. "Quiet! Do you want me to explain things or not?"

Even though Tayton was the only one I could see, I could feel the furious energy vanish from the air.

Jaron spoke loudly over the others. "Go on, Noll. And no one interrupt her."

My gaze flicked quickly to the specter standing across from my cell. *Ailill can't hear what I say on those strange book pages. But the specters can hear, right? Does he somehow hear through their ears?* I opened my mouth. "Some of you already know about this, but there's a cavern—"

The door to my cell opened, the specter producing a key from his inner coat pocket and pushing his way in before I could finish my sentence. Tayton stood, eyeing the specter warily. "Now wait a minute."

The specter grabbed my forearm and dragged me out of the cell.

"Where are you taking her?" asked Tayton.

I could finally see into the cells on either side of me, the line of worried faces pressed up against the bars. I had only an instant to meet each of their eyes as the specter locked the door to my cell behind us and placed the key back in his coat pocket.

"What are you doing?" demanded Darwyn. "Don't tell me she's forbidden to talk about this!"

"Well, if that isn't proof that Noll speaks the truth," added Master Tailor, "I don't know what is."

"No!" Jaron gripped the bars and shook them wildly in vain. "Not when we're so close. Not when—"

But I had just enough time to send Jurij a warning glance amidst all the shouting and cursing letting loose from the cells. *Don't talk about what I told you. At least not yet.* I was dragged out the door and back into the chillingly cold third-floor hall.

I tugged against the specter's grip on my arm, but I

had no hope of resisting. "Ailill!" I dug my heels into the floor. "I mean *you*, not him! Let me go!"

The specter hesitated, and I saw something strange flicker across the redness of his eyes. He was old, this one. Older than many of them, now that I looked closely. Washed pale with time. A shade of a long-forgotten man.

"I'm sorry," I said, and I meant it.

His fingers loosened, and I recognized something of the lord in his quieter moments. Regret. Longing.

His mouth opened.

"Leave us."

It wasn't the specter Ailill who'd spoken. The specter dropped his hand from my arm and turned, retreating into the darkness at the other end of the hallway, not even sparing me one last glance. He passed the current lord in black, pale but still breathing. Ailill stood, his arms crossed, in front of the throne room. He looked me over from head to toe and nodded. "Come in here." He vanished inside the throne room, leaving me alone in the hallway.

He gives an order, and I'm to obey? He once had to do the same when I spoke, but he did everything he could to resist me. He should have known I could do the same. He'd left me completely on my own in the castle. I could just walk right by, go after that specter about to speak, or walk out the front door, come back with an army.

But no. I'd tried that once before and wasn't pleased with the results. Besides, I had no doubt the specters would appear from the shadows to stop me if I tried.

I tossed my shoulders back and followed Ailill into the throne room. He had let all but one torch extinguish, so I could barely make him out atop the throne. If not for the glisten of the golden bangle he let dance over his fingers, I might not have known he was there at all.

"I tried sparing your friends the harshest of punishments. I truly did."

I hadn't spent all of this time with Ailill—*parrying* with Ailill—not to be able to divine the meaning hidden beneath those words. "Of course. That's why we were unceremoniously dumped into your cells for life." I marched toward the throne, closing the distance between us. "And now? What harsher punishments await us?"

The golden bangle stopped twirling on Ailill's fingers. "Us? No, you are exempt from any further punishment, I gather."

"You gather?"

Ailill let the golden bangle slide over his hand to his arm. I was reminded revoltingly of his brother Elric. "This is not a game, Noll. I spared your friends from death, and then you try to condemn them to it."

"I didn't think it was a game. It never is that simple between us." I jutted my chin out and climbed the step to the raised platform so I could look down on him as I spoke. Elgar glistened faintly as I did. I pointed at it. "Where did you find that?"

Ailill looked up at it briefly, then turned away. "I cannot tell you."

Convenient. "All right. Keep your secrets. But may I ask what would have condemned them to death?"

He rolled his eyes and looked away. "You told them you were the first goddess."

I dug my nails into the palm of my injured hand, ignoring the pain. "But... wasn't I?"

He rested his elbows on the throne's armrests and placed his fingertips together. "I suppose you were. In this village, at least."

"In *this* village?" I thought about the village in the past, how I felt like it both was and was not my own.

"And then you were going to give them a map to the heart of the village, let them find their way there if I ever felt gracious enough to let them out of here."

I didn't really think he was planning to let them out, but I let that comment slide. "The cavern?" I decided not to point out that Jurij and Luuk already knew about it, although he must have known as much.

"The pool there." He tilted his head slightly. "Surely you remember the beat of the heart beneath its waters? You rode its heartbeats to the past. I was as sure of that as I was that you were the first goddess returned, that day you first trespassed in my castle."

"So why didn't you tell me?"

"Tell you what? That you had doomed the entire village to its wretched existence? You clearly had not yet traveled to the past. Would you have believed me?"

"No. Maybe not," I admitted. "But it would have been better to hear that than be pushed and pulled around, thinking you were nothing more than a heartless monster."

Ailill threw his hands in the air. "Again, back to that. Certainly. You would have just considered me a ranting madman. One who kept entirely to himself and then droned on about a past long ago where you cursed mankind. Would you have fallen in love with that?"

In love? "Were you ever concerned about me falling in love with you?"

Ailill slapped the armrest with one hand. "You doubt that? After all you now know about me?" My heart felt almost like it'd stopped beating. Then the hope that lingered there in that breath between beats floated away as Ailill shook his head and turned away. "After a hundred or more lifetimes, I was ready to be done with this curse. And I would not get there by vanishing the moment you saw my face."

Of course. He wanted me to love him to free his own soul. Not because he loved me. "But that's what happened anyway in the end, isn't it?"

Ailill shrugged. "I had given up by then. It was not the first time I had. But I had hoped it would be the last."

I felt a sharp pain in my chest, even if I couldn't stop the anger that invaded my body every time I stood near him. "You lived this long only to give up? It shouldn't have mattered what I thought of you! That's no reason to give up on living."

Ailill laughed harshly, but I knew it wasn't because I'd said anything amusing. "I am surprised to hear you talk so! You, who became a shell of herself at the idea of her beloved marrying her sister. A beloved you were not even compelled to love, a beloved you had hope of one day no longer desiring."

I squeezed my arms tight across my chest, swallowing back tears. "How would you know how I was before Jurij and Elfriede's Returning? I thought you weren't 'always watching' after all. You seemed surprised when I first arrived in the castle."

Ailill pointed to the book on the stand and nodded. Without waiting for his instructions, I walked over and flipped it open. A man sat beside the fire in his home, a woman at his side, a child at his feet. Whether one of the few remaining families from the curse or a new one formed in the days after, I couldn't say. I flipped again to a random page, seeing Darwyn's mother sweeping out her bakery, a smile on her face, her lips moving. She must have been talking to someone off page. *Roslyn*. The two had found happiness in their new arrangement, as friends and bakerwomen. It seemed like weeks ago, but it was really just earlier that evening.

"I did look," said Ailill from behind me. "I watched this village evolve for countless years on those pages. A mere echo of what was going on out there, but all I would be able to see."

I didn't say anything. I turned a page again and saw a man sleeping in a bed. Another page had a man and woman clinking their mugs together and drinking a toast. After a few moments, Vena appeared on the page, dropping off more mugs on the table between them.

"I saw my sister on those pages," continued Ailill. "Silently, she worked. Organizing the village after the curse. Guiding the women to gain more confidence. Blessing newfound families." I heard him sigh. "She never created one of her own. Not that it surprised me. She did not seem the type to forget, and there would be no man worthy of her forgiveness, even if he was altered."

I turned the page again, trying not to think about Avery's bloodlust and trying to imagine her settling down as a leader. I couldn't picture her with her own children, either.

"She never came for me." Something in Ailill's voice seemed about to crack. "I wondered if she even knew I was alive. Or if she even cared."

I stopped. "But they must have known they were left with a lord?"

Ailill waved a hand. "They knew the castle shook when they looked at it. They were scared. Or maybe they did not think they had left behind anything worth going back for."

"But your servants—"

"Did not yet exist." He drummed his fingers on the throne's armrest and smiled, haltingly. "I had not died yet. They could have sent their men after me, but no one thought to. They could have come even if the ground shook, but Avery did not try."

"I added the earthquakes to protect you. I was worried after Avery stabbed your—stabbed *him*. I thought she might hurt you."

"Who knows? To me, that would have been preferable to isolation. Even if she had killed me, I would have sprung to life once more."

"I... I'm sorry." I turned back to the book, more out of shame than a real need to flip through its pages.

"Sorry for the earthquakes that kept my sister from me, or sorry for the whole appalling mess you made of things?"

I flipped to another page. My mother. Alone in bed. Her brows furrowed even in slumber. Alive because of him. "Both," I said at last.

"Of course—" Ailill stopped himself. It was as if he had expected me to say "neither" and had readied himself for the argument we almost always had. "Well. I do not expect Avery would have sought me out regardless."

Mother tossed and turned in bed. I felt bad that even her dreams couldn't offer her peace. I saw the foot of Elfriede's bed in the image. Her sheets were all crumpled.

Ailill continued his story. "I grew older, clinging to that book, living for a time off food stores my brother and father had prepared for some unknown purpose. And when it ran out, I had the food they gave—well... I had food at least. I saw my sister die. I watched as everyone I ever knew faded into thin air. And when the day at last came for me to join them..." He stopped, and his leather attire squeaked uncomfortably in the silence behind me. "Well. I came back. This time with a pale old man for company."

I traced my finger across the dancing ink on the page, wondering what it'd be like to only see those you love on its pages, to watch them fading away until you were left with nothing but strangers. I wanted to ask so many questions, but I wasn't sure if dredging up memories of what I'd done would set my friends free. I wasn't even sure what was so important about keeping the cavern's "heart" a secret that he would summon me to stand beside him even after all our fighting.

Ailill's voice was closer when he spoke again. "In any case. The story repeated itself, only with strangers filling that book's pages. And repeated itself. And repeated itself, only, the women fell into a comfortable routine of being objects of worship after a few ages. There was no need for anyone to organize the village. 'The lord' was the leader. The leader they hardly needed or cared about. But their lack of caring emboldened me. I stopped relying on food from the same sources and sent the servants out shopping. I had no lack of copper with which to pay for it. My father had stockpiled quite a bit, and his father and grandfather before him." An arm clothed in black reached over my shoulder, and a dark-gloved hand rested a mere hair's breadth from mine. He turned the page. "I had the servants collect all the weapons, tossed aside in trunks and sheds, forgotten generations earlier. Nobody alive recognized their purpose or cared that we took them. I made sure the idea of swords faded into the realm of myth, so person would never harm person again. An ideal world for all, in a way. Just take the free will of all men away and imprison me. Life was very peaceful."

I thought of Elgar, guiltily, and wondered how he'd found the blade at all, when I'd left it in a tree for Jaron to find for me. The sword seemed to exist outside of reason, like there were two in the village at once, one over Ailill's throne and the other in the tree.

Before I could ask, Ailill spoke again. "Eventually, I stopped caring." He turned the page. This one showed the crowded tavern, Vena running across the book, men's heads thrown back in laughter. The page followed a man with his arm around a woman's waist, his other hand holding hers as they swung around the crowded room dancing, tripping, and nearly tumbling over with laughter. "I would open the book on occasion, but I tended to find it hurt too much to look. To pretend I meant anything to the people in these pages."

It was my father. My *father* dancing with some other woman. Who was she? I couldn't put a name to her face, but I really didn't care. To see the look of delight on my father's features when he held a woman besides my mother made me gasp and turn away.

By turning, I found myself perfectly positioned in Ailill's arms. The torchlight danced and flickered across his brown hair. His dark eyes bore into mine, and I felt his arm shift behind me, move ever closer to the center of my back.

"Do you blame me for so seldom looking?"

"No." I swallowed and tore my eyes away. My hands gripped the sides of my skirt. I was unsure what to do with them. How to move away—or if I even wanted to. Ailill dropped his arm and took a step back, taking with him a raging blaze of something powerful between us I hadn't even realized he'd brought with him.

A glint of light caught my attention on the floor just beside the stand. I bent down and picked it up—it was the coin I'd lost. I held it out between Ailill and me, letting the firelight dance off its luster. "When you took that bangle away," I said, nodding at the bangle around his arm, "you said it would have saved me from a lifetime in prison. So what does this coin, or any golden copper, mean?"

Ailill ran a hand over his bangle. "It means you have the right to know. To see. To rule over this village."

I twisted the coin this way and that, not believing that even something so bright and beautiful could give me the right to that. "Like your bangle?" I asked, thinking of the one Elric wore.

The corner of Ailill's lips twitched. "And the dozens of others like it." He removed the bangle and held it out in front of him in echo of my stance with the coin. "I got so bored with receiving them, I started to use them for practical purposes." He smiled, and I thought of how the golden rings held the veil over the table aloft, how they clattered as they fell to the ground when I ordered him to rip it. "And then I began to leave the remainder behind. I thought it dangerous to populate one village with over a hundred such tokens, solely because I was sent back time after time after time."

I gripped the coin tightly in my palm and lowered my hand. "You keep talking about our village as if there are others."

Ailill smiled again, and it didn't feel like he was mocking me. More like he was impressed his pet could perform new tricks. He slid the bangle back over his arm and gestured around with both hands. "We are surrounded by mountains, Olivière. Everywhere you look, there are mountains." He stepped back, walking toward his throne. "And people are born, and live, and die in this village, and they never seem to think about what is on the other side of them."

"But..." I frowned. "How can there be? The mountains end? And other people live there?"

Ailill sat back on his throne, crossing his legs so one ankle rested on the other knee. "Not quite, but close enough."

"So why haven't any of these people noticed us?"

"Who says they have not?" Ailill gestured at the book behind me. "Where do you think I came by such a tome, a book that shows the people of this village at play?"

"*At play*? Is that what our lives are to someone like you? Just a game?"

Ailill rested his fingertips together, always looking somehow both bored and in charge whenever he sat there. "There are greater forces than a simple lord in a single village, Olivière. Even one who frustratingly will not die." His eyes seemed to search the ceiling, as if looking for a person who might be listening. "And whether my vexing immortality is still in place remains to be seen."

"What do you mean? Because you found your goddess, you..." I stopped. It was only my not being born yet that had kept him alive.

Ailill shook his head and waved a hand. "Do not worry yourself. I might be freed from the curse at last. It is exactly what I wanted for many, many years."

I gripped the coin harder and felt its smooth edges push into my skin. "But you can't die!"

Ailill raised his eyebrows. "I am touched you care." His voice betrayed his meaning, his sarcasm back in full force, dripping over the sentiment.

"I *do* care!" I stomped a foot, feeling like the little elf queen not getting her way. "Must you continue to be so frustrating?"

Ailill stood and stepped down the platform. "My sentiments exactly."

"I caused this. I caused all of this, I know." I looked up as Ailill stopped moving, the surprise clearly written on his face. "I want you to have a chance to live this time."

Ailill froze but said nothing.

"I want all of the men to have a chance to choose what makes them happy. And the women understand that the happiness they had before was never *really* happiness. Not when there wasn't a choice. Although I don't want things to go back to the way they were, either. *Everyone* in the village deserves to be treated well."

"Olivière—"

"No, let me speak! For once, just let me talk without misunderstanding and berating me. Give me some answers!" I threw my hands up. "The hole behind the throne. That leads to this place beyond the mountains?"

Ailill took a step closer, his hand outstretched. "Yes, but—"

"And knowing about that is the danger?" I held out my coin again. "Unless you hold a golden copper, knowing that there's a world beyond the mountains somehow justifies imprisonment? For *life*?"

"Olivière, *yes*, but not now." Ailill brushed past, laying his hand on my shoulder for the gentlest of shoves.

My eyebrows furrowed at his look of concern. "What is..." The last word died on my tongue.

The moving ink drawing of the tavern had erupted into chaos. Man after man came to blows with each other, some with bare fists, others with broken glasses or even chairs raised over their heads. Things moved so quickly, tables turning, plates crashing, the silent fury screaming across the page, and I couldn't find my father. The page was supposed to be centered on him.

Ailill furrowed his brow, one hand marking his place while his other raced through the pages. "I was afraid something like this might happen."

"Like what?" I asked stupidly. "A fight in the tavern?" It looked worrying, but it was nothing like the battle I'd caused in the village of the past.

Ailill continued to scan the pages. "Too much freedom. Sometimes men cannot be trusted with it." He grunted. "As you have seen." He stopped flipping the pages, and his eyes widened.

"What is it?" I asked, leaning in beside him for a better look.

A man I didn't recognize plunged a shard of glass into another man's back. The second man crumbled, his head lolling forward and then his body vanishing, only his clothing cluttering the floor.

I gasped. "Someone might have *died*! We have to stop them! Find whose page that was! Find out if he was killed or hurt or..."

Ailill let the pages fall back, leaving the page he'd held open, the page belonging to my father. Bright red burst onto the paper, the first shade of color I'd seen on any of the pages. It dripped down, like spilled ink. Like blood. And then the page went blank before vanishing in a surge of bright violet.

"FATHER!" I screamed, clawing at the book. It was he who was stabbed on that other man's page. He who crumpled. Ailill's arms slipped around me, his hands clutched together at my abdomen. Tears streamed down my face. Endless, white-hot tears.

Ailill's cheek pressed against my temple. It was warm, not at all like the cold marble I remembered. "They watch us now," he whispered, barely audible over the sobs choking out past my throat. His lips brushed close against my skin, like the flutter of petals in a breeze against my cheek as I lay in the lily fields. *Lily fields.* I'd associated those, that feeling of serenity, with Jurij for so long.

"They are always watching." He took a deep breath. "But we cannot let them win."

Chapter Twenty-Four

I STRODE OUT OF THE throne room before I could even think.

"Olivière, where are you going?" Ailill grabbed me by the shoulder and spun me around. He cradled the book in which I'd watched my father. I'd watched his page burn.

Father's not dead. He's not! But I couldn't just stand there. I had to know.

Ailill frowned. "Do you intend to run all the way to the tavern?"

My stomach hurt, and my throat felt dry. I didn't know what I intended. I was going to head down the stairs and just run until I got there. Until I could prove to myself it wasn't true. My eyes wandered over Ailill's shoulder to the door leading to the cells.

I spun out of Ailill's grip toward my friends. "I have to go!"

"Now what are you planning?" asked Ailill as he walked quickly along beside me. "The door is that way."

"Aren't we going to free them?" I gestured at the door to the cells. "They could help. They know the crowd at the tavern."

Ailill didn't respond to my question. "We will take the carriage. It will prove faster."

I started. "You'll come with me?"

There was a slight bob to Ailill's throat. "Of course."

"But you never leave the castle." I frowned. "Hardly ever, that is."

"This is too important." He muttered something to himself about how "the Ailills would restrain them" and disappeared down the staircase to the second floor.

Several specters appeared from the dungeon and walked past me at a brisk pace, following after him. I may as well have been invisible. One bumped into me with an echoing clatter as he passed and didn't even slow down.

I stood there a moment longer, staring at the dungeon door they hadn't even closed behind them.

My father needed me. Because he couldn't be dead. It had to be some mistake. But he wasn't the only one who needed me.

Something glistened from the floor beside my feet, and I bent to pick it up. The specter who'd brushed past me had dropped the cell key. It was almost like he was asking me to free them while Ailill was distracted.

ŋ ŋ ŋ

The book on my lap jostled with the bump of the carriage, and I was afraid my tight grip on its edges would make the thing crumble beneath my fingers. Up close, it wasn't really in the best of shape—although when I considered how old it was, I was surprised it hadn't faded to dust years before. My fingers traced over the scene of the tavern men fighting, from Vena's point of view, as she and Elweard cowered behind the counter, their arms wrapped tightly around one another.

I wanted to throw up. My mind was racing. I hadn't felt this anxious, this *awake*, since the day I'd led Avery and the other women to Elric in the castle. And thinking about that, I realized no one in this village—in this present-day village—had seen physical fighting before.

Ailill tapped his knee with his fingers, displaying worry for the first time in all the time I'd known him as an adult. "The Ailills can restrain them," he said, for the tenth time at least. "They will have to."

I flipped the pages until I found one with a better view of the brawl. It followed a man I didn't know as he threw a punch and then received one.

Ailill had been talking to himself since we'd left the throne room. He touched the fingers on one hand as if he were counting. "There are a 104 of them. Some more frail and older than others." The specters, I assumed. Even though some certainly looked older than others, I hadn't suspected any were "frail." "There are 564 men in the village, minus the seven currently in the cells."

I stopped flipping through the book to glare at him. His knowledge of exactly how many men were in his village would have impressed me—assuming it was right—if it wasn't compounded by the fact that he still intended to keep my friends in his prison.

"I will not have them bring swords," continued Ailill. "The longer the people go without thinking about those, the better." He ran a gloved hand over his face. "But just because I secured all the swords in the fifth life does not mean they cannot turn their tools into instruments of death." He laughed sourly. "I seem to remember women made great use of pitchforks and axes at one point."

I swallowed, too distraught to think of the mob of violent women, instead thinking of the glass shard in Father's back. I turned the book back to where Father's page had been. I felt the page that had been behind it, the tanner's wife, asleep in her bed. Completely free of the pain and worries that filled my chest.

Because I couldn't quite believe Father was dead. Page or no page, I had to be mistaken. Or if not, then I'd just have to undo it. Somehow. Someway. I'd been into the past before.

"Olivière?"

His voice brought me back to the moment. "Does this mean my father is dead?" I tapped the woman's page.

"Olivière," said Ailill, softer than was his usual custom. "The book shows the truth of the village. When a page burns, that means the villager has vanished into... Well, he moves on from this life."

"*No!*" I slammed a palm against the book. "You burnt Master Tailor's page, and he didn't die."

"Burning the page is not the same as the page burning itself. My act only returned the page to its bindings."

"I know! I saw it. I..." I didn't know what I was going to say. The next word caught in my throat, suffocating me. Breathing hurt. Thinking hurt. I'd lost my mother once, and that pain had numbed me for months. Father and I had never been as close, but that brought its own kind of pain. We'd never properly talked since men became free. What kind of man was he really? All I'd have to remember him— the *real* him not bound by devotion to Mother—was that night I brought Arrow back and our chance meeting in the tavern, when he'd reminded me of the father who'd blamed me for Mother's illness.

"Olivière." Ailill's soothing voice melted the cold panic and confusion ringing in my ears. He got up from where he sat across from me, his back hunched, his arms out to steady himself as the carriage flew down the path. He slid in beside me, our thighs pressed close together on the too-small seat. His arm flew around me, and before I knew it, I was cradling the book to my chest and pressing my head against his shoulder. It took me a moment to realize the great heaving sobs I heard were coming from my own throat, that my tears were dyeing his black jerkin even darker with dampness.

"He can't be dead." My voice cracked. "I just saw him. And I thought my mother dead once, and she wasn't."

"She was in my care." Ailill's gloved fingers ran through the back of my hair. "And I have no such power left. He has already vanished."

I leaned away and took his hand in mine, dropping the book to my lap. He swallowed, perhaps hurt that I'd pulled back from him yet again. But I took the glove off and gripped his hand tighter, running my finger—the injured finger now almost entirely without poultice—over his smooth, pale skin. I wanted to feel that healing touch. He'd used it once on me, on a splintered finger. He could use it again. He could fix my hand and save my father. But even if he couldn't...

"I could save him," I said, determined. "The pond will have to accept me and take me back in time. I'll make it." My eyes burned as tears continued falling.

Ailill threaded his fingers through mine. "Olivière, you cannot let your thoughts take you to such dark places. You cannot turn to that power. Please. You do not understand what you were dealing with when you fell through that pond before. They toyed with you."

I wanted to scream. "Who are *they*?"

"I... cannot tell you."

"Fine." This whole exchange reminded me of how frustrated Jurij must have been when he was the one asking questions and I was the one not giving answers. "Then what do you mean, they toyed with me? By sending me into the past?"

He didn't answer. I clutched the book again to my chest with one hand. It was a wonder Jurij hadn't taken me by the shoulders and *shaken* the answer out of me, because that's what I was considering doing now.

Is this what those women who assaulted their men after the edict dissolving marriages felt? The desire to hurt even those you love just because they don't act exactly how you want them to? Violence is a scary thing. The little elf queen knew nothing of it. "Ailill," I said, willing my heartbeat to slow, "what happened to you during that month you were gone? Why does no one seem to remember it but me?"

"Does a dreamer remember his dream after he has finally wakened from it?" An echo of a smile glinted across Ailill's face briefly, but it was hollow. "They toy with me, too. With all of us."

"Is it these people who are really the ones 'always watching'? Are we nothing but—" The carriage ground to a halt, and I flew forward. With the book cradled to my chest, I couldn't stop myself from falling.

But Ailill was there to catch me. He gripped my shoulders, saying nothing of it as he tore his eyes from me to look out the carriage window. "It is too soon. I told them not to stop but for any injured parties we come across." Alarm colored his face as he gently pushed me back upright and swung the carriage door open, jumping to the ground without even waiting for a specter to assist him.

I pulled the book away from my chest. I'd bent a page, and now Mother's face was halfway revealed. I pulled it out and smoothed down the creases, realizing with a jolt that I saw an ink figure I'd never seen before—Ailill—running across her page. I left the book on the seat and jumped out of the carriage after him.

"Where have they taken her?" Mother looked up. "Noll!" She ran past Ailill to pull me against her chest, choking back sobs. Did she know about Father? "Elfriede's missing." She pulled back and wiped her eyes with a shaking hand. "Forgive me, your lordship." She curtsied unsteadily. "I should have greeted you. I've just been so frantic." Lines had deepened across her face. The past few hours had aged her.

Ailill nodded curtly, his hands behind his back. What I once would have taken for rudeness I understood now was simply his mask for discomfort. He was so unused to interacting with others, now that I thought about it.

"Since when?" I asked, thinking about how I'd seen my sister in bed on the book's page just a short while earlier. No, hours earlier. And she'd been awake, looking worried or frightened.

"I don't know!" Mom threw her hands out as her eyes clenched, tears running down her face. "A few hours maybe. I was asleep. Or, I was trying to sleep. I should have heard her leave. But I just woke up, and she wasn't there." She cradled her face in her hands. "I came out here to find her, and then I saw the carriage and—oh, *goddess*." Her gaze ran over the two lines of specters at rest behind the carriage, and she sobbed. "Something has happened, hasn't it?"

"Yes," I said, unsure of how to tell her. "But not with Elfriede." I swallowed. I didn't really know she wasn't involved. The pages showed such a mess of chaos at the tavern.

The pages.

Ailill gestured to the specters and pointed toward the village. The servants continued their march toward the tavern, splitting to walk around the carriage, my mother, and me. I let go of Mother, eager to slip back to the carriage. *Why now? Why did Elfriede have to go tonight, of all nights?* I tapped my foot anxiously, willing the men to hurry up so I could get back to the book in the carriage.

I heard Ailill speak from behind me. "Why do you think your daughter has gone against her will?"

I'd forgotten she said something about people taking her.

"It's not that she'd go against her will. It's just..." She grabbed me by the shoulders, pulling me away from the line of specters between me and the carriage. "I've tried to help her get over things, Noll. It's been so hard. She took it so much harder than I thought she would." She hiccupped. "And all this time, I had my own problems to worry about with your father."

I met Ailill's gaze at that, and his eyes fell immediately to the ground. The last of the specters filed past, leaving only one atop the carriage, his hands gripping the black horses' reins. Ailill slipped inside the carriage, and

I felt relieved that someone was going to get the book to find Elfriede.

"And I was worried about *you*, Noll." Mother sniffed. "It's just I thought you might be doing all right. Handling the change better than anyone. Maybe even finding some happiness with Jurij." She broke down again. "I'm sorry, your lordship, I shouldn't speak in front of you so. It's just been so hard keeping this family together. I thought maybe just *one* of us would find some happiness. But perhaps it wasn't with him after all. Noll, are you and the lord a coupling again? I didn't even stop to think what you were doing together. I..."

I wondered if Mother would be happy at the thought, or if she'd come to understand what had passed between us, how she'd been his hostage while lost in slumber. But he'd healed her... I had to clench Mother's arms tightly to keep her from falling to the ground. I looked to see if Ailill had heard what Mother had said—especially how everyone assumed I would run right back to Jurij despite all I'd been through—but his attention was on the open book in his hands as he stepped out of the carriage, his brow furrowed.

"We should go," he said, his voice fraught with tension.

"What is it?" I asked, suddenly scared that I'd lost my sister and my father in the same evening. *She couldn't be at the tavern, could she? Looking for Jaron? For Father? Did it matter?* I was going to set it right. Somehow.

Ailill flipped a few pages, not bothering to explain anything to Mother, who could barely contain her sobs. "The fight has gotten worse."

Mother's jaw hung open. "A fight?"

I shook her gently, snapping her back to reality. "Not with Elfriede. Right?" I looked to Ailill for confirmation, and he just nodded, scanning one page after the other. "Is Elfriede all right? Ailill?"

His head snapped up at the sound of his name. The

crease between his eyebrows softened as he took a step closer to me. If things weren't so chaotic, if I weren't so mad at him over my friends, if I weren't so angry about my father, so determined to get to the cavern to undo everything, I'd have melted under the softness of his gaze.

"Your sister is with her friends," he said, snapping the book shut and pulling it back just as I reached out to grab it from him. I'd wanted to see for myself. He stared earnestly at me. "Noll, go back inside and wait with your mother. I will return for you when I have finished with the fight at the tavern. Then we will go fetch your sister and put your mother's mind at ease together."

"The tavern?" interrupted Mother. "What do you mean *fight*?"

I grimaced. The only fights she knew were ones people fought with words alone, or from stories about legendary kings and queens who fought with swords that were just imaginary items.

Ailill replied to her for me. "People have gotten hurt." He stepped back toward the carriage, gesturing up at the sole specter that remained. He twisted around to face us again. "Stay here."

Mother wrenched out of my grip. "No! Your father's probably there. I thought Elfriede might be there, too. She... that is, many of the girls like to visit... someone."

"Jaron was with me. He's back at the castle." I took a deep breath, not ready to explain all of that just yet.

"With you? Oh, Noll." Mother's irises glistened with moisture. "Not you too. What about... ?" She eyed Ailill warily, perhaps afraid to finish the sentence with a name. Unsure which name to finish it with.

Ailill nodded toward her, ignoring Mother's train of thought. "Elfriede is not at the tavern. Please. Go inside."

"Then where is she?" I demanded. I tried to snatch the book from his hand, but he tossed it into the carriage. "Why aren't you letting me—"

"Olivière, I will explain everything upon my return."

One of his hands gripped the edge of the open carriage door, and the other, the hand still missing a glove, reached out to cradle my head. "I must go. Promise me you will stay."

I shook my head. "I'll go with you."

Mother latched onto my arm, pulling me farther away from Ailill's soft hold. "How does he know this? What's going on? And what about your father?"

I swallowed.

"Olivière!" called Ailill, reaching out to shut the door. "I will go ahead. You escort your mother to safety indoors."

"No, wait! Ailill!" I looked between my hysterical mother and the closed carriage door as it drove by. My eyes met the specter's briefly, pleading. He returned the gaze but continued onward.

I wanted to run after him and make sure no one else got hurt. But wasn't this the opportunity I'd wanted? Ailill had been against me entering the pool again. If Mother hadn't flagged down the carriage, I wouldn't have had this chance.

But Mother was crumpled into a heap on the ground beside me. I couldn't take her with me to the cavern. And I couldn't risk her running to the tavern and putting herself in harm's way. Not after everything. Not after Father.

"Come on," I said, crouching down and lifting Mother's arm to drape it around my shoulders. "You have to tell me what's going on with Elfriede."

η η η

The chaos wasn't contained to the tavern alone. Out of old, rusty habit, I thanked the first goddess there weren't people stabbing each other in the village streets—remembering then, that I was thanking myself, and a whole lot of good that would do. Men and women alike were running to and fro, shouting at one another. Man pushing aside woman, woman pushing aside man, children ducking into doorways. What had spurred them all out of their homes to compound the problem, I wasn't sure—but then I realized. The parade of specters. The hermit lord's black carriage. That kind of sight was bound to attract notice.

Please, Ailill, let us not have made it all worse.

There was at least enough room on the roads to push through the village's center and make my way toward the old commune, and from there to Alvilda's and Siofra's home nearby. But dragging my reluctant mother along made the journey far too slow.

"Why?" she sobbed, mumbling that word to herself for the hundredth time. "Why did it all come to this?"

"Mother," I spat at last, frustrated with trying to maneuver her around a small crowd of children who'd come out to see what was happening. One cradled a wooden squirrel to her chest, and my heart warmed, despite the state of the village. "You have it wrong about me and Jaron. I'm not coupling with Jurij, either." I couldn't bring myself to mention Ailill.

"Why did you let him move in with you then?" asked Mother quietly, as if she'd barely heard me.

"That doesn't mean we were a coupling!" It seemed like the older women in the village couldn't let go of that idea. "I know how I once felt, but he's not even the same man anymore. I'm not the same woman. But we're still friends." I sighed, relieved as Mother stopped resisting. "I wanted him back with Elfriede."

Mother stopped and pulled away. "I didn't."

"Why?" I backed into the wall of the nearest building as two frightened women passed by.

"I wanted her to find love. Real love." Mother cradled her arms against her chest. "Love that kept on going, even against all odds. Even against all hope. I thought what you had with Jurij was a good example of that."

"Mother, you were the one counseling me to wait for my own man."

Mother shook her head and raised her voice. "That was before all this!" She threw her arms out at the people wandering the streets, many hurrying toward the commotion. "Before the lord set the men's hearts free!"

"Ailill didn't..." But he *did* in a way. Though only because I'd let him. I sighed, remembering Ailill's warning that knowing I was the first goddess, or at least knowing *how* I was the first goddess, could condemn someone to death. I wasn't even sure he meant death by his own hands anymore. All of that talk about the world beyond the mountains, and *they*, and the golden copper somehow connecting it all. I couldn't tell Mother, even if it *were* an appropriate time.

I'd told Jurij. I hadn't given him all the details, but I'd told him more than the others. And maybe he'd told the rest of them since. But even if he hadn't, Jurij knew.

I had to get to the cavern and undo tonight. All of it. Those small moments with Ailill were nothing in comparison. My own desires were nothing.

Still, he held my hand.

"Mother." I grabbed her by the hand and dragged her forward. "Now's not the time. Please come with me to Alvilda's. I'll look for Elfriede," I lied. "But I have to go."

The door to the nearest building burst open, and I had to drag Mother back to avoid her getting hit. Darwyn's mother came out. We were standing in front of the bakery.

"Aubree! Noll!"

My grip slipped from my mother's hand. Mistress Baker looked terrified. "I can't find them! Any of them!"

Mother slid in beside the hysterical woman, dropping her own panic with the appearance of someone else in need of comfort. "What is it? Who?"

Mistress Baker pointed down the road. "People are talking about something going on at the tavern. I couldn't get close enough to get in there. Some of my boys have been spending a lot of time there." Tears streamed down her cheeks. "I thought I'd at least wake Roslyn, to help me get in there. But she's gone, too!"

My stomach lurched. *"She is with her friends."* What could the girls be up to? Why tonight of all nights? Ailill hadn't seemed as concerned about them as he was about the tavern. *But why did he refuse to show me?* "Darwyn and Sindri are all right," I told her. "They're not at the tavern."

Mistress Baker laid a hand on her chest, exhaling a deep sigh of relief, even if her lips still wavered. "You're sure?"

"Yes." I dug my nails into my palm. I felt I'd made a terrible mistake, even if it seemed the best choice at the time. *Please, do what I told you.*

Mistress Baker took me at my word and ran her fingers over Mother's arm. "But Roslyn! And my other boys. I can't be sure they were at the tavern. I know they didn't visit it as often as Darwyn and Sindri." She swallowed. "I know Merek at least would be with his wife. They stayed together after all of that."

Mother took Mistress Baker's hand in hers. "Roslyn must be with Elfriede. The lord said she was with her friends."

"The lord?" Mistress Baker seemed confused, then relieved, until she read the distress across Mother's features. "And where are they?"

"Noll!"

Alvilda and Siofra ran toward us, not from the direction of their home, where I'd hoped to drop off Mother, but from the center of the village.

"We can't find Nissa!" sputtered Siofra as they ground to a halt beside us. She doubled over slightly, fighting to catch her breath.

"We thought maybe she'd gone to be with Coll and Luuk," added Alvilda. "But they weren't home." She glanced back at the chaos behind us. "And now we hear there was some problem at the tavern."

Here I go again. "Master Tailor and Luuk weren't there. And neither was Jurij. They were all with me—at the castle, before this all started. But I don't know where any of the girls are."

If any of the women had questions about what I was doing with such a large group of men at the forbidden castle, they likely didn't think it the right time to ask. The relief that loosened some of the furrows on their faces was temporary, filled with a new worry about the women whom I couldn't vouch for.

Siofra pinched her lips. "Nissa might be with Roslyn."

"I didn't know Roslyn and Nissa were friends."

Mother looked embarrassed. "They are. Elfriede felt sorry for her after Luuk left her, and she and the others just sort of took to her. The girls have been spending a lot of time at our house. A sort of gathering for young rejected women."

The women all exchanged glances, and I felt pointedly left out. I'd felt that way longer than any of them imagined. Well, besides Alvilda and Siofra, perhaps. But that had worked out for them in the end.

Alvilda wrapped an arm around Siofra and pulled her closer. Siofra's head lulled gently onto the taller woman's shoulder. She looked about to pass out. "Nissa's been saying something recently," said Siofra quietly. She rotated her head to look up at Alvilda. "A place to battle monsters?"

Alvilda nodded, mulling over what she'd said. "She was too young to get along with those girls the way she wanted. She kept wanting to show them something. A place she used to battle monsters."

"With a pool!" added Mother as she slammed her fist into her other palm. "That shined with red, glowing light! I thought she'd made it up. Noll often did the same at that age."

My heart practically stopped. I didn't know Nissa

had gone that far into the cavern. But the cavern. Where I was headed. Where Ailill was not keen to let me go.

It makes perfect sense now why he wouldn't let me see her page. But if the place was such a danger for me, why so little concern for my sister?

Mistress Baker frowned. "Roslyn mentioned... No, but why? She at least had reason to be happy now! Even without that no-good son of mine."

"Thea, what is it?" asked Mother, more concerned than ever.

Mistress Baker's eyes widened. "When I offered to take her back, she cried. She said she and her friends had almost given up hope—that they'd considered succumbing to the glow, and just letting it all go! I didn't know." She choked. "I didn't think that meant they'd drown themselves!"

And even if that wasn't what they'd intended, they might very well find themselves the recipients of a death sentence. Ailill's mysterious "they" who lived far beyond the mountains. Always watching. Toying with me.

Please, let the pool have closed its heart.

Chapter Twenty-Five

HERDING A GROUP OF HYSTERICAL women to a secret, dark cavern wasn't the best idea. But there was no way I was going to convince Mother and Mistress Baker to stay behind now. Alvilda or even Siofra might prove helpful in talking some sense into Elfriede and her friends, but I was sure Mother and Mistress Baker were just a breath away from losing themselves completely.

So how am I going to dive into the pool without them noticing? How will I get the glow to accept me? I'd just have to figure it out once I got there. If I successfully changed the past, then none of it would matter. I'd make sure to stop Elfriede from even leaving the house, and none of us would be in the cavern this evening.

At least with Mistress Baker to care for and a goal in mind, Mother seemed to steel herself a little better. Her tight grip around Mistress Baker's shoulders kept them both steady as we marched back out of the city and into the woods. Away from the tavern. Away from Ailill and the danger he thought more pressing than the cavern.

He's got over a hundred specters to help him calm things down. He can do it. But even if he couldn't, I could. I could save Father and stop Elfriede. Maybe save Jurij, too. And never put Ailill in danger in the first place.

"This way," I said, pointing to the bush bent from all

the times we'd pushed past it to get to the cavern a short distance ahead. The women followed me with only Mistress Baker's occasional sobs to punctuate the chirps and hoots of the animals in the darkness. Mistress Baker could only find two candles to light our way, and she tried to light them with shaking hands before Alvilda took over. I tapped my foot impatiently. I just wanted to be there and make sure it was all just a misunderstanding. And take them all away from the cavern so I could do what I needed to do.

It was unsettling, leaving the murmurs and shouts of the chaotic village behind us. But something about what Ailill had told me, the threat of someone other than him "always watching," made me certain Elfriede, Roslyn, and Nissa were the more pressing matter.

"Here it is." I held my candle up to give them a better look at the mouth of the cavern. "Watch your step. There are stalagmites all over the ground." I nodded at Alvilda as she followed behind me. "Take the back. Light as much of the ground as you can with your candle."

We didn't speak for several more minutes as we made our way slowly through the cavern. More than once, one of the women stumbled, but there were no complaints, no suggestions we stop to rest as we plowed forward. The whistling emptiness was invaded by a faint trickle of water.

"The pool's up ahead," I said, clearing my throat. The light that should have been violet poked into the darkness, as red as the blood on Father's page. There was no way the page had been lying. Father was dead. And I couldn't tell Mother. I wouldn't need to, if I could change the past.

Father. Part of me worried I couldn't do this. That I'd never get to know the real him. I'd failed to thus far. I'd just seen glimpses of him, been reminded of the time he drank to forget the pain of Mother being trapped in Ailill's castle, and turned away.

Darwyn had even asked you to save him. To save "both" of them. I frowned. I never knew who else he'd been referring to. Jurij? Or was it the lord? But why would he care about the lord? It had to have been Jurij. But my mind had gone instantly to Ailill, my thoughts never more than a step away from him. Somehow, that had become the case.

My chest clenched at the image of Ailill's castle in my mind. Rotten and in disarray. And he'd been taking so many deliveries of wine and ale from the tavern.

He'd looked thin when I saw him. Almost like he was trying to wither away.

The trickle was drowned out by a splash, and Mother screamed. She let go of Mistress Baker's arms and pushed past, running forward.

"Mother, wait!" I couldn't reach her. Even when she tripped and stumbled, the brightening red glow was enough to give her confidence in her steps.

I picked up my skirt with one hand and ran after her, not caring that the candle extinguished as I did. Not thinking of the women I left behind.

As the pool came into view, I gasped. The useless candle slipped to the ground.

"What are you *doing* here?" I shrieked, running toward the large gathering of people at the water's edge. "I told you to hide in my shack!"

Jaron turned his head, not moving from where he stood, casually leaning on a stick. "We discussed it and thought it might get a little crowded in there. Best make use of our freedom while we have it, right? It's not like we'll be able to effectively hide from him anywhere."

I frowned, my gaze falling over the men I'd freed from the castle's cells just before I'd joined Ailill in the carriage.

I'd wanted them to hide. To stay away from the tavern and just get out of there, so I could reason with Ailill once the whole thing blew over. I should have warned them to stay away from this place.

Mother bent down by the water. "Get out of there!" She tugged on Nissa until they both fell on the sediment.

Nissa laughed as she rolled over, dripping wet. Mother was furious.

"Darwyn! Sindri!" Mistress Baker reached out to hug them both. Before they could even process that their mother stood beside them or think to reciprocate the hug, she pulled back. "Roslyn!" She pushed past them to draw the young woman into her arms.

Roslyn smiled and hugged her, twittering like a sweet little bird. "Goodmother!" She laughed and pulled away, covering her mouth. "I suppose it's just Thea now, isn't it?"

Mistress Baker's lips grew taut, and she stuck a finger in Roslyn's face. "I was worried sick about you! I thought you were in the tavern—and then I was sure you'd drowned yourself!"

"*Drowned* herself?" Nissa stood, brushing off the front of her skirt. Siofra brushed past Master Tailor with a spiteful glance, as if he had anything to do with Nissa being there. Finding Luuk a short distance away, she led Nissa to him and put her arms around them both. Luuk looked embarrassed and shifted away, patting the side of his leg.

Mistress Baker looked at all of the faces around her, perhaps more confused than I was. "What's going on here then?"

"Nothing!" said Sindri. He also looked uncomfortable, and he'd spoken his protestation of innocence too quickly. "Jurij said we should see something here. And when we got here, we found the women. Swimming."

Elfriede and Marden sat at the edge of the water, whispering to each other. Their clothes were damp, as if they'd slipped them on hastily and they'd gotten soaked due to the wet undergarments beneath. Mother joined them.

I just about jumped out of my skin as someone's arm entwined through mine. I turned, expecting Jurij or Ailill, but it was Roslyn, smiling. "We've been here a few times, swimming."

I wanted to rip my arm away from hers, but I couldn't blame her oblivious peacefulness if she truly didn't know what was happening. "At night?"

Roslyn shrugged. "Sure. Why not? Everyone expects so much of us during the day." She dropped my arm and motioned for Jurij. "And I wanted to celebrate today. And maybe just help ease the pain of your happiness a bit for your sister."

Jurij didn't take the cue to stand beside me. His glare was cold, and he dropped his eyes, focusing on his side, at which he clutched something.

"Well, that was stupid," said Alvilda, stopping beside her brother and looking him once over. "And dangerous. Especially tonight."

"We didn't know they were here," protested Master Tailor.

"Tonight?" cut in Roslyn, her sweet voice wavering. "What's going on tonight?"

Every man's eyes dropped down to his side. Every man's but Jaron's. *But I didn't tell them about the tavern. I didn't want to put them in harm's way.* Jaron stood straighter, no longer leaning on his stick. He lifted it up in the air, letting the red light of the pool bounce off it.

It was a sword! All of the men had scabbards tied around their waists. Every one of them. Even Luuk.

"Tonight the men decided it was time to get some answers," said Jaron. I couldn't sense malice in his words, but the sword he held aloft gave me dreadful feelings of nostalgia. There was a time when men acted much like he was acting, not even realizing the menace of their actions. Jaron slid his sword back into the scabbard at his side and nodded. Roslyn screamed as Darwyn and Tayton shoved her aside and slipped their arms through mine, gripping me tightly.

Jaron smiled. He looked almost friendly. "And Noll here has some answers."

Chapter Twenty-Six

I STRUGGLED TO BE FREE of Darwyn and Tayton, sending them both my angriest glare. Neither looked down, and neither caved much to my resistance, so I went slack.

It wasn't like I wanted to keep it all secret. But I'd have to find a way to explain my hesitation.

"What is the meaning of this?" demanded Alvilda, striding toward me.

But before she could get much closer, Master Tailor stepped around her, pushing his hands against her chest. "Stand back, Alvilda."

Alvilda's eyebrows furrowed, and her face soured, like she'd eaten something rotten. "No! Step aside, Coll, or so help me, I'll—"

"You'll what?" interrupted Jaron, his casual stride to stand beside Master Tailor belying any ill intent. "Command him to stand down? Send him to the commune to rot?" The corner of his mouth twitched. "You don't have any power here, Alvilda. Not anymore."

Alvilda spat at the ground near his feet. "You think I was any happier knowing I couldn't be with Siofra thanks to you meddling men? Don't blame *me* for the rules of this village."

"Blame Noll." Jurij's voice was quiet. Elfriede lifted

her head as he stood beside me. It was the first time I'd seen her move at all since we'd arrived.

All eyes were on me. Even the women's, and they looked more surprised than angry.

I glanced warily at the glow of the red pool beside us. "This isn't the time."

"You had weeks, *months*, to pick a better time." Jaron stepped closer. "We waited long enough for Jurij to get the truth out of you. His way didn't work."

I eyed Jurij curiously. "His way?"

The lump at the base of Jurij's throat bobbed, and he looked away. "I thought if you loved me, you'd tell me everything you knew."

I supposed it was lucky Darwyn and Tayton had such tight grips on me because I imagined myself punching him across the face. "You liar! All you've ever done is lie to me! You pretended to be my friend! You pretended to love me. You no-good—"

Jurij spun around, bringing his face closer than ever. "I wasn't lying! I loved you. You gave me my freedom, and then you pushed me away." He turned away and wouldn't look at me again.

"*She* gave you your freedom?" echoed Mistress Baker, oblivious to the intensity of the conversation.

"People are hurt at the tavern!" I shouted, drowning out Mistress Baker's question. "There's been a fight—a *real* fight, in which people spill each other's blood—and the lord and his servants had to rush out to stop it." I gulped, not expecting the sudden wave of emotion that slammed into me. I had to stop myself from letting tears fall. "And I... I've got to take care of it. I told you all to wait out of harm's way." I eyed Roslyn and Elfriede. "And then *you* all had to have this little pity gathering at the worst time."

"*Pity* gathering?" Elfriede shot up, practically knocking Mother down as she did. "How dare you belittle us?" She marched toward me, clenching her fists.

"Oh. Because you've been through so much just

because your men left you," I growled. "Excuse me while I reserve my sympathy."

"Enough!" Jurij's voice reverberated off the cavern ceiling. He looked from Elfriede to me and back again. "Both of you." He sighed and ran a hand through his short hair. "I'm tired of being the cause of fights between you."

I rolled my eyes. Since when had he cared about that? Maybe he couldn't help it before, but he could now.

Jaron stepped between us sisters, nudging Jurij aside. "We know about the fight at the tavern." Jaron nodded at Darwyn and Tayton, and they let me go, even if they still stood within easy reach. I pulled my arms away to make the point that I didn't appreciate being held in place. What was the point of holding me down anyway? Were they worried I'd run, or a specter would step out from the shadows to whisk me away?

I stopped. "You *knew* about the tavern?"

Jaron looked smug and patted the sword at his side. "The boys told me about those games you used to play. A queen and her retainers battling monsters with tools called swords meant to destroy your foes. We realized people could fight each other with or without these tools." He gestured toward the scabbard at his waist, which I noticed was slightly askew and over his stomach, not at all the tight and practiced way the men of the distant past had worn them over their hips. "Of course we didn't expect to find a whole stash of these things in the castle after you let us free. But we didn't need them for our fellow village men, anyway. Fists would do."

"What are you saying?" asked Mistress Baker, her voice wavering.

Jaron shrugged. "We planned the fight in the tavern. If we failed to return after we investigated the castle, Gideon agreed to provide a distraction that might summon the lord and his men away."

"You *planned* that?" I felt hot tears burning my cheeks, but I couldn't stop them. "Father's dead because of your plans!"

The air went still, the stifling thickness of the cavern with so many people in it threatening to suffocate us all. Even Jaron's smugness slipped just a bit. "How do you—"

"No!" Mother screamed. She broke down into sobs, far worse than when she feared Elfriede had gone missing.

I took a step toward her, but Darwyn and Tayton clutched my forearms to stop me. I glared at them and by the time I turned back, Jaron was crouched beside Mother, patting her back. "Aubree, she must be mistaken. Don't get yourself so worked up."

"The pages!" I screamed, roaring to life. "Father died in ink and silhouette before my eyes. And more men and women could too." I strained my shoulders, struggling to free myself. "What were you thinking? You figured out men could harm one another, but you didn't consider how easy it would be for that harm to become permanent? Even fatal?"

Jurij rubbed his scar and watched as Elfriede crouched beside Mother and took her into her arms. The red of the pool flickered across the tears streaming down my sister's face. Jaron backed away, watching the two sobbing women like they were some monster he'd unleashed upon the world. Perhaps their tears were.

Alvilda frowned. "What are you talking about? Pages?"

I stopped fighting, and I felt my captors relax. They still didn't let me go. "Ailill watches us through pages in a book."

Alvilda raised an eyebrow. "Okay..."

"Well, if *you* had shared what you knew with us earlier, it wouldn't have come to this!" Jaron took the distraction from my weeping family as an excuse to wag a finger in my direction. I felt a sudden wave of anger for this stupid man and his stupid plan, which put my father and so many more in danger. And now he wouldn't even let me be with my family. Marden took my place patting Elfriede on the back, and Roslyn brushed past Jaron to join them,

Mistress Baker trembling and following after her. Even Siofra let go of the children's hands and directed them over toward Mother and Elfriede.

"Don't blame this on me!" I snarled. None of the men but Jaron would look at me. That said all I needed to know; they did indeed blame me. *But how much has Jurij told them?* I swallowed, wondering if I was just imagining the red of the pool growing brighter and deeper in color. Was it time? Could I go back? Could I stop myself from even hinting to Jurij while I was at it? "The lot of you schemed without me, trying to drag me into your foolish plans, coming up with the stupidest of ways to find out something you don't even need to know!"

"Don't need to know?" Jaron practically spat as he grunted in frustration.

"Why can't it be enough for you that you're free? Do you really need to know why?"

Jaron patted the hilt of the sword at his side. "That's easy for you to say since you know everything!"

"I *don't* know everything!" The water seethed red, echoing my anger. "And if I told you what I know, I could put you all in danger!"

Jurij snapped back to the moment, tearing his focus from the huddle of grieving women. "Danger?" he asked, anxious, disbelieving. "From whom?"

"Who else?"

Ailill.

The specters that filed into the cavern from the darkness were so silent, not a single person had noticed them approaching. They split into two lines, settling in behind the group on either side, blocking us all from the path back to the entrance.

Falling into place at the center of the half circle of specters, Ailill stepped out from the darkness, tugging at the bottom of his glove as if he were just slipping it back on.

He's all right! I couldn't believe how relieved I felt. There were tears in his clothing. His boots were scuffed and dirty. His hair was a bit mussed and out of place. There was a dark bruise on his cheek, and a thin line, no thicker or deeper than a cat's scratch, across part of his throat that smeared red across the delicate paleness of his skin.

He didn't seem to notice me studying him as he forced a smile. "I had wondered where you all slipped off to." He gestured slightly, and the specters moved forward, each reaching for the nearest person. "Perhaps you can find the answers you seek in the life beyond." The specters lifted their arms and reached forward as one, easily tearing the swords from the scabbards the men wore too loosely at their hips.

The specters raised the swords above their heads with both hands, all pointed down at the men.

Ailill crossed his arms and nodded. "Proceed."

"No!" I screeched.

Chapter Twenty-Seven

THE SPECTERS STOPPED AS ONE, the blades hovering dangerously over the men's heads and backs.

Their sudden hesitation gave the men enough time to pull away. Sindri, Darwyn, Tayton, and Master Tailor formed a half circle with their backs to the water. Even Alvilda stood beside her brother, her hands clenched at her sides. Siofra pulled Luuk out of the way, and she and the rest of the women, my mother and Elfriede included, stood in a half circle around Luuk and Nissa, whom they pushed toward the water's edge.

I was worried they were making a mistake, trusting in that water to save them. I didn't want them anywhere near it. I had no idea how I could go back through time with so many people around.

Now that Darwyn and Tayton had abandoned their posts at my sides to form their protective barrier, I was free. Jaron stood at the center of that group, his blade clumsily drawn. The specters hadn't disarmed him or Jurij, who'd been further inward when they arrived. I scanned the statue-like crowd of ghastly pale figures. There should have been enough of them to take the blades from Jaron and Jurij. But there weren't. Not in the cavern anyway.

"What happened to the rest of the specters?" My heart thundered wildly at the idea of vanished specters and dead men, more lives to go back and save.

"Specters?" Ailill echoed my word as he stepped forward, hands clutched behind his back. "Oh. I keep forgetting what you call us."

Us? I supposed Ailill considered himself as one with them in a way. Although he seemed convinced with the curse broken, he wouldn't find himself joining them.

"They are detaining the rabble-rousers from what is left of the tavern."

"What's *left* of it?" repeated Alvilda. "What did you do to it?" I was afraid she'd launch herself at the nearest specter, but Master Tailor grabbed her forearm and pulled her back with a warning glance.

Ailill cocked his head. "*I* did not do anything. It was the men of this village who started the fire."

"Fire?" spat Jaron. "I never told them to start a fire!"

Ailill raised an eyebrow and nodded at the nearest specter. They all lowered their weapons, holding them at their sides. "But you told them to start a fight, I assume?" He chuckled darkly. "I should have guessed. I only wonder how you managed to get out of the cells while I was distracted."

I shifted uncomfortably and decided to stand beside Jurij. We alone were between the specters and the line of villagers. "I let them out." I eyed the nearest specter, as if I really had a hope of identifying which of them had dropped the key or which had almost spoken to me. *Are the specters truly one and the same?* "One of the Ailills dropped the key."

Ailill scanned his specters, struggling to contain a smile, my comment eliciting amusement when I expected anger. "Interesting," he said, almost as if expecting the culprit to speak up. For, now that I thought about it, the idea of these perfectly trained statues doing anything on accident was absurd. I'd either found a rogue specter—and the thought that one had tried to speak to me led credence to that theory—or I'd played right into Ailill's plans, which his lack of utter anger and disgust might attest to.

Both ideas seemed wrong. Possible, but wrong. I'd never known a specter to act without Ailill's instruction, or at least a general sense of what he'd wanted. But it made so little sense to me that this would be what he wanted.

Ailill gave up on his fruitless search for the suspect and clasped his hands together in front of him. He studied us, staring over my head at the line of people behind me. Or at the deep red glow of the pond he insisted they should know nothing about.

I used the silence as an opportunity to ask what I'd been dreading. "Ailill." His head snapped toward me, a mixture of surprise and delight on his face. "My father?"

"Olivière, you knew from the pages..." He stopped, his eyes drawn back to the pool. "He was gone. I asked the tavern masters. He was one among a dozen or so who vanished in the battle. I am sorry."

As I thought. All the more reason I had to make this work.

A scream of rage echoed around the cavern as Mother launched herself at the specter who had threatened Luuk, her arms flailing.

"Mother, no!" I shouted.

"Aubree!" I heard again and again.

I pushed past Jurij, determined to stop her, afraid of her getting anywhere near a specter with a blade. But Mother turned sharply, running right toward me. I stopped, surprised, but Mother kept advancing, tears running down her cheeks. She was going to try to punish somebody for this. If she somehow thought I was to blame, if she, like everyone else, just wanted to lay the blame on me without giving me the chance to fix it, then I'd let her. I'd tried. I tried staying away from everyone. I tried letting solitude be my penance for my sin. I was tired of trying.

An arm clamped down across my chest, dragging me backward. I tried to turn, but the force was too great. I kicked.

"Now, hold on, Aubree!" Jaron! Jaron the flirt, the

instigator, the all-around troublemaker I'd considered more of a friend when he hadn't an original thought in his head. His left arm was clenched tight across my chest, his right hand still holding the sword awkwardly at his side. The tip of the blade poked into my skirt, ruffling it as he fought to hold me.

Mother kept running, and Jaron did the unthinkable. He raised his sword so the tip pointed at my neck. "Aubree, stop!"

Mother froze just a short distance from us. "Jaron, let her go! How could you?" She choked on her sobs. Like a coward, he'd used me as a shield. As though my mother's fists could possibly harm him as much as he and the rest of the men had harmed the people in the tavern.

"I'll let her go," he panted, but I didn't feel at all comforted. I struggled to keep my feet firmly planted, but he was dragging me so that I rested on my toes. "I just want you to calm down and listen."

Mother shrieked. "*Listen*? Your foolishness killed my husband!"

"Your *former* husband," pointed out Jaron, a correction not at all appropriate given the circumstances.

Mother's face grew dark as her eyes widened. "I don't care! I loved him even still!" She looked like she was barely restraining herself from leaping at him. "I wish I'd never loved you! I hate you!"

Jaron's grip slackened somewhat, and I almost twisted away, feeling the prick of the blade on my throat. But he tightened his grip again and backed up, turning his head to and fro. Everyone around him was suddenly an enemy, even if no one else had made a move. He turned us both so I could see Ailill again, but he was gone. *Gone.* Impossibly gone. In desperation, my eyes darted to Jurij. He looked from me, to Jaron, to my mother, and back. Frozen in place. His hand on his sword's hilt.

The specters were just a blur of white at the edge of the darkness. Not a single one moved forward to stop him.

Jaron dragged us back through the circle, even as Alvilda swooped out to lay a hand on Mother's shoulder. "What are you doing?" she sneered. "Jaron, let Noll go right now!"

"Ha!" spat Jaron. "You can't order me around, Alvilda! Not anymore!"

"This isn't about that, Jaron!" Master Tailor stepped beside his sister. "Great goddess, man! What are you doing? Let the girl go!"

"I'm not doing anything!" He swung his sword out, pointing it at everyone in sight. "I just want you to listen. Calmly."

"You're the one who's not calm!" said Tayton. He took a step forward, swinging his clenched fist. "We didn't want to hurt her!"

"Tayton, *no!*" shouted Darwyn, grabbing onto his shoulder.

"No one move." Jaron flicked the sword back to my throat. It hurt. I could feel the warmth trickling down my skin. I didn't dare breathe.

"All right," said Jaron after a moment of silence. He dragged me slowly backward until I felt the water lapping at my feet, and he froze, probably realizing he couldn't retreat any farther without falling into the pool.

"All right," repeated Jaron. His breath fluttered across the top of my head. "Start talking, Noll. Tell us everything. Explain to them why I had to go to such lengths. And then we'll all go home. We'll be fine."

"My father is *dead*, Jaron." I expected my voice to be strengthened by anger, but I practically choked on the words. "And so are a number of others."

"No," said Jaron, in denial. "He's lying. You hear me?" He waved his sword away from me, pointing it across the crowd. "The lord just doesn't want us to know the truth."

I brought my heel down as hard as I could on his toes.

"Gargh!" He bounced back, trying to maintain a grip on me, his sword hand wobbling.

I kicked back again, aiming for his shin, twisting my leg around his to drag us both down. I fumbled, and he brought the sword toward me, but I squirmed away and eventually wound my leg through his, using my fall to take him with me.

I heard a man's guttural scream from some distance away as I fell, but it was drowned out by the splash of the water, and then the thud of my head against the sediment. The roar of the movement in the water made everything else impossible to hear.

Everything else but the beat of the heart. I twisted free of Jaron, who flailed beside me, and set out for deeper waters, to the point where neither of us could stand up. My head throbbed, and my vision blurred. I was overwhelmed by the red. The burning, fiery red from the heart in the water. The thump of the heartbeat. The threat of drowning.

Time seemed to stop, and I reached out for it. I wanted that red to go away, and I tried willing back the violet light that had been more inviting. I floated in place close to the sediment, telling the orb I needed to go to the past.

And then, whether I imagined it or not, I heard my name whispered. *"Olivière."*

The red bled into a dark violet. *Yes! Take me back. Let me undo this!*

I reached out again, but it was gone, the red drowning out the violet once more, a pair of hands grabbing my wrists and tugging me upward.

I tried to scream, to shout "No!" But when I opened my mouth, I invited in the water. It tasted sour, like the scent of copper. I closed my mouth and kicked, feeling the pressure of the water in my chest.

"Olivière!" This time my name wasn't so clear, but I felt a tugging at my wrists. I floated right up beside my captor.

My eyes were blurry, thanks to the water and my throbbing head. But he was dressed all in black, his pale face inches from mine.

I opened my mouth, "Ailill" spilling out across my tongue but sounding like only a gurgle of water. Why was he stopping me? I knew he hadn't wanted me to use the pool, but couldn't he see I had to? I wasn't going to let this evening happen.

I panicked, throwing my head back, and Ailill kicked, bringing us back to the surface after what seemed like forever but couldn't have been more than a moment.

We broke through the surface, and I vomited water. Ailill hugged me close to him, resting my chin over his shoulder and pounding on my back so I could throw up the rest of the water I'd swallowed. What should have been the quiet trickling of the cavern walls was filled with splashing and shouting. I couldn't focus. I concentrated on breathing, on the way I felt so close to Ailill. I felt warm. Safe. Even though my head told me I was neither of those things.

I had barely started breathing again when Ailill dropped his hand and swam backward, dragging me with him. "No!" he barked. "Stay back."

A mess of bodies slammed into us, almost knocking me under.

"Leave her alone!"

"Damn you!"

The words were halted between splashes and gasps of breath as two—no, three, four—men splashed through the water, a tumble of limbs.

"Just stop!"

A glint of red reflected off a gilded blade. The tip poked out from the water, driven upward with a powerful swimming kick. There was no way I could avoid it. I froze, telling myself to swim away, to duck under, anything. *Get out of the way!*

But as my eyes fixated on the blade, liquid red wrapped around my legs like a rope of solid blood. All the shouting died in my ears, and I heard only the echoing heartbeat of the water below. I couldn't move. The red of the pool had restrained me. *"OLIVIÈRE!"* It wasn't calling me. It was angry with me. *Why? Because I'd tried to order it? Because of what I'd done the last time I went through it?* Whatever the reason, it would drown me, one way or the other.

"Olivi—gah!"

The tip of the blade shot up, stopping a hair's breadth from the base of my throat, and I lurched away. The blade had come through Ailill's chest, and now it dripped, dripped, dripped blood into the glowing red water.

"AILILL!" I grabbed his upper arms, struggling to keep him from sinking. The squeeze of the red light on my legs faded, for what good it did now. I had to kick to stay afloat, but I was panicked. I couldn't let him move, not with the blade still struck through his chest.

Struck through his chest from behind, just like Elric had been when I led the rebellion to stop the men of the old village. And then I'd decided that I was a fool for playing at battle. That I never wanted to see bloodshed again.

Ailill's lips oozed with blood, but he tried to smile. It wasn't a cruel smile. No, it was the most genuine smile I'd ever seen across his face. "I love... when you say... my name." He spat out a river of blood, his head lurching forward.

"AILILL!" I screamed again, not sure what to do. Lift him off the blade? Swim to the sediment? *What can I do? How can I save him?* "No, no, no, no, you can't—"

Though I clenched his arms so hard I might have left bruises, his body collapsed, leaving me holding nothing but black leather.

"NO!" I shouted again, but he was gone. Vanished into death. The very last death.

And behind where he'd been, still clutching the hilt of the blade that dripped red with blood, was Jurij, his mouth agape.

Chapter Twenty-Eight

"YOU!" I SCREAMED. "HOW COULD you? How could..." I swam forward, screaming nonsense, ignoring the blade that hung limply from Jurij's grip. I pounded my fists into the water, one hand still clutching Ailill's jerkin.

Jurij pulled the blade out of my path and then tossed it, letting it succumb to the heartbeat of the water. He swam backward, holding his hands out to stop my approach. "Noll, wait! Noll, listen! I didn't mean to."

"You didn't mean to? You were swinging around a weapon, and you didn't *mean* to?" I reached him, snarling, and tried to clobber him, but I faltered when I hiccupped and choked on the flowing streams of tears. I could barely keep myself afloat. "Who were you *trying* to kill then, *me*?"

Jurij swam backward out of my reach, the coward, and I just got my second wind to surge after him when Darwyn and Tayton appeared on either side of me, holding me in place.

"Calm down, Noll!" shouted Darwyn, but he got a splash of water from my foot in his face.

"Let's get to the sediment," said Tayton. He leaned his head back to avoid another flurry of kicks. "Noll, *Noll*. Let's go."

"No!" I said, determined to dive back under, but they

overpowered me. I reached out toward the red glow, willing it to turn violet, but it refused. It burned.

You are not welcome here. The echoing voice in my mind was so harsh, so final, I knew at once that my last chance to go back to the past was beyond me. There would be no undoing this night, no matter how hard I tried. It was like Ailill's death was final not just for him, but for all hope of miracles.

The water surged like a great gust of wind shot through it, and I flew back, hearing screams echo throughout the cavern. When hands grabbed my arms again, I stopped resisting and was dragged out of the water toward the sediment.

"What was that?" Alvilda's voice rang out.

The surge calmed into ripples behind me. But my heart sank. If I dove in, the pool would send me right back out. But maybe once I got clear of all of these people, I could try. And try. As many times as necessary.

You're a fool. Father and Ailill are gone, and all your power to stop it is gone with them.

As soon as I broke free of the blood-stained water, Mother and—to my surprise—Elfriede swooped in on either side of me, wrapping me in their embraces.

"Oh, Noll!" Mother rubbed my head and cradled me, her tears falling onto my forehead. "Noll, I was so worried."

I pushed her away, and fury that shouldn't have been directed at her must have been plain on my face. She nodded at Elfriede, and they gave me space. I pounded the sediment as they moved back and stared at the jerkin in my raw and bleeding fist.

"Where are they?" I stood on wobbly legs, gently shoving Elfriede when she swooped in to help me stand. "Jaron! Jurij!"

I blinked, clearing the drops of water that still clung to my lashes and ignoring the pain that throbbed at the back of my head. I looked around, trying to bring the many—too many—figures into focus. And then I noticed the piles of white clothing in a half circle around the length of the pool's sediment.

"No!" I screamed again, walking toward the nearest pile, shoving aside several people who tried to stop me, who let me go despite my weak pushes and faltering steps. I collapsed, laying Ailill's black jerkin next to the white jacket.

I traced my fingers over both. Even though the black one was dark and wet, they had the same embroidery of roses and thorns. My fingers stopped on one of the white jacket's blooms. On the black one, there was a hole framed in dark, dark blood.

"Where are they?" I snarled again, turning around to face the group. Master Tailor stood beside Alvilda, and between them Jaron sat cross-legged on the ground, his arms tied behind him with his own scabbard belt. Siofra stood off to the side with Luuk and Nissa, her arm around Jurij's shoulders.

"Why?" I asked, leaping to my feet so ferociously I almost fell over. "Why did you kill him?" I didn't know where to direct my anger, who was more to blame. But I stepped toward Jurij, passing by Jaron to beg for answers from the man I'd once loved more than anything.

He was reluctant to look at me, and Siofra let go of him to stand between us. "Now, Noll, you couldn't see what was going on."

I gripped the jerkin to my chest. "I don't care! He killed him."

Jurij's head snapped up. "Is that such an awful thing? He was going to imprison us for life. And you said yourself you didn't want to be with him before the curse broke, and he forced you to be with him anyway."

"I was working on the imprisonment! And it wasn't all his fault. You don't understand!"

"Apparently not." Jurij looked down. "I thought you loved *me*."

"I told you—"

He waved a hand. "I know. You don't. Not like that.

Not anymore. Well, maybe I'm tired of loving where love isn't wanted."

"So you killed Ailill? Because I didn't love you?"

He didn't answer.

Siofra placed a hand on my shoulder. "He didn't mean to, Noll. It was such a mess. They were all trying to get Jaron away from you. To rescue you. You weren't coming up, and we were worried you'd hit your head."

I choked. "But why did you bring your sword into the water?"

Jurij's eyes narrowed. "I wasn't thinking. I just saw a chance to save you. I dove in."

I shook my head. "You launched up with the blade extended. Were you trying to kill me? Jaron?" I paused. "Why did all of you get swords at all? Who were you going to harm with them?"

Jurij clenched his jaw. The flames may have been gone, but his eyes burned with their own fire, glistening from the red glow of the pool. "The lord and his servants," he answered after a moment's hesitation. "If it came to that."

He brushed past his mother and me, moving down the path to the entrance and disappearing into the darkness.

η η η

There was no sign of Jurij, the Tailors, or any of my friends. Everyone's plan to calm me down by keeping me back in the cavern a while longer, while the lot of them ran away with their tails between their legs, seemed to have worked.

But they couldn't hide from me forever. Not if they didn't know there was a place beyond the mountains. Besides, they never got the answers they sacrificed so much to find.

And if some "they" watching us beyond the mountains wanted to punish people who knew about their existence, then that was fine with me. Ailill had told me the gold coin saved me, marked me as one fit for ruling. But I wasn't imagining things when the red light in the pool held me paralyzed as the blade approached. I was done trying to protect them. I was done trying to protect myself.

As Marden and Roslyn broke through the last of the trees and bushes to the path that ran through the forest, I fingered my sash. The golden coin was still there.

"Noll?" asked Mother, her arm around my back. I took another step forward.

"His carriage is still here!" exclaimed Marden. "No horses, though."

I froze.

Elfriede stopped at my side, reaching out a hand. "Noll—"

"I'll be fine," I said, waving her away. "Just leave me be."

Elfriede looked hesitant, but Mother let me go and wove her arm through Elfriede's, gently tugging her away. "Come see us when you're ready, Noll. We have... mournings to arrange."

They joined Roslyn and Marden on the path toward the village, leaving me beside the carriage. The first light of dawn trickled through the leaves above me.

As if I could forget that I'd lost both Father and Ailill. As if I could forget the lord's smile as he vanished from my arms, leaving me before I could say what it was I truly wanted to say.

But this time, at least, he hadn't vanished from existence. The clothes. The carriage. Even the castle might still be standing. This time, I wouldn't be the only one who knew him.

I lurched forward, leaning against the open carriage doorframe to keep from collapsing. I looked at the emptiness inside for what felt like forever, taking in the blackness of everything, the memories both painful and longing. There was one thing that wasn't black. A book with open pages.

I dragged myself inside the carriage, crawling on hands and knees. I held on to the jerkin even as I picked up the book, dragging it over my lap.

I saw myself, sitting on a carriage seat, looking down at a book on my lap. My fist still clutched the jerkin to my chest.

The ink smeared as tears dripped onto the page. But the water quickly dried and the ink was smooth, only to be drowned again and again.

The book grew hot in my lap, and the back glowed bright with violet light.

With wavering fingers, I turned the pages to the source of the light. My other hand clutched the leather so hard my wound reopened and my finger bled. But I kept clutching. I kept willing myself to breathe.

A half-formed page wound out of nothingness, fibers in the paper as clear as thread stitching, only without the needles. When at last the page was complete, the light faded, and I was left staring at a blank, yellowing page, one that seemed as old as the rest of them, even if I'd just witnessed its creation.

It was the castle throne room, complete with that hole in the wall where the throne should have been. The throne was already pushed aside.

Out stepped man after man after man. Their hands clutched behind their backs, their faces so similar, their ages varied, although most were older, far older-looking than one would think could walk so upright. They filed out of the hole and off the page. I counted. A hundred and four... a hundred and five.

And that last specter's face was young, perhaps in his twenties. He paused, and I saw Ailill, *my* Ailill staring out at me.

My fingers traced over his form. His jerkin wasn't

colored in black ink. It had to be white. My Ailill was a specter.

He stepped aside, and behind him came another specter. No. His face was dark, shaded lightly with ink that only gave an impression of color against the yellow of the page. His clothing was even darker, the blackness of night, like the jerkin I held tight in my hand. And he looked younger. Not as young as the Ailill I'd known many years in the past. But a man newly grown. Seventeen, perhaps, just a little more life to his eyes, just a little more roundness to his cheeks.

And on his arm, he wore a bangle.

Acknowledgements

YOU'D THINK AFTER THE LENGTH of the acknowledgements in the first book, I'd have thanked everyone I know by now. The second verse is much like the first, but it's worth saying again.

Thank you, Bethany Robison, for your great suggestions and amazing work on my manuscript—and for keeping all those details straight from book one to book two. Annie Cosby, thank you for your keen editing eye and your sharp insight.

Thanks again to Meet Cute Photography's Rachel Conway Schieffelbein, model Sakinah Caradine, and Makeready Design's Allison Martin for coming together to make these incredible new covers.

Thank you to the #WO2016 group of authors, whom I can rely on for encouragement, advice and some pretty awesome Twitter chats, and the #WIPMarathon members who've cheered me on for three years now. Writing and marketing is a lot more fun with all of you!

Thanks as always to Melissa Giorgio, my beta reader, best friend, and fellow YA author. You're always the first to read my work, and I appreciate everything you do to support me, from reading to tagging along to my signing to passing out promotional materials to your friends.

Thank you, Cameron, my partner of over a decade,

for always believing in me and being so proud of my work. I'm so happy you support me at every turn!

Thank you, Mom, Sara, and Anthony, for continuing to be cheerleaders for my work. I feel so lucky to have had so many fans right from the start.

And last but not least—thank you so much to my readers! I've appreciated every comment or email I've received from you, and I feel humbled you've come back to read more of Noll's story. I can only write because of your support!

About the Author

AMY MCNULTY IS A FREELANCE writer and editor from Wisconsin with an honors degree in English. She was first published in a national scholarly journal (*The Concord Review*) while in high school and currently writes professionally about everything from business marketing to anime. In her down time, you can find her crafting stories with dastardly villains and antiheroes set in fantastical medieval settings.

Find Amy at amymcnulty.com and on social media as McNultyAmy (Twitter), Amy McNulty, Author (Facebook), McNulty.Amy (Instagram), AuthorAmyMc (Pinterest), AmyMcNulty (Wattpad), and AuthorAmyMcNulty (Tumblr). Sign up for her monthly newsletter to receive news and exclusive information about her current and upcoming projects. Please visit her Goodreads and Amazon author pages and leave a review!

A Preview from Nobody's Pawn

Chapter One

I CLUTCHED THE BOOK TO my chest, the open page crinkling as I moved. I was afraid to look at it, afraid to see that I'd just imagined the throne room exploding to life. My damp dress raised bumps on my skin, which the cool morning breeze of an autumn day did nothing to alleviate. Even as the sunlight trickled through the leaves overhead, there was no hope of warming. No hope of going back to how things were just a day before.

My first thought had been to run to my friends, to run to Jurij when I saw the movement on the pages—but then my breath caught. Jurij had *killed* him. He might have returned—at least, that was what I wanted to see, to confirm with my own eyes—but that wouldn't change the fact that Jurij had driven his sword clear through his back. No, I couldn't go to Jurij. I couldn't go to any of the men, to those fools who'd destroyed the tavern and my father along with it.

I'd considered telling Mother at least what I'd seen. In my hazy thoughts of the previous few hours, I didn't remember if I'd have to explain to her what the book was, and how I'd known what had happened. But she had Father's death to come to terms with, and as I'd flipped through the book to find her page—my hand keeping my place on that last page, I couldn't risk losing that page—I saw her standing in our home besides the wood, Elfriede at her side, their faces both contorted as the full awareness of what we'd lost sunk over them. I could see the tears even in the black ink, see the puzzlement on Arrow's face as he looked up at them, but my eyes weren't drawn to their tears for long. Jurij walked onto the page and flung his arms around my sister.

I slammed the book shut, losing my place. Panicked, I flung it back open to the last page, and it was still there. It still followed the drawing of the young man who was and was not Ailill.

"Ailill." I said his name to the dawn, to the empty path through the woods before me. "Ailill, you didn't die for the last time. You came back. I know it." I squeezed the book harder to my chest, afraid to check, afraid to see if the page would turn red with blood and fire, like it had with my father's. I tried not to think of how it was selfish of me to want that. How he'd practically said he was ready to die at last after this life, how I was the one who'd doomed him to all his many lives.

My boot squished into the soft dirt, and I felt the sash around my waist loosen. I was prepared to trod on it as it flitted to the ground, but the heavy weight that hit my foot drew my attention. I paused as a trickle of sunlight glinted off the ground and caught my eye. The golden copper. It had stayed in my sash through all that time in the cavern pool, through almost drowning.

Still clutching the book, I crouched to pick the copper up. I held it out above my head and it caught the light. Before I'd realized it, I'd arrived at the black castle that nestled against the eastern mountains. Fear spread throughout my body at the thought that the gate doors might not open for me. I clenched the coin in my fist, feeling the weight of carrying the book with one hand but refusing to let the coin go. *Let me in*, I thought, and the gates parted quietly.

They hadn't even finished opening before I squeezed through them and stepped inside. "Ailill?" I called out, not caring how hollow the echo of my voice sounded in the entryway. *The throne room*, I thought, heading toward the stairway and coming face-to-face with a specter.

"I..." The sentence caught in my throat. I wanted to embrace the specter, but it would be too strange. They were back. It was proof he was, too. I studied the specter, the weak light pouring into the room through the open door not enough to fully make out his face. "I need to see Ailill," I said at last.

The specter said nothing. He was joined by a wave of other specters descending the staircase. They fanned out on either side of me, ignoring me, some even bumping me aside.

"Where are you going?" I asked, fully aware that none of them would answer. I stepped back, letting the specter who had blocked my path join the group, and I found myself tracing my steps back toward the doorway to make room for the flurry of movement. The sunlight from the doorway wasn't enough to make the entryway light up entirely, and no torches were lit, making the already usually dark room difficult to navigate. But the group of specters knew exactly what they were doing as they lined up in two parallel lines between the exit and the doorway at the back. They stilled all at once, their hands behind their backs, their legs slightly parted.

Sunlight streamed in from the doorway to the garden at the center of the castle, the place that had been my sanctuary all those months before. The dueling sunbeams from that door and from the open doorway behind me lit up the line of specters just enough that I could make out their stern, unmoving faces. My eyes roved over them and came to a halt at the end of the line.

"Ailill...?" I asked, my throat parched. "Ailill?" I crossed the room, ignoring the line of specters to reach the one who'd caught my attention.

I knew they were all "Ailill" in one way or another, but this specter—this young face, this disheveled hair—was mine. I was sure of it. "Ailill," I said again, reaching out to touch the white hair that cascaded off his shoulder with two fingers, leaving the coin clutched in the remaining three. "You're a specter now." I shook my head, remembering he never called them that.

"You're one of them. A servant." The hair that ought to have been deep brown was brittle in my hand. The eyes that ought to have been dark brown were red, and they focused over my head, not looking at me even as I fondled him. I gripped the hair harder, and the book dropped from my other hand to the floor. It echoed loudly in the entryway as I grabbed hold of Ailill's shoulders.

"Talk to me!" I said, my cheeks burning. Tears I hadn't even noticed cascaded down my face. "Say something!" I pounded his chest, determined to get a reaction out of him, not caring when the coin fell to the ground beside the book with a clatter. I'd never outright assaulted one of them. Surely there came a point at which they reacted. "Ailill—"

I felt a tap on my shoulder, and I turned. One of the specters had broken the line, and he held his hand out to me, his palm open.

"What?" I snapped, rubbing a haze of tears out of my eyes. This specter seemed familiar—what a farce, they *all* seemed familiar, and since they were all shades of the same man, I knew why. I couldn't shake the feeling that I knew this one more personally than the others. He was older than my Ailill, but not too old, perhaps a couple of decades older. This specter was looking at me, his red eyes boring through me. I hesitated and took his hand, which was holding the golden copper I'd dropped. "Thanks," I muttered. I reached for the book tucked beneath the specter's arm, and he drew back. I stared at him in shock. "I need that."

He fell back in line, carrying the book with him.

"Ailill," I started, not knowing what else to call him, "give that back! I only dropped it a moment—"

"May I ask how many times you are going to call me before you come inside the garden? Surely it has not escaped your notice that these men are clearly leading you here."

I froze, my hand still extended toward the specter who had taken the book from me. My ears picked up the trickle of the water fountain from the garden. I *knew* that voice. It felt a little off, perhaps, too calm, too blithe, but he had spoken.

"Ailill!"

A young man—perhaps a year or two older or younger than me—leaned against the door frame to the garden, his arms crossed against his chest, one leg crossed in front of the other.

"As you have said. Many times now." He nodded at me. "Come join me. I believe you have a lot to tell me."

He turned, crossing past the rose bushes—the bushes no longer withering, no longer dying, even with the chill of winter soon upon us—and sitting at the nearest stone bench. My eyes flitted over the rest of the garden. The entire place looked so much more cared-for than it had the last time I'd seen it, months before when I'd first sought out Ailill after the curse had broken. The benches were upright, and there wasn't a speck of brush out of place to litter the walkway or the table. Even the fountain spurted clear water, and the broken statue of the boy crying was conspicuously missing.

"Come," repeated the young man, gesturing to the bench on the other side of him. On the table was a chess game, and I remembered the matches I'd had with Ailill, and the brother I'd mistaken for him. I clutched the coin harder.

"Do not bother to hide that," said the young man, nodding. "You bring gold into my castle, and you stand there, your mouth agape, as if you do not know what it means."

"Gold?" I repeated, opening my hand to look at the coin I held there tightly. "The golden coin?" Some instinct compelled me not to betray my ignorance. *Ailill told me this token gave me the right to know...* I straightened my back and stepped in farther.

"Of course I know," I lied, trying to put that confidence into my shaky, soggy steps. I stopped suddenly, my eyes scanning the man's face. Of course. This was why he was shaded darker in the book; he came back, but he was no longer faded. He was born again, but younger—only slightly younger—but how? Why at this age? This was Ailill, as dark and as beautiful as any man in the village—no, even more so. I gasped. "Ailill!"

He shook his head, and the corner of his lips upturned into a smile that set my body on fire. "As you have said," he repeated. He gestured to the chess board. "Then come. Join me. I should enjoy a game with a lady in on the bet, my future bride."

Look for the third and final chapter of The Never Veil Series October 25th, 2016! Add it to your Goodreads to-read list today.

Men can love, but they can also hate. Noll knows too well that the men in her village have adjusted poorly to the freedom of their hearts, but she hopes to bring peace back to her community. With the lord's return, Noll feels confident that together, they can work to settle down the villagers, but in his rebirth, he remembers only one thing about her: that she caused the curse that tortured him for a millennium in the first place.

Determined to start anew, Noll must accept that, romantically, she and the lord are better without one another, but she'll need his help to uncover what's really behind all of the suffering in her village. Escorted to a land beyond the mountains, Noll uncovers the truth about her village and the strange occurrences in which she's had a hand. When someone who loves her discovers the same things and betrays her, Noll feels powerless to stop her village's fate. By learning to forgive and seek forgiveness, Noll finally understands true love of a free heart—along with true sacrifice.

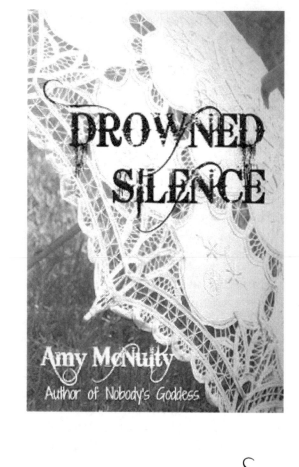

DROWNED SILENCE EXCERPT

Read an excerpt from my short story collection, *Drowned Silence*. It's available exclusively in its entirety on Wattpad, where it has received over 63,000 reads and was a featured pick in the Wattpad Teen Fiction genre for six months. Add it to your Goodreads to-read list today!

"YOU DON'T SMELL HALF BAD for someone who can't shower."

Of all the things Dylan Kushner could have said to Kelsey Wade to fill the silence, the comment about her odor was probably among the stupidest. But he'd already tried the "Mr. Castaneda's class blows, right?" that had opened successfully with his last research partner, and which led into his perfect imitation of Mr. Castaneda droning on and on about dead people through a perpetually-clogged-up nose. He might have tried what he'd asked a number of people this week, "What's your costume for Randi's Halloween party tomorrow?" but Dylan knew he didn't need to see the crickets chirping on Kelsey's Facebook friends list (did she even *use* Facebook?) to figure out no one was going to be inviting Kelsey anywhere—even if Randi was her sister. ("We're *not* twins, god. Why do people always think that?" Randi had made it clear she was a whole eleven months older than Kelsey the only time Dylan had bothered to ask. It probably didn't help that their parents had waited to enroll Randi and Kelsey in the same grade back in kindergarten, something Randi said they thought would be "cute," saying the word "cute" like it was a synonym for "nauseating.")

So Dylan had sat there, watching Kelsey fumble through that bag of hers—it wasn't a purse, or even a backpack; it was something like one of those sparkly small bags the girls brought with them to dances, the kinds that only had room for a tampon and lipstick and whatever else girls absolutely needed even just for a few hours. But it wasn't sparkly. It was made of some old fabric that Kelsey might have torn off of her grandmother's—scratch that, *great*-grandmother's couch. And because she wasn't speaking, he thought of everything he knew about her— *weird*, quiet, *weird*, Randi's sister, maybe a little hot, just a little, in a *weird* way, uh, allergic to water—and asked her if it was true that she broke out in hives if water touched her, and if that's why she got out of swimming. She hadn't answered—just sort of nodded—but he kept going. "How can you be allergic to water? Isn't that like being allergic to air? Do you die if you drink?"

And it was the first thing he'd asked that actually got her to open her mouth.

"Obviously not, moron."

Dylan took the insult in stride, considering who it was coming from. "But I thought I saw this thing on YouTube once about a woman who was even allergic to *drinking* water—"

Kelsey had bent under her chair to retrieve the pile of books she kept in book straps that resembled a couple of belts. "Well, that's not what I have. Just the skin contact thing."

That's when the line popped out: "You don't smell half bad for someone who can't shower."

Kelsey's darkly-shadowed eyes didn't open fully, but they did grow just a centimeter wider—enough to shoot Dylan a highly unamused look. Dylan cleared his throat a few times and started tapping his finger against the table. Kelsey did nothing to alleviate the building silence. All Dylan had for comfort were the soft murmurs of the other research teams around the library, but of course, he'd been stuck with the partner who walked straight toward the back corner, the farthest possible from other human contact. He'd had no choice but to follow, shrugging his shoulders apologetically to Ryan and Ashley, who'd beckoned him to the empty seat at the end of their table by the window.

Kelsey pulled a little jar of ink out of her handbag and an actual quill—a bird feather with a pointed end. She laid a stack of unlined paper atop the desk and unstrapped her pile of books, positioning a thick encyclopedia beside her jar of ink.

Dylan couldn't help it. The words came tumbling out of his mouth. "You don't... seriously need to use that, do you?"

Kelsey shrugged and pawed her encyclopedia volume, letting the cover fall open with a great thud. "This is history. There's nothing they didn't know about Martin Luther before the Internet that they suddenly know now."

"Sure." Dylan wasn't quite sure he believed that statement, since Mr. Castaneda had emphasized the importance of historical theory as much as historical fact, and surely the Internet was home to a few thousand more theories on pretty much anyone in history, ancient or not. But that wasn't actually what he'd meant. He pointed to the feather quill. "I meant that." He dug his tablet out of his backpack and placed it next to Kelsey's encyclopedia. It was less than half the width and easily a hundredth the thickness of Kelsey's outdated research tool. Dylan brought up his word processor app. "You can take notes on a tablet without lugging a little pot around filled with a laundry disaster waiting to happen."

Kelsey didn't look at Dylan; the only indication she'd even heard him was the slight twitch of her eyebrow. She licked a finger and turned a page. "Inkwell."

"What?"

Kelsey rolled her eyes. "The 'little pot' is called an inkwell."

Dylan took a breath. "Okaaaay..." When Kelsey didn't respond, Dylan shrugged, figuring that was the end of that conversation. He grabbed his tablet, googling "Martin Luther" and sorting through a few pages of the much more recent civil rights leader before finding the Wiki on the 16th century German monk. He began skimming the entry, drifting dangerously close to sleep. He shook his head to clear it and reached for the bottle he'd tucked in his backpack's pocket for drinks.

"I don't like using anything invented after the 19th century."

Dylan nearly spit out his swig of Lemon Lime Gatorade. Kelsey still hadn't turned to face him, instead carefully removing the cork from her pot—*inkwell*—and dipping the quill in.

"Oh," said Dylan, after a moment's uncomfortable silence. He screwed the cap back on his Gatorade and slid it back into the backpack, rummaging around and finding what he was looking for at the bottom. He shifted aside some old Kleenex and scrap paper and what felt like possibly an old forgotten sandwich in a Ziploc bag. He tossed the ballpoint pen on the table. The freebie marked with his mom's bank rolled and came to stop against Kelsey's elbow. Kelsey's hand stopped, the tip of her quill pooling ink onto her paper with each passing moment.

"What. Is. That?" Kelsey's eyes shifted slightly to meet Dylan's expectant glare.

"A.... ballpoint pen?" Dylan suddenly wasn't very sure.

Kelsey sniffed. "No thank you." She picked her quill back up and dipped it in the pot, continuing her slow scrawl across the blank page.

Dylan reached for the pen awkwardly, his fingers brushing Kelsey's puffy black sleeve as he retrieved it. "I've seen you using pens in class before," he muttered.

"Those are fountain pens."

"Okay." Dylan scratched the back of his head while tapping the ballpoint pen on the tabletop, eliciting another sideways glare from Kelsey's heavily made-up eyes. "Ballpoint pens weren't around in the 19th century?"

Kelsey's shoulders stiffened. She dipped the quill again. "No."

Dylan chewed his bottom lip. He didn't really care, but— "I think you're wrong about that."

The corner of Kelsey's deep-red lips twitched, but she kept writing. "Are you a pen expert?"

"No, but—" Dylan slid his tablet closer, entering "ballpoint pen" into Wikipedia. He tapped the screen with the top of his rarely-used pen. "Ha! The first patent was in 1888."

Kelsey's quill stopped moving. "It wasn't widely in use."

"Ah," said Dylan, putting as much sarcasm into the one syllable as he could muster. "I suppose the knee-high skirt was a regular fashion trend by then, though?"

Kelsey's hand moved to shift her short petticoat and layered skirt more securely over her white-tights-covered knees. Dylan could tell she was sort of dressed old-fashioned-like—and by *old-fashioned*, he meant like something out of *A Christmas Carol*, not the poofy '80s fashions his parents wore in prom photos—but he knew he was right about the skirt length. Probably the knee-high boots she paired them with, too.

"It's Gothic Lolita," said Kelsey. She dipped her quill again and ran her left hand over her book. Dylan wondered why she didn't worry about dragging the long, flowing sleeves over her ink-stained paper, but she was wearing black. It probably just blended right in.

"And that was a fashion style in the 1800s?"

Kelsey sighed. One of the pale pink curls framing her face escaped from underneath the frilly lace black headband she wore. "No. But it's close enough to make me feel comfortable."

Dylan nodded and rolled the side of the pen over his upper lip. "Uh huh. And a ballpoint pen isn't. Got it."

Kelsey lay her quill down gently, keeping the white feather out of the still-glistening ink. "Are you going to pick on me all day or are we going to so some research?"

Dylan shrugged and laid down his pen, picking up his tablet and whisking his fingers across the screen. "Since you'll take about twenty times longer than me to research with your *inkwell* and book, I figure I have some time to—"

"Some time to what, Mr. Kushner? May I ask exactly how much work you've gotten done so far?" Mr. Castaneda appeared like Batman—a portly, cardigan-wearing Batman—out of the shadows and stood in front of the table, his arms crossed. Kelsey continued to write her calligraphy

247

undisturbed, but Dylan dropped his tablet, causing a number of people to glance over at the thud.

"Uh—" Dylan's usually ever-moving tongue suddenly failed him.

"We've started the basic research," answered Kelsey, not completely untruthfully.

Mr. Castaneda leaned over the table to examine Kelsey's paper. He nodded. "Don't make a mess, Miss Wade."

Kelsey crossed a 't' with an especially prolonged flourish of her hand. "I won't."

"All right." Mr. Castaneda looked at Dylan. "You two have Martin Luther. So what are you going to do for your presentation?"

Dylan ran through the possible answers in his head, feeling the weight of every second of silence that followed. Kelsey kept scratching at her paper and dipping her quill in ink. A clock ticked somewhere off in the library. He could even hear the hum through the walls—the heating system, maybe, which popped and crackled annoyingly every few seconds, like some workman was crawling through the walls and continuously dropping his tools down the air vent. He started spacing out, no longer hearing any of the possible excuses he could come up with.

Kelsey finally released Dylan from the agonizing silence. "We're not sure yet."

Mr. Castaneda rapped his knuckles on the table and started walking away. "Get to it. I expect you to present *fully prepared* on Monday."

Dylan watched the teacher retreat to the next table of students, taking the looming threat of silence with him. Dylan bent to grab his bottle of Gatorade and took a drink to calm himself.

"Are you coming to Randi's *thing* tomorrow?"

Dylan snapped back to his presentation partner. She'd stopped writing and looked at him expectantly, the quill in her hand dripping ink from its tip onto the paper. "Are *you* going?" he asked.

Kelsey sighed and lay her quill down. "I *live* there, genius."

"Yeah. I know." Dylan had to stop himself from pointing out he figured Kelsey would be as welcome in her own home during a party thrown by Randi as a ballpoint pen would be welcomed by Kelsey. Dylan cleared his head, smirking. "Yeah. Yeah, I am." He lifted both hands in the air in his best impression of Frankenstein's monster, even with the Gatorade bottle in hand. "I'm wearing a Frankenstein mask. You going as a modern teen in jeans and a sweater or something?"

"Ha ha." Kelsey put the cork back in the top of her inkwell, shut her book closed and stacked it with the others. "We can finish then. I'll look for the oh-so-original green skin and bolt coming out of your head."

Dylan took another swig. "I'll search for the uptight girl looking like she stepped out of a Dickens book."

Kelsey pinched her lips and finished tying her book strap. "I'd avoid her, if I were you." She gathered the papers, blowing on the slowly-drying ink. She folded the pages, stuffing them into her handbag as she stood.

Dylan gestured his bottle lazily in her direction. "Wait, you couldn't possibly want to *work* on this during a *party*—"

"Watch out!" shouted Kelsey. She took a step back, but she fumbled, reaching out to grab the table to steady herself. Dylan instinctively tried to grab her hand, dropping the bottle of Gatorade on the table. The remaining liquid leaked out, covering Kelsey's pale hand in bright green liquid.

Kelsey shrieked and pulled back her hand, shaking it. Dylan could hear the moving chairs behind him. The curious murmurs.

"Kelsey, I'm sorry." He reached out to the hand she cradled like it was wounded. He thought he saw—well, that was ridiculous. If her allergy was as bad as she said, her hand might have been bright red with hives, but the discolored skin Dylan saw was green, maybe even yellowy.

The color of his Gatorade, of course.

Kelsey tucked her discolored hand under her other arm as she slung the book strap full of books over her shoulder. She clutched the handbag with the same hand. "Forget it."

"Miss Wade, is everything all right?" Mr. Castaneda had returned, incapable of standing in front of any student without his arms crossed over his chest.

Kelsey wouldn't look up. Her arm twitched. "Yes. I'm sorry for screaming."

Mr. Castaneda sniffled, speaking low. "This is the *library*." He looked down. "What a mess! Miss Wade, I warned you about your archaic methods of note-taking!"

If Kelsey wondered how Mr. Castaneda confused Gatorade with ink, she said nothing. "I know, I'm sorr—"

Dylan stood and stuck a hand out in front of Kelsey. "I'm sorry, Mr. Castaneda. It was me. I spilled it and—" He looked at Kelsey, who refused to look back at him. "I got her hand wet. I think her allergy is acting up. Can you let her go to the nurse?"

Kelsey's eyes met Dylan's, and for the first time, Dylan thought she saw something other than annoyance in her expression. Mr. Castaneda fumbled and waved a hand. "Yes, yes, of course." He pointed at Dylan. "I expect you to clean this up, Mr. Kushner. Ask the librarian for paper towels."

"Sure." Dylan nodded at Kelsey, and she tore her eyes away. She looked about to speak but squeezed her arm to her chest tighter and left without saying anything more. Dylan glanced once more at the mess he'd made.

The puddle of Gatorade had turned brown and murky. At first glance, it was almost black.

The ruckus over, the library grew disturbingly quiet.

Living in a home dripping with silent tension, lonely teen Dylan finds refuge at school—until Kelsey is assigned to be his class project partner. Kelsey, the school outcast, is allergic to water, dresses in Gothic Lolita fashion and refuses to use technology from past the 19th century, which makes working together difficult to say the least.

Invited to Kelsey's house during her sister's Halloween party, Dylan uncovers a frightening connection between Kelsey and a death that took place on her property years before.

A serialized YA contemporary horror short story from the author of The Never Veil Series and *Fall Far from the Tree*. Available exclusively on Wattpad and through Instafreebie.

CPSIA information can be obtained
at www.ICGtesting.com
Printed in the USA
LVOW10s1147291117
557886LV00024B/934/P